THE MAN WHO ATE THE SUN

Michael Whitworth

ISBN: 9798642991404 (paperback)

First eBook edition May 2020

For my family

Chapter 1

By the time I was thirty-five, I'd stolen, blackmailed and killed. I hadn't planned it; it had just happened. The manifestation of my lost hopes. I was an inconsequential man, and that's the thing which surprised me the most. I'd thought I was destined for such great things. It wasn't how I'd pictured my future, all those years ago, as I climbed the steps to the town hall, strolling happily between my mother and father on a hot summer's day.

It was 1976, the year of the heatwave. Sixty-six days of sun. Concorde had made its maiden flight, and my father had been promoted at the bank. He'd celebrated by buying a new car, a mustard coloured Datsun, and suddenly the world seemed to overflow with possibilities.

In keeping with our newfound station in life, gone were the weekend trips to the football and days out at the beach. We now visited museums and the town hall, to see exhibitions and to learn about things. About our past, when all that really concerned us was the future. I remember this day specifically, because my parents were laughing. Both of them, at the same time. Years of familiarity had made the utterings of affection feel awkward, until finally they'd disappeared altogether. Sarcastic comments and small digs were now the only ways they knew to express their love. But today was different.

We'd been wandering around town for what seemed like hours and had achieved pretty much all of the goals my mother had set earlier that morning. A combination of the heat, an empty stomach and a constant running between my parents had made me feel ill, so we'd stopped off at a cafe for a drink of water and a bite to eat. My parents had been out the night before and had started the day in good humour. When my mother had suggested we do some shopping, followed by a trip to the town hall, my father had agreed immediately. My opinion had not been sought.

I still couldn't understand why I came on these trips. It wasn't what I wanted, and not something my friends did either. So as we entered the town hall and stepped into the cavernous marbled foyer, I was wholly unprepared for what lay in store, the riot of colour and shape that assailed me from every side. There, hanging from walls and hastily assembled stands, were pictures and posters portraying everything a ten-year-old could possibly imagine: huge buildings and aeroplanes, rockets and computers, submarines and spaceships. By each one was a small picture of a man or woman, with a brief description of who they were. I learned that day about Edison and Bell, Tesla and Kwolek, and the eagerness I showed, as I made my way from one stand to the next, had made my parents smile.

On the way home that day, in my father's new car, I spoke of Grace Hooper and Garret Morgan and my mother had laughed, telling me to slow down and to breathe. But I was excited. Excited about all the great things I would achieve and how interesting my life was going to be.

My father suggested we stop off at the local ice cream shop and I cheered, making my mother laugh even more.

Inside the shop, sitting at a small metal table by the window, overlooking the sea, my father explained that all those people had done great things. They had made people's lives better and had changed the world. My mother leaned over and kissed me, at the same time removing a small spot of chocolate ice cream from my face.

'Don't you wish you'd done great things?' I asked, looking at my parents. I still remember my father's smile.

'But we did, Thomas,' he said. 'We made you, and that's the greatest thing of all.'

Chapter 2

Dreams, hopes and reality. These are the three stages of life. Children have dreams, and young people have hopes for the future. As adults, we have reality.

It was 2001, twenty-five years later, and I was working in an office. I was bored, overworked and alone.

It had been an awful start to the morning. I'd woken up early, next to a stranger, and my muscles ached. The throbbing in my head was like a drum beating, and despite a shower and a shave, I looked little better than I felt. On the train, I'd been sandwiched between two heavily sweating men, both of whom remained for the duration of my journey. One of the men had opened a newspaper, so close to my face that I could smell the ink. I'd thought I was going to be sick.

It was going to be a long day.

Emerging from the station, I was greeted by bright morning sunshine. There was a cool breeze blowing from the Thames, and I breathed in deeply, unbuttoning my shirt collar so that the cool air came rushing into my shirt. It's small pleasures like these that can make a bad day almost bearable. A short stroll across London Bridge and I'd be at the office.

As I walked, the streets around me teemed with grey pinstriped suits and Louboutin shoes. Designer handbags and leather briefcases swarmed from the Underground, and I started to feel dizzy. So I stopped, placing my backpack against a wall, and I waited. It was several minutes before I set off again.

To the right was St. Paul's, my favourite building in the city, and to the left was Tower Bridge and HMS Belfast. It was usually such a pleasant way to start the day, but today was not a typical day. In the distance, tall stone office blocks pointed to the sky like accusatory fingers, and it was all I could do not to give up and turn back. But a few more minutes and I'd be there, ready for another week. A week, I was later to realise, that would change my life.

Finally, at ten o'clock, I made my way through the large double doors of my office. There were many empty desks, and I smiled to myself. At least I wasn't the only one feeling rough. By the water fountain, several of my colleagues stood in silence, hair uncombed, their faces pallid and expressionless. There'd been an office party the night before, and as far as could recall, it had gone off well. I remembered everything until around ten o'clock. After that, I wasn't too sure. I wasn't even sure that I wanted to know. I suddenly remembered the woman I'd woken up next to that morning. Her name, how we'd got there, what had happened, I had no idea. I wouldn't have to wait long to find out.

Moments later, there was a knock at the door and in came Mary, my assistant, carrying a pile of papers and unopened correspondence. Dressed in a white cotton shirt and black skirt, she looked the opposite of how I felt—refreshed, happy and looking forward to the day. She'd worked for me for a couple of years now, but unfortunately was about to move jobs. I'd be sad to see her go.

'Would you like a coffee, Thomas?' she inquired, her face radiant as she placed the papers onto my desk. I'd seen her at the party last night, but she hadn't drunk much and had left early. Just as any sensible person would have done. But I'm not a sensible person.

'You look like you need something to perk you up,' she said. I smiled at her but said nothing. 'Henry and James have been looking forward to seeing you all morning,' she continued. 'They're bursting to ask you about something. Shall I tell them to come in?'

Henry and James were not sensible people either.

'No, thank you, Mary,' I said. 'In an hour or so maybe. Tell them I'm busy. And no, I don't want a drink, thank you.' The door closed quietly. And leaning back in my chair, I immediately fell asleep.

When I awoke, it was eleven o'clock, and I'd drooled onto my lapel. I had nothing to clean it with, so I used one of the papers Mary had brought in, then screwed it up and threw it into the bin. No one would know, and even if they did, they probably wouldn't care.

My first priority was to get some water. My throat was incredibly dry, so pushing back my chair, I made my way to the door and asked Mary if she could find me a bottle of water. As uncomfortable as the feeling of dehydration was, at least my hangover had gone. While I waited in my office for Mary, I sat back in my chair, enjoying the post-hangover high now sweeping over me. Suddenly, I was feeling much better.

For a few moments, I tried to remember what had taken place the evening before. As hard as I tried, I could recall very little. No doubt Henry and James would take great pleasure in jogging my memory, with a few of their customary embellishments.

It wasn't long before there was a knock at the door, and in came Mary, a bottle of water in her hand. She glided over to my desk, the soles of her shoes leaving small indentations in the thick office carpet, and at that moment she looked like an angel. A water-carrying angel.

'I'm glad to see you're looking better,' she said. 'It must have been quite a night, judging from your appearance this morning.' She paused slightly and smiled. 'And from what everyone's been saying in the office.'

Raising an eyebrow, I asked her what had been said, and her face reddened.

'I never listen to office gossip,' I remarked, enjoying her discomfort. Of course, that was untrue. 'I think I'll have that coffee now, thanks. And you can send in Henry and James, please.' Without looking at me, she made her way to the door. Just before she left, she turned around.

'It's not the gossip I take much notice of,' she said, 'but the photos are pretty convincing.' And with a smile, she disappeared.

Her departure was immediately followed by another knock at the door. I wondered if Mary had perhaps forgotten something, but before I could see, in came Henry and James, Henry half turned, like a crab, as he watched Mary disappear.

Henry was the company lawyer, a red-faced man in his early forties, though with the posture of someone much older. He was old school. He wore a suit, even at home, and his shirts were white. Always white. Twice divorced, he was an incorrigible flirt, and most recently he'd been flirting with Mary. It was the very definition of one-way traffic, and I wondered if it had played a part in her decision to leave. I'd asked her once, and she'd laughed, so I supposed not. For a wealthy man, he was incredibly tight. Everything went through expenses, and more than once, I'd been called in to explain his spending. But he was good at his job, so no one really cared.

James was the opposite. In his late twenties, he headed up the firm's trading desks. In his bow tie and brightly coloured braces, he would gamble the firm's future each day, and for the most part, he won. At six feet, he towered over Henry, and his sticklike frame made him look ungainly, as if he were about to topple over. He knew little about business, so had been promoted rapidly, to the point where he now ran the whole area. But despite his outward flamboyance, I'd always found him quite shy.

And then there was me. Socially awkward, perhaps. Lacking in patience, definitely. The three of us were an odd fit, but we got on. Very well actually. I liked Henry and James a lot, and they were, without a doubt, my closest male friends.

And so it was that the three of us sat at my desk, me on one side, Henry and James on the other. They were smiling.

'Photographs, please,' I said, holding out my hand. Henry reached into his jacket pocket and passed me a small brown envelope. It was the kind of envelope you would associate with a bribe, and I wondered where he'd got it. All the office envelopes were white. The two of them sat there motionless, as I opened the envelope and casually flicked through its contents. The pictures were clear, as if taken by a professional.

'Christ,' I sighed as I looked at the final photograph. 'Was I really that drunk?'

'Quite a lot worse actually,' replied Henry, which wasn't helpful. 'And that was before twelve.'

'What happened at twelve?' I asked, almost afraid of what I might hear.

'I've no idea,' he admitted. 'I'd passed out by then.'

'Me too,' added James, who by now was grinning broadly.

I put the photographs back into the envelope and returned them to Henry.

'The thing I don't understand,' I said, 'is that you're both in the photos with me. So, who took them?'

James shrugged.

'It was Terry from sales,' remarked Henry. I had no idea who that was.

'Who's that?' I asked.

He shook his head. 'No idea. He came over to me this morning and handed me the envelope.' I decided to find out who this Terry person was.

We were interrupted by a knock at the door. To this point, Henry had been slouching in his chair, but when Mary walked in, he sat bolt upright, as if he had a pole down his back.

'Mary,' he cooed. 'You look lovely today.' I looked over at James, and he smiled at me, then rolled his eyes and silently pretended to be sick.

'I thought you two gentlemen would also like a coffee,' she said, bending over to put the tray on the table. She winked at me, and I felt like laughing.

'Jesus Christ!' moaned Henry as she left. He was actually sweating. 'I think I've put my back out.'

For the next half an hour, we sat chatting about the party, filling in the blanks for each other as best we could. I was sure Henry was making most of it up, but I was in no position to challenge him.

'I hope that you haven't forgotten Potter's party tomorrow,' said James, as the two of them got up to leave. 'All invited.'

Of course, I'd forgotten. Nigel Potter was the company accountant, a huge, fat man who sprayed spittle as he spoke. His parties were an annual event, and I enjoyed them very much. But at that moment, more drinking was the last thing I needed.

'I don't know if I'm up to it,' I said, hoping they would understand, but knowing that they wouldn't. 'Mary can go in my place.'

'She already is!' laughed Henry. I wasn't getting out of it that easily. 'Besides, it wouldn't look good if she went and you didn't. You know what these things are like. I don't think she'll go if you don't go.'

I smiled, and it was an admission of defeat. I knew that Henry wanted to go, chiefly because of Mary, but I also knew that Mary was afraid of Potter, a trait she shared with the majority of the female workforce. He was a bit of a letch. More than a bit actually.

'I'll see,' I said and looked at my watch. This was the cue for Henry and James to depart, leaving me to contemplate the prospect of the party gloomily. By five o'clock I'd accomplished very little, so I decided to call it a day. Collecting my jacket, I left the room and said goodbye to Mary.

Once in the open air, I realised how stuffy it had been in the office, so I decided to take a short walk before heading for the Underground. The sun was hiding behind a large cloud, and the heat was more bearable than it had been in the morning. In this part of London, even out of doors, the air couldn't be described as fresh. It had been so long since I'd been outside of London that I'd almost got used to it. Born in the north of Lancashire, I'd rather taken fresh air for granted. Since then, I'd lived in some of the most industrialised cities in the world: Tokyo, Shanghai, New York, and now London. I often wondered why I'd come to London at all. I'd heard that people came to London to escape, and perhaps that's why I'd come too. As I walked, the streets began to fill with local office workers, making their way home after another routine day at work. But today was Friday, so they didn't appear quite as miserable as usual. Soon it would be rush hour, and with it the pavements would disappear, as people swarmed from office buildings like termites in search of food. I quickened my pace, and very soon, I was disappearing underground. In another half an hour, I would be home.

By the time I arrived back, it was beginning to get dark. Several of the streetlights along my road had flickered into life, revealing rows of pristine new flats, where once an old terrace had been. The terraced houses had been demolished around ten years ago to make room for the increasingly massive influx of workers into the area. I couldn't help thinking that with their disappearance, something essential had vanished, a tight-knit community replaced by a multitude of strangers. Making my way up the concrete steps to my door, I noted for the umpteenth time that the door needed painting and as I fumbled with my key, I added yet another scratch to its glossy black surface.

Inside, my flat was in total disarray, with half-empty pizza boxes covering the floor. An empty cigarette packet lay opened in the corner and on the windowsill stood a single shoe. One of mine, at least, but I couldn't see the other. A couple of glasses lay on the floor, one half-full, the other on its side, next to a large wine stain. No prizes for guessing which had been mine. Having picked them up, I placed a nearby rug over the stain. The carpet could be cleaned later. And as I made my way towards the kitchen, I noticed the answering machine blinking at me from its place next to the TV. I turned it on, let out a huge weary yawn, and set about the reconstruction of my home. The answer machine beeped.

'Hi, it's Anna. It's about six, and I was just wondering what you had planned for this evening. If you get home before nine, give me a call. Hope you're feeling better.' Recollections came flooding back. So it was Anna who'd stayed over last night. I felt ashamed, knowing that I had no intention of calling her. As there was a possibility she might ring again, I kept the answering machine on. I'd bravely make my excuses only when absolutely necessary.

Within an hour, the flat was looking respectable. It was a nice place, and I'd been lucky to get it for such a reasonable price. Though quite small, it was in most respects a typical London flat, and being unsure how long I planned to stay in London, I'd decided to rent, rather than buy. That had been eight years ago. A large portion of my monthly savings had gone on buying things for it, but when I looked around, I couldn't really see where all the money had gone. The computer maybe. The dining table and chairs, the coffee machine, the treadmill. All things which I'd thought essential. Now they just sat there, taking up space. A bit like me.

Having made something to eat, eaten it, and then washed out the plastic microwave pot it had come in, it was nearly nine o'clock. Which just so happened to be my favourite part of the day - television time. The TV was another thing I'd spent a lot of money on, but unlike the other items, it had been a good buy. So had the coffee table and sofa, to be honest. So not everything had been a waste.

For the next two hours, I could forget about work, life and other people. I could just sit there getting older while the TV fed me information about things I would never see and people I would never meet. Two hours of escape.

That evening's television was a dazzling mix of repeats and minority interest programmes, ranging from quiz shows to old sitcoms, and finally to a foreign film. I'd seen the film before and remembered it as a kind of soft porn masquerading as French period drama. Something about a lowly farm worker who falls for the daughter of his boss. Or was it his wife? I couldn't remember, but either way, it didn't end up well. At least I didn't think it did. I'd been drunk when I'd watched it previously, so it could, in fact, have been a completely different film. Regardless, I decided to watch it again. Or for the first time. I made a cup of tea, then settled down for the evening.

No sooner had I sat down than there was a knock at the door and in walked Sarah, a friend of mine, who often turned up unexpectedly.

'Come in!' I called, but she already had.

'Thank you,' she said with a laugh, 'I shall. You really are too kind.' All mohair jumper and Doctor Marten boots, she strolled over and plonked herself unceremoniously on the sofa beside me, forcing me to place my tea on the coffee table in case I spilt it. Noticing the tea, Sarah reached over and took two noisy slurps before placing it back down, dark red lipstick clearly visible on the rim. I told her she could have it, I'd only just made it, and she thanked me as I went to the kitchen to make another. Discovering that I was out of clean cups, I took one from the sink and gave it a rinse before drying it on the old Butlins tea towel hanging from the oven handle. I'd owned the towel since I was a child and it had been bought for me by my parents one summer holiday. Looking back, it seemed an odd gift to buy a six-year-old child, but at the time, it had seemed so perfectly natural.

When I got back into the living room a few minutes later, Sarah was quietly watching the television, her boots off and her stockinged feet propped lazily on my coffee table.

'Are you watching porn, Thomas?' she asked casually.

Moving over to sit next to her, I took a drink from my tea and shook my head. 'A film,' I said, and she snorted into her cup.

'I think you will find that this is porn,' she retorted. 'So this is what you get up to when you're not entertaining.'

'It's a Channel 4 film,' I corrected her, pointing it out in the TV magazine which lay opened on the coffee table next to her feet.

'Oh, yeah,' she said at last, 'I think I've seen this one.' She paused for a moment, and I could see that she was trying to remember something. 'Or at least something very similar.'

We watched to film for another forty minutes, at which point we decided that it wasn't the film we remembered, though the storyline seemed the same.

It had become increasingly clear to me during the course of the film that something was on Sarah's mind. She was usually so much chattier than this. I'd known her since my arrival in London, and we'd become good friends, such that she was about as much of a confidant as I had. Her visits were seldom unwelcome, though they did tend to coincide with arguments with her boyfriend and so could become quite heavy. At that moment, I wasn't in the mood for a heavy conversation, so I asked her if she wanted another drink.

'Of course,' she laughed. 'When have you ever known me to turn down a cup of tea?'

'Never!' I replied from the kitchen.

'I'll pretend I didn't hear that,' she said. 'Anyway, tell me all about last night. What happened?'

'What do you think?'

'You got drunk and woke up next to some girl you don't even remember meeting. You've felt terrible all day. And judging from the answering machine, you're afraid of her ringing.'

'Close,' I said. 'How do you know?'

She laughed. 'It's an old story, Thomas. I don't pretend to

understand you, but I know you better than most.' She rambled on for a few minutes, as I made her tea, though I wasn't really listening by this point.

'When are you going to finally settle down, Thomas?' she said as I re-entered the room, and the concerned look on her face took me by surprise. I shrugged and replied that maybe I didn't want to settle down, but I could see she didn't believe me. Sarah thought all problems could be solved by a good relationship, even though her own seemed far from ideal. As with all things, it wasn't so simple as that, but I knew there was no convincing her, so I kept my mouth shut.

I changed the subject, and for a while, we talked about trivial things, the kind of things that fill a space, and the words are unimportant.

And as the credits rolled, Sarah finally spoke of her latest argument with Gerald, the boyfriend, which seemed to me to be the same as the last argument. I told her that it would all turn out fine, as it had done many times before, and she smiled and thanked me for being such a good friend. She was reassured, because that's what I did. I reassured other people.

Finally, she decided it was time to leave. It was midnight, and I needed my bed. Saturday was going to be another long day.

Chapter 3

I awoke the next morning a new man. Whereas the day before I'd crawled out of bed, today I bounded. Whereas yesterday I'd been repulsed by thoughts of alcohol and parties, today I looked forward to them. It was Saturday, and I was going to enjoy it. Even if it killed me.

There are two main types of routine: firstly, those imposed by others, such as work. This type is unenjoyable and followed due to lack of choice; secondly, those imposed by oneself, such as a visit to the pub. This type is enjoyable and done happily. My weekend routine most definitely fell into the second category. I liked to wake up early, at around half past nine, make a quick breakfast and then go out. By going out, I would walk a couple of hundred metres to the local shopping precinct, go to my usual cafe, read a newspaper and watch the world go by. This was my relaxation, my way of recharging after a long week of work. It was rare for me to miss it. This particular Saturday, I was looking forward to it more than ever.

Once I'd finished breakfast, I slipped into my weekend clothes and set off. My weekend clothes consisted of jeans and a polo shirt. I had numerous versions of the same shirt, differing only in colour. Once I found something I liked, there was no point experimenting further. The jeans were interchangeable with other trousers. I'd never found denim comfortable anyway. During the summer months, I usually wore shorts, which I found the most comfortable. I would have worn them all year round if that had been socially acceptable. But it wasn't, so I didn't.

It was hot outside, so I put on grey shorts to go with my blue polo shirt. Overhead, the sky was clear, and the sun blazed down, searing long shadows into the pavement. Its glare bounced off the dusty streets, making me squint. The road was empty, except for a few cars, and I walked quickly from one cracked paving stone to the next, until finally, I turned the corner onto the path which led to the shops. As I approached, I could see and hear people at the end of the path, first one or two, then large groups, making their way from bookstore to coffee shop, nail salon to bank. It was always bustling on a Saturday, but with the sun out, it was much busier than usual.

The general shape of the area was that of a large square, with several paths fanning out like a vast spider's web. In the middle sat an expanse of bleached white concrete, with a small fountain at the centre providing makeshift seating for families with ice creams, and groups of teenagers with long hair and pimples. On the outside were a variety of shops, by far the most popular of which were the coffee shops and bookstores, with their colourful awnings and comfortable chairs. And it was in that direction that I headed, dodging through the press of shoppers and disappearing into the welcoming coolness of Cafe Piccolo.

Inside, I headed straight for my usual table by the window, from where I could see the entire square. Someone must have only just left, as there was a half-drunk mug of coffee and a newspaper on the table. I picked up the coffee and placed it on a table nearby. The paper, with its headlines of job losses and heatwaves, I kept for myself. And for the next few minutes, I sat there, looking out of the window, doing and thinking about nothing, just watching the world pass me by.

Outside the cafe, it was like a silent movie, bedlam with no sound. The usual people were there, sitting and standing in the same places they occupied every Saturday. In the coffee shop opposite, a local franchise of a large American company, small groups of middle-aged men and women sat in their expensive clothes drinking decaf lattes and skinny flat whites. They would drive home in large cars to flats much like mine, too expensive and too small for their needs and with no room to park.

Next door was a bookshop, one of the few still in business outside of the large retail parks and shopping centres. It was a place I liked very much, but rarely visited, its large bookcases reminding me of all the books I'd promised myself to read but had never found the time. Outside, under a giant red awning, were several small tables, surrounded by students from the nearby halls of residence, drinking coffee and scrawling notes onto the pages of their shiny textbooks.

In contrast to these, between the shops and the fountain sat a large group of homeless people. They were the one constant in the area, through sunshine and rain, and I'd come to recognise several of them over time. Furthest away from me was a tall man with a huge grey beard, his back against the fountain and a purple blanket around his legs, despite the heat. I knew him from his usual spot outside the tube station, where he would sit each morning, as hundreds of people walked past, as if he were invisible. I'd spotted him one day in smart clothes, inside one of the local banks, paying in money and wearing brightly polished shoes. People were talking to him then, and it had made me feel angry.

In the middle of the group was a younger man with a dog. The dog was always by his side and was a terror to the shoppers, snapping and barking at them as they passed. The man himself looked ill, though I had no idea if he actually was. He wore a dirty grey shirt and old jeans, tied at the waist by a piece of cord, and for some reason, I was a little afraid of him. I told myself that it was due to the dog.

As I watched, my mind turned to my own situation. I wondered which group I'd fit into. On the face of it, I should be chatting with friends and drinking latte, but that wasn't me. If I was honest, I didn't really like other people, and the idea of idle chat over coffee seemed horrendous. But neither was I the studious type either. I'd never been that. I'd done okay at university and had enjoyed myself too, but I would never have classed myself as a hard worker. It had seemed far too much trouble, and it still did. So that left me on the street, sitting in dirty clothes with a brown paper bag and a dog. No, definitely not that. Perhaps I just didn't fit in.

By the time the waiter came over, I was craving a coffee, so I ordered one, black. And even though I'd eaten breakfast less than an hour earlier, I also ordered two slices of toast and butter. I was feeling melancholy, something which always happened when I started to think about myself, the person who I'd hoped I would be, and the person I was. 'Beautiful People Beautiful Problems', or so the song went. It's easy to have problems, much harder to find solutions.

There was a commotion in the square outside, and I looked out to see someone arguing with the ill-looking man. He was pointing furiously at the dog, and at the same time indicating a tear in his trousers. I smiled as the homeless man shrugged and patted his dog. He really couldn't have cared less about the man's torn trousers. I thought that perhaps the angry man was going to hit him, but then the bearded man stood up, and he disappeared, the dog barking triumphantly as he retreated.

I finished my coffee and took a last bite from the toast. As I left the square, I watched as the two homeless men talked to each other, laughing as the dog spun around, its tail wagging furiously. For some reason, the whole thing made me happy, and my mind turned to the party that evening. I was quite looking forward to it now. Whistling to myself, I slowly walked back to my flat.

Potter's parties tended to be formal dress affairs, as quite a few of the firm's top brass would show up. The free drink and mountains of food never failed to draw in the crowds, attracted by the prospect of getting something for nothing. So it was that I took my dinner suit out of the cupboard, hung it on the door and set off for the bathroom. It was seven o'clock, and all I'd eaten that day was a small breakfast and the toast at the Piccolo. I wondered if I had enough willpower to wait until the party.

Twenty minutes later, I was sitting at the kitchen table in front of a large bowl of steaming spaghetti, pretty much the only thing I could make with any confidence. The aroma of spices filled my nostrils, and I ate with the abandon of a person accustomed to eating alone.

The party was due to start at eight-thirty. This allowed me a few minutes to shower before having to get ready. The telephone had been continuously ringing the last hour or so, but I knew that it was probably Henry, ringing to remind me of the party, or rather to remind me to go. I hadn't bothered to answer. When the phone rang again, I smiled and imagined the state Henry must be in, wondering whether or not I was going to turn up. It rang a few more times, then went dead. By the time I'd dried myself, shaved and cleaned my teeth, it was past eight o'clock. I was going to be late.

Moving into the living room, I put on some music. My music system was an ancient black plastic box given to me by an old girlfriend many years earlier, when such things were still referred to as 'music centres'. It was probably the only good thing to have come from the relationship. It had two cassette decks, but I only had one cassette, and that cassette was already in the machine. I pressed the play button and waited. The Pointer Sisters, 'I'm So Excited'. I played that song every time before going out, and it had become part of my preparations. Singing along to the chorus as I stood in front of the mirror, I fiddled with my bow tie, trying my best to get both sides the same length. In the end, I gave up. No one would notice, except Henry. Hair combed, jacket brushed, at last, everything was done. The doorbell rang, and the taxi driver shouted through the letterbox. I waited for a moment to give him time to get back to his car, then turned off the lights and made my way outside.

The taxi journey was going to take a while, so I sat back and watched the sights go by. I often thought of London as a far more beautiful place at night. Disraeli had once declared it the modern Babylon. That sounded pretty cool to me.

It was nine-twenty by the time I arrived. Nigel Potter's flat was situated on the top floor of a fashionable new apartment block, overlooking the river. He was an overtly ostentatious man, flaunting his wealth in a way that left many of us feeling uncomfortable. He described himself as 'big' which in reality meant 'fat'. Years of sitting at a desk, coupled with a vocal dislike for exercise, meant that his figure had grown at roughly the same rate as his wage packet. And while almost universally disliked, he considered himself irresistible. Money can make us believe the most outlandish of untruths.

I decided to walk up to the flat. Six floors. It was going to be stuffy, so I wanted to make the most of the fresh air while I still had the opportunity. The whitewashed stone staircase, spiralling the outside of the building afforded beautiful views of the City, so it was a slow climb, as I stopped at each floor to take in the night-time scenery. On the lower levels, I passed a handful colleagues, smoking and chatting, and we exchanged nods as I passed, but as I approached the sixth floor, I came across more and more people, sitting on the stairs, drinks in hand and already showing signs of drunkenness. Near the top of the stairs, leaning unsteadily against the wall was Graham, an athletically built marketing manager who had joined the firm at roughly the same time as me. He was on his own, staring blankly over the polished metal railings.

'Thomas, how are you?' he slurred. I smiled and shook his hand. Graham had been in my squash league several years earlier, before I gave up playing, and had beaten me easily every time we played. I recalled clearly how he'd gloated with each victory. He could probably have beaten me now, even in his current state, and the thought made me want to push him over the railings. I pictured him tumbling over and over into the night, as the hard car park rose up to greet him. Given his current state, however, there was a fair chance he'd topple over of his own accord, so I patted him on the back and wished him well.

A moment or so later, I found myself standing in front of a pale white door, the sound of music and laughter drifting from inside. Small scratches surrounded the keyhole, and there was a smell of vomit coming from somewhere nearby. I straightened my bow tie and gave the door four solid raps. It took a while before it was opened, but when it did, I found myself facing the bloated figure of my host.

'Here you are at last,' he spluttered. 'I wasn't sure if you could make it after yesterday. You looked awful.' When I said nothing, he waved his hand in the general direction of the party. 'Anyway, come in, there are a few people here who are keen to meet you.' I could sense the unspoken 'though I don't know why'. He smiled and patted me on the back, a little more forcefully than was necessary. Just to reinforce that he was the senior person here, in case I'd forgotten. With that, he disappeared, leaving me to brush a drop of spittle from my lapel.

I was about an hour late and the flat, though extremely large, was already full. I estimated there to be between ninety and a hundred people. Not bad considering there were only eighty people in the office. Many faces were immediately recognisable, though a few I'd never seen before. Most of the company directors were there, their plates piled high with food, and drinking generous measures of whiskey. With them were the middle managers, laughing loudly at every joke. Two of the foreign managers had also turned up: Dieter, from the German office, faithfully guarding his own portion of the room; and Paolo, from Milan, gesticulating wildly and laughing with two colleagues I didn't know. A friend had once told me that there are two types of Italians, those who wear Armani suits and drink expensive wine, and those who wear string vests and eat chillies. Paolo was drinking wine.

Before going in any further, I took the opportunity to have a look around. It really was a big place. The main living room was in the centre, off which, and overlooking it, sat a raised open plan kitchen and separate dining room. Doors to either side led to the bedrooms and at the back, through a large wall of glass, was the balcony, with its view over the Thames. I couldn't help but wonder how Potter could afford such a place. Surely he didn't make that much more than me. There were paintings along each wall, mostly abstract, and I noted with interest that there were no photographs. No pictures of his childhood, his family or indeed anything with which to shed a more personal light.

As I walked further into the room, I was greeted by several people I knew, though not well enough for comfortable conversation. This was the part of the evening I hated most, having to make polite small talk before finding an excuse to leave. In the distance, I caught sight of James, making his way unsteadily over, a glass of red wine in each hand.

'There you are,' he said. 'You're a bit late, aren't you?'

I apologised and took one of the drinks. It appeared that James had been here since the start and had been one of the first to arrive. As a result, he'd already consumed a fair amount of alcohol. Gulping down his drink, he took great pains to tell me he'd be taking it easy going forward. He then took hold of my arm and led me towards the other side of the room. 'Come with me,' he said. 'There's someone over here who's been waiting for you to come all night.'

We slowly made our way through the guests, eventually arriving at a large group of men gathered together in a tight semi-circle. Suddenly, from out of the group popped Henry, a flustered expression on his face.

'Are you okay, Henry?' I asked, a little concerned. 'You look like you've seen a ghost.' While James choked on his drink, Henry took a handkerchief from his jacket pocket and carefully mopped his brow.

'She'll be the death of me, I tell you!' he wailed. Seeing that

I didn't understand, he added: 'You've never seen anything like it, old boy!' He pointed back to the group before emptying the remainder of his large glass of wine.

Through the gap created by Henry's exit, I could clearly see Mary, and at once, I understood. Dressed in a blue summer dress and with her hair hanging loose about her shoulders, she was unrecognisable from the bookish persona she adopted at work. There was a confidence and an ease I hadn't seen before, and it hadn't gone unnoticed, judging by the number of young men surrounding her. At my side I could have sworn I heard Henry growling. James chuckled, draping a reassuring arm around his shoulder.

'God help me!' moaned Henry, as he emerged from his reverie. 'If only I could get all those arses away from her.' I said nothing. Suddenly, she looked over and smiled, and I was embarrassed at having been caught staring, but then she waved, and the men around her stopped talking, turning to see who was there.

'Perhaps someone should go and save her,' laughed James.

'Perhaps someone should,' I replied, and the three of us stepped forward.

Arriving at the group, we were met with half-hearted greetings, and it was clear that our company wasn't welcome. Nevertheless, it was equally clear that we were going nowhere.

'I believe you've acquainted yourselves with my assistant,' I said, to their evident surprise. 'Now, if you don't mind, I have some business to discuss with her.' The message was clear, and despite the odd grumble, the four of us soon found ourselves alone.

'You certainly seem to have made an impression on my colleagues,' I said. Mary smiled and shrugged her shoulders.

'Would you like a drink, Mary?' interrupted Henry. He then repeated the question to me. We thanked him, and he disappeared, James trailing behind unsteadily.

'I didn't think you were coming,' said Mary. 'I was thinking of going, but Henry kept saying that you'd be here any minute.'

'It's fortunate I came then,' I laughed. 'How are you enjoying yourself?'

'Well, it's been an experience,' she smiled. 'I've been stuck with Potter for the most part. And Henry.' Here she paused for a moment and looked at my jacket. 'Looks like you've been talking to Potter too,' she laughed. I looked down and noticed two spots of fluid on my lapel.

'Maybe they're Henry's,' I chuckled and brushed them off with a handkerchief. Potter's tended to be much larger anyway. We spoke generally for a while, and I asked her if she was bothered by all the attention she'd been getting. She replied that she wasn't. It had been a stupid question, and I wished I hadn't asked it. But, before I had time to say anything else, Henry returned, drinks in hand. He seemed quite worked up about something and wasted no time in blurting out the news. It was rumoured that Sir Ian Walker, the chairman of the company, would be turning up at the party, and though I replied that the same rumour circulated every year, he felt that this time it may be different. Potter and the other senior managers were extremely excited. If indeed it did turn out to be the case, I could understand the agitation, as Sir Ian rarely dirtied his hands on the rest of us. This, in itself, was enough for me to dislike him, or at least the idea of him, but the accompanying grovelling was something I could really do without. Mary seemed oblivious and watched on smiling, as all around us, our colleagues scuttled about like ants on a hot summer day.

'Should be interesting,' I laughed and took a drink.

It seemed as though half of the guests had disappeared to

check their appearance. Henry had vanished too. Alone, Mary and I talked and drank. It was the first time that I'd met her socially, and I was enjoying myself. We were both a little tipsy and enjoyed watching everyone scampering around.

'Is it really that important?' she asked. I replied that to some people it was.

We didn't have to wait long to discover the truth behind the rumour. After ten minutes or so, there was a knock at the door, and Potter wobbled off to open it. As he returned, a momentary hush enveloped the room. Following him, in place of the expected chairman, was a heavily drunk James. He'd been sick outside. One or two of the guests started to laugh, more out of relief than amusement, and I grinned, while Mary tried to cover a smile with her hand. Henry, wherever he was, would have disapproved greatly. Ten minutes later, there was another knock, but this time no one paid attention. Once again, Potter teetered over to the door. But before he reached it, in strode Sir Ian and his wife. In the corner, a glass shattered on the floor.

It was the first time I'd seen the chairman's wife, and it appeared that the rumours were true. She was really quite beautiful. Probably about the same age as me, so that would be about half Sir Ian's age. With her long black hair tied back tightly into a single ponytail, it made me think of a dominatrix, a thought which I tried quickly to get out of my head. Rather unsuccessfully, as it turned out. Her green eyes were both beautiful and piercing, shifting smoothly from face to face as she walked through the room. And around her slim waist was Sir Ian's meaty hand, guarding her carefully against the unwanted attention of his inferiors. An overly protective attitude which was well known throughout the company, so no one would have dared to approach her anyway.

The two of them had no sooner set foot in the room than

they were surrounded by London's finest. Potter himself was busy watering everyone in sight, and most of my peers were falling over themselves to get close. Mary playfully pushed me in their direction, and I steadfastly held my ground. I'd never been comfortable in such situations, so I decided to leave it to the others. And that's the way it stayed for the next half hour, Mary and me quietly chatting while the rest of the world howled with laughter at Sir Ian's anecdotes. The peace didn't last. As I was about to get another drink, out of the crowd popped Peter Carney, Head of Finance, who advised me to introduce myself to Sir Ian and his wife.

'No thank you,' I replied, though I knew it was pointless. Peter would hear nothing of it, and after further refusals, we took our leave of Mary and headed over. I looked back at her pleadingly as we disappeared across the thick patterned carpet, and she smiled then turned away. No sooner had I left, than she was once again engulfed by a tide of black dinner suits.

Though I felt like a prisoner being led to gallows, dragging my heels and trying desperately to think of an escape, I later realised that I was wrong. I was walking toward my future that night. And the meeting with Sir Ian was to change my life.

On my arrival, the group parted slightly. I was relatively junior to most of the people there, but they'd always treated me well and, at least openly, were quite friendly. I introduced myself to the chairman and his wife, and we talked for several minutes. I found out that his wife's name was Yasmine, which I'm sure most people knew already, though not me. She smiled at me, an intense sort of smile, which would usually have made me look away. Tonight, however, after a few drinks, I was in no mood to be intimidated. When Sir Ian finally stopped talking to a bald man by his side, he turned his attention to me, and it quickly became apparent why I'd been called over. Inwardly, at least, I let out a groan.

An executive from the New York office was coming to London on a short secondment. Around two months in total, which to me didn't seem short at all. You could do a lot in two months. My job was to show her the London operations and generally to help her settle in. In short, it was babysitting. My mind wandered to the times when I had babysat as a teenager, stealing in girlfriends and alcohol when the parents went out. Somehow, I doubted this would be the same. They dressed it up, of course, making it sound like a great opportunity, and another string to my bow, whatever that meant. But I didn't want another string to my bow. I wanted girlfriends and alcohol, and naive parents who paid me five pounds to get drunk. No, this wasn't going to be like that at all.

I could feel myself getting angry and fearing that I'd say something I may later regret, I searched for an opportunity to leave, excusing myself when one finally came. As I went, I noticed a look of surprise on the chairman's face, and one of amusement on his wife's.

Mary's admirers once again dispersed as I strolled up. She seemed pleased to see me. 'That was quick,' she said. 'I thought you'd be there all night. How was it?'

'Fine,' I shrugged before helping myself to another drink. Seeing the look on my face, she asked what was wrong.

'Oh, nothing,' I sighed. I didn't want to talk about it. 'Let's drink.'

We talked together for a couple more hours, at which point Mary said that she was tired and wanted to leave. I offered to escort her home, and she smiled, then refused my kind offer. After kissing me on the cheek, she left, so I headed for the balcony. I needed some air.

The party was now in full swing, and I was glad of some time to myself. I'd been talking to Mary for so long that things had pretty much passed me by. The balcony offered an attractive panorama of a large part of the City. In the distance was the NatWest Tower, the Lloyds Building and the Houses of Parliament. And there amongst them all was my old friend St. Paul's Cathedral, stark against the night sky. Illuminated by the moonlight, it rendered the neighbouring buildings dark and nondescript. It was magnificent, and I envied Potter that he could have such a view.

I wasn't sure how long it had been, but I suddenly found myself standing next to Henry. He was looking unsteady, and I wondered how he'd managed to creep up on me so quietly. In his right hand was a large glass of red wine and a cigar, and in his left a bottle of beer, which he offered to me.

'You look like you could do with this,' he said, before taking a huge drag from the cigar. A ball of white smoke drifted lazily into the air, before disappearing over the edge of the balcony and into the night. 'I take it your chat with the big man was not to your liking?'

His use of the term 'big man' made me laugh, so unusual did it sound coming from him, and this in turn made Henry laugh too.

'That's more like it,' he said, patting me on the shoulder. A length of ash tumbled from his cigar onto my suit. I brushed it off as he apologised, then I explained to him what had taken place. I filled him in on my upcoming assignment and how much it annoyed me, given that it was nothing to do with my role. He nodded sympathetically, which only made me feel worse. When I'd finished, he thought for a moment then patted me on the shoulder again, this time making sure that his cigar was in the other hand.

'You never know,' he said, trying to cheer me up. 'She

30

might be a looker!'

'Yeah,' I sighed, 'because that's how it works, isn't it?'

He shook his head sadly. It definitely didn't work like that. Unable to find any positives in the situation, Henry decided to head off in search of more wine. I told him that I'd join him soon.

After a few minutes and frequent deep breaths, I felt ready to go back to the party and was just about to go back inside, when I felt a gently restraining hand on my shoulder. I turned to see who it was. It was dark outside, and against the lighting of the flat, all I could see was a rough silhouette. A silhouette with a long ponytail.

'Lady Walker,' I said. 'This is a surprise.'

'Is it?' she replied with a smile. I glanced around the balcony, noting with discomfort that the two of us were entirely alone. It was not a good position to be in, given her husband's nature, so I decided to leave.

'Lady Walker...' I said, as I prepared to make my excuses.

'Please,' she said. 'Call me Yasmine.' As she moved into the light, dominatrix images unhelpfully flooded back.

'Yasmine,' I said. 'I don't wish to sound rude, but I was just about to go back inside for a drink.' With that, I shuffled along the balcony towards the door.

'I'm not going to bite you, Thomas,' she laughed. 'You looked a bit annoyed earlier, so I thought I'd come to see how you are. You were pretty keen to get away, to be honest.' She paused for a moment. 'I can't say I blame you. I always find these things a bit of a bore too.'

There was another pause, this time slightly longer, as she looked at me. My mind went back to the French film I'd watched with Sarah, and I pictured the young man with his boss's wife. Things hadn't ended well for him.

'Look, we're leaving soon,' she continued. 'We didn't get

the chance to tell you before, but we're having a welcoming party for your American colleague on Tuesday. I hope you can make it.' Before I had time to say anything, she moved away.

'Okay,' I said into the darkness, but she was already gone.

By the time I got back inside, Yasmine and Sir Ian had left. The whole room seemed to be breathing a sigh of relief. And as people congratulated themselves on their feats of ingratiation, I caught sight of James slumped in a chair by the door. The red wine stain on the front of his white shirt signalled that his night was over. I went over to him to ask if he was okay, but all I received was a nod and a few slurred words, which I couldn't make out. As I stood there unsure what to do with him, over came Henry, unsteadily weaving his way through the crowd, his route marked by wine-stained dinner jackets and dresses. He seemed to be looking for something.

'Where's Mary?' he asked immediately upon his arrival. Like James, his speech was slurred, but I was an expert at deciphering Henry's drunken ramblings.

'She left about half an hour ago,' I said. 'I don't think she felt too well.' He didn't seem at all pleased. He looked around for a while, as if not believing what I'd told him, then suddenly he tumbled to the floor. More stains on Potter's carpet, I thought happily, then helped him to his feet.

'I saw you talking to her,' he grinned, and I frowned, not sure who he was talking about. 'Lady Walker,' he added, tapping his nose several times with his index finger, as it were top secret information. I smiled at him, still tapping his nose, and I shrugged, as if to say there was nothing to tell. It felt odd looking at the state of him and James, and I was thankful that I'd taken it easy that night. Drunkenness seems far less attractive when you yourself are not drunk. I looked around the room, now only half full, and I could see that those who remained were much like my two friends. I turned back to Henry, to see if he wanted to leave, but when I did, I found him spread-eagled on Potter's sofa. And this time he didn't get up. His night was over too.

There wasn't much left for me at the party, now that Mary, James and Henry had effectively gone. So I finished my drink while surveying the devastation of Potter's flat, with its broken table and overturned chairs. On several of his large leather sofas, people were already sleeping, one of them snoring so loudly, that I wondered if he was ill. I decided it was time to go.

And so it was that I found myself in Potter's bedroom searching for my coat. The room was full of portable coat racks, making things much more complicated than I'd hoped. Empty boxes of wine and champagne littered the floor and I stumbled more than once before finding a coat which looked vaguely like mine. I checked the pockets for my keys and on finding them, headed for the door. But just as I was about to leave, a small noise came from the far corner, the sound of bottles clinking together, so I turned around and went over for a look. And there to my surprise, behind one of the coat racks was a young man, in his early twenties, busily filling his pockets with bottles of champagne.

'And what might you be doing?' I asked him calmly. It occurred to me that I sounded like an old man, and I wished I'd said something else. Something a little cooler.

Shaking uncontrollably, the young man emerged from the shadows, his movement hindered by the sheer number of bottles he had in his pockets. For some reason, I felt sorry for him, waddling over to me like a penguin in his dinner suit, and if I hadn't been so surprised, I would probably have burst out laughing. But I didn't laugh. He was stealing after all, albeit from Potter.

I'd expected him to come out with some sort of excuse, some reason to explain why it was okay to be in someone else's house, stealing their belongings. But he didn't, and I felt disappointed in him. Hadn't he prepared for the eventuality of being caught? Instead, he stood there in silence, and I wanted to shout at him.

'Perhaps you could explain what's going on,' I said, again wishing I didn't sound quite so old.

'There's not really too much I can say,' said the young man. 'I was trying to steal Potter's booze.' He looked at me defiantly, and I noticed that he'd stopped shaking. 'Everyone else is doing it,' he added, by way of validation.

'Everyone else is vomiting in his plant pots too,' I explained. 'Do you want to do that as well?'

He smiled at me and shook his head. My thoughts switched to Potter, remembering that he'd often complained of missing champagne after his parties. I'd always assumed he was making it up, and it was actually quite amusing to find out that he was being robbed. By his own colleagues.

I'd once again lost my train of thought, so for want of something to say, I asked him his name, and he replied that it was Leaf.

'You're joking, right?' I laughed. 'As in tea leaf?'

But he didn't laugh with me. 'It's from the Scandinavian name Leif,' he replied. 'My parents are from Norway.'

'Nor-way you're getting away with this then!' I said, but Leaf didn't so much as smile at my joke. I don't think Leaf had much of a sense of humour.

'I beg your pardon?' he asked, a look of genuine puzzlement on his face.

'Never mind,' I replied hurriedly. 'Anyway Leaf, why steal the champagne? It's not even that good.'

'Oh, no,' he replied. 'That's not why I do it. It's the possibility of being caught that's the fun.' He smiled at me then. 'You don't think I usually sweat this much, do you?'

I hadn't noticed that he was sweating, but now that he'd mentioned it, I couldn't help but see the damp patches across his chest and under his arms. That really is a lot of sweat, I thought to myself.

'It's exciting!' he continued, laughing nervously. 'And it's not too often that I get to do anything that is.'

'Stealing drink is exciting?' I asked.

'Not just drink,' he replied. 'And not just stealing. Anything risky.' He paused for a while, trying to gauge my expression. 'Of course, I don't expect to get caught, but that's always a risk.'

I stared at him blankly.

'What are you going to do?' asked Leaf, starting to shake once more. But I was miles away again, trying to understand what could be so exciting about stealing. We were all looking for excitement but was that really the best way? I decided I'd drunk too much to think about it.

'What are you going to do?' he asked again nervously, and my attention came back to him.

'Nothing,' I said and left the room.

Chapter 4

I woke up early the next morning feeling relatively fresh, though with a pressing need for some water. I was still feeling tired, but that wasn't uncommon for me. I always felt exhausted after waking up, even when I'd slept all day. I needed some time to come to.

After a few stretches and several yawns, I got out of bed and headed for the kitchen. Coffee normally helped. I turned on the tap and left it running, something which my father would have found hugely wasteful. I'd never really seen the problem. Surely the water just went back into the system, down the plughole, into the sewage, then a bit of cleaning and back into the tap. I'd also read that stationary water collected germs, so it was best to run the tap first. My father wouldn't have believed that either.

I turned on the radio and listened to some music. It was probably five minutes before I remembered the tap. No chance of there being any standing water, at least. Filling the kettle, just full enough for one cup, I turned it on then looked for a mug. My kettle was ancient, and there were small chunks of limescale floating around at the bottom. It wasn't very healthy, so I'd been looking at one of those new glass kettles, but they were still quite expensive. I'd wait until the price came down. I didn't mind spending a small fortune on alcohol and restaurants, but a few extra pounds on a healthier kettle seemed extravagant.

As the scent of coffee filled the room, the weatherman on the radio told me that it was going to be hot. I got to thinking about the events of the previous evening, specifically the role I was being asked to play with our American colleague. Last night I'd felt irritated, now I felt worse. I was going to have to spend weeks with another person, and I didn't even do that with my friends. I knew that if someone else had been picked, they would probably have taken it differently, but someone else hadn't been picked; I had. At that moment, I really disliked Sir Ian Walker. And what made it worse was the fact that there was nothing I could do about it. I decided that if Yasmine Walker showed me the slightest attention when we next met, I would flirt with her just to annoy him. It was all I could think of, and it was incredibly childish.

Then I went back to bed.

I was feeling tired again when I woke up, so I did a few more stretches. My mind returned to the night before, but this time I focussed on James and Henry. Then I started to smile. The state of them! No doubt they would be mortified on Monday. And I could only imagine how rotten they must be feeling.

As I was picturing them, I remembered the young champagne thief, and the things he'd said about excitement and taking risks. I did need some excitement in my life, but crime really wasn't the solution. I'd have to think of something else. Something more me.

I think I dozed off for a few minutes after that.

By the time I eventually got out of bed, it was early afternoon. My muscles had stiffened up, and I hobbled into the bathroom for a shower. I was normally what people referred to as a functional bather, that is, someone who has a shower to get clean, rather than to relax and enjoy the experience. But today, I stood there for a long time, hot water cascading over me, so that by the time I got out, the skin on my fingers was wrinkled, like a prune. I stared at my fingertips, wondering if this was how they'd look when I was old. If I got old. My current lifestyle didn't guarantee it.

Finally, I dried myself and got dressed, and before long, I was doing the household jobs I'd put off all week. The bins, some cleaning, the usual stuff. It wasn't something I liked doing, but it had to be done. And it took less than an hour, the beauty of living alone and in a small flat. Feeling pleased with myself, I sat down to indulge in one of my favourite pastimes, reading. As a student, I'd never found much time to read books, outside of those prescribed for the course, despite being blessed with a ridiculous amount of free time. Studying languages, there'd been the opportunity to read novels by foreign authors, but all those books had been required reading. Requirement always removes enjoyment. Today, I was a keen reader, and so I walked over to the window and picked up my book.

I spent the next few minutes staring out of the window, as my mind wandered, and the book remained closed. Across the street, in one of the newer flats, a young woman was doing some painting. She had short brown hair and was wearing dungarees. She obviously had some music on, because she kept stopping to dance, waving her paintbrush in the air, like a torch. The music from my radio must have been much slower than what she was listening to, and her moves appeared odd and out of rhythm. I wanted to laugh, as she threw back her head and sang, even though my own music had just finished. But just then, she noticed me and not knowing what to do, I smiled at her and waved. She smiled back and then covered her face with her hands as if she was embarrassed, but I bet she was thinking how creepy I was.

I then watched a middle-aged couple, travelling the length of the street in the direction of the shops, chatting away as they walked, hand in hand. The man was laughing at something his partner had said. He was dressed in a grey suit, and the woman wore an overcoat despite the heat. They seemed to be walking in slow motion. A couple of minutes later two teenagers appeared at the top of the street and very soon they'd caught up with the first couple. The teenagers, a boy and a girl, wore bright T-shirts and ripped jeans, and huge headphones rocked back and forth on their bobbing heads, in time to their music. As they arrived at the middle-aged couple, they slowed down, so as not to rush them and that made me smile, the four of them now merged into what could easily have been mistaken for a family. Then they turned the corner and disappeared, and it was as if the street had been empty all along.

At just turned four o'clock, Sarah burst through the door. Despite an initial annoyance at her abrupt entry, I was unable to stay angry for long. Her quirky smile always made sure of that. After asking her to shut the door, I put down the unopened book and invited her to sit down. She'd cut her hair, and it was now blue, and much shorter than before.

'Do you never lock the door?' she inquired, with a look of fake concern.

'I've never felt the need,' I laughed, looking at her hair more closely. She didn't seem to notice.

'Well, may I suggest that you do,' she said, throwing

herself dramatically onto the sofa. 'You may get burgled.'

'In an ideal world, that would never be a problem,' I replied.

'Well, I'm sorry to have to tell you this,' she smiled. 'But we don't live in an ideal world.'

'Unfortunately not,' I muttered and went to the kitchen to make a drink. When I returned, I sat next to her. She had adopted a sombre expression, and I sighed to myself. I knew what was coming.

'I've broken it off with Gerald,' she announced.

'Was it the hair?' I asked, and she looked confused.

'What?'

'Nothing,' I replied. So it wasn't the hair. 'Please. Carry on.'

'Well, he's getting worse,' she continued, totally ignoring what I'd said. 'He just doesn't take me seriously!'

I could feel the sides of my mouth beginning to twitch, so I scratched at my cheek, as though I had an itch. I didn't really like Gerald, but I did have some sympathy for him. Much as I loved Sarah, I imagined she would be incredibly hard to live with.

I listened attentively, at least initially, as she detailed the most recent example of his poor behaviour, all the while wondering how it must be for Gerald living with her day in day out. It would be tiring, trying to live up to her idea of the perfect relationship. Perhaps that's why I'd remained single. Just trying to look after myself had always been hard work. Add in someone else, and I wasn't sure I could cope.

Experience had taught me that Sarah would eventually wear herself out, and sure enough, after three-quarters of an hour, she appeared to have arrived at the summing up stage. Then finally, she finished.

'What do you think?' she asked. I was at a loss. I'd been

daydreaming for the final twenty minutes of what she was saying.

'I think it's a very complex situation,' I said thoughtfully. Sarah enjoyed being associated with anything complicated, and I was confident this was the best response. Smiling enthusiastically, she said that she agreed, it was indeed a very complex situation. I gave her a hug and told her that everything would be fine, then I headed into the kitchen for some drinks. I returned a couple of minutes later carrying two glasses of wine. Sarah took one of the glasses and drained it, promptly helping herself to the second glass. I went back for the bottle.

'Tell me about last night,' she said. 'Who was the lucky girl?'

She seemed disappointed when I told her that I'd returned on my own. For someone so keen on me settling down, she held an unhealthy interest in short-term relationships. I then explained the events of the evening, making sure not to miss anything, as she was a stickler for detail when it came to gossip. When I mentioned Sir Ian and Yasmine, Sarah's face took on a look of concern.

'I'd be careful about Yasmine Walker if I were you,' she warned. 'She's well known and carries a lot of clout.' She paused for a second, before flashing me a playful smile. 'And if you try anything there, it may well be more than your job that you lose if her husband finds out!' Not a very pleasant thought.

I then mentioned Leaf, though not what he'd been doing.

'Odd name,' I said. 'Leaf.'

'It's from the Scandinavian name Leif,' she replied.

'How do you know that?' I asked, wondering if it was only me who didn't know.

'I used to fancy Leif Garrett,' she said, smiling wistfully.

I'd never heard of him.

During the course of our conversation that evening, Sarah finished off the bottle of wine, while I stuck to one small glass. The more she drank, the more delving her questions became. From any other person it would have been intrusive and meddlesome, but with her, it was somehow different. She genuinely cared about me, and I cared about her, though we'd have been mortified to admit it to one another. In the past, I'd tended to brush off her more personal questions with a sarcastic comment or a joke, but for some reason, on this evening, I found myself answering. And answering with honesty. She listened intently, and when she was satisfied that I'd responded to all of her questions with sincerity, her conclusion was candid—I was an unhappy person.

And I laughed. But Sarah didn't.

'How on earth do you come to that conclusion, Sarah?' I asked, as she sat staring at the inky remains of her wine. She looked sad, as if what she'd said had brought about a truth that she didn't want to believe. I reassured her that I was fine, but she shook her head.

'No, Thomas, you're not.'

Of course, she was right.

The alarm went off at seven-thirty. I hadn't slept too well, and I made my way grumbling to the shower. I promised myself an early night soon, and after performing the usual ablutions, eating a bite of breakfast and drinking a strong cup of coffee, I set off. I didn't like Monday mornings, and today I liked them less than ever. My tube ride was the usual cacophony of noise, the carriage swaying while I squeezed myself into the corner. I closed my eyes and waited for it to end. Then finally, an hour later, I emerged through the cavernous doorway of the station, and headed into the bright early morning sunshine of London, to start yet another week.

During the journey, I'd become increasingly aware of the rumbling sounds emanating from my stomach, so I decided to break with my usual habit of avoiding the sandwich bars surrounding my office. Over the years, dozens had sprung up, along with coffee shops, transforming what had once been little more than a quiet thoroughfare to my office. Sights and sounds mixed effortlessly with the smell of roasted meats and the rich aromas of coffee.

I opted for Cafe Raffaele, for no other reason than I'd known someone by that name a few years previously. Joining the queue, I spent the next few minutes peering through the glass-fronted display at the vast assortment of sandwich fillings: cheese and mango chutney, tuna mayo, BBQ pulled chicken, goat's cheese and bacon. The choice was overwhelming. Whenever I was working over lunch and sandwiches were sent for, I'd always ordered prawn cocktail, on brown bread. Not because I liked it so much, but because I couldn't be bothered to think of anything else. However, as I'd made an effort to go into the shop myself that day, I decided it was time to try something new. Chicken, bacon and mushroom or prawn and avocado, spicy Mexican sausage or blue cheese and ham? I sighed inwardly.

'Prawn cocktail,' I said. 'On brown bread, please. And a coffee.' I just wanted to get out of there.

The lady at the till smiled at me, the sort of smile that is only produced by the prospect of money, and after a short calculation, she announced that I owed her eight pounds fifty. Even by London standards, that was extortionate. But not every battle is worth fighting, so I returned her smile and handed over the money.

As I left the shop, carrying a small sandwich bag in one hand and a cup of coffee in the other, I passed a colleague.

We nodded to each other, and I realised that I didn't know his name. It occurred to me that I knew very few of my colleagues by name, and I wondered if that was normal. In the end, I decided that it probably was.

By the time I reached the office, the heat from the coffee cup had started to burn my hand, and I regretted not using the protective sleeve that I'd been offered. I hurried past reception with the sandwich bag between my teeth, and as I waited by the lifts, I swapped the cup from one hand to the other.

The lobby by the lifts was starting to fill up, and it wasn't long before Paolo arrived, in his impeccably fitted suit. 'Beautiful woman,' he said, grinning broadly as he patted me on the back. I wasn't sure exactly who he was talking about, so I thought it best to say nothing. When the lift arrived, we both got in, and at the third floor Paolo got out. As the doors were closing, he turned to me and smiled once again. 'Beautiful woman,' he repeated, and with that, he was gone.

I liked Paolo, but his limited English did tend to be unnerving at times. Probably much better than my Italian though. I wondered whether the 'beautiful woman' was Mary or Yasmine. I hoped it was Mary.

The first thing I noticed on entering the office was that Mary wasn't at her desk, and that was unusual as she always arrived before me. I didn't get in particularly late, but Mary was always the first to arrive. I assumed that she found it easier to work when I wasn't around. Or Henry. I asked one of her friends where she was and was told that she'd gone to see HR, so would be in at around ten. I sighed and went to my room, aware that Mary's trip to personnel could only mean one thing - her move had come through. Soon she'd be gone, and I'd have to find my way around the filing system again. At least until her replacement arrived. I felt anxious at the prospect, as well as embarrassed by my lack of knowledge of the essential workings of my office. Wandering over to the window, I stood staring at the comings and goings outside.

One of the best things about my office, aside from the fact that it allowed me privacy from my colleagues, was that it afforded an excellent view of the street below. Recently I'd found myself at the window a lot, staring blankly outside, trying to pluck up enthusiasm for my work. This morning, even though I hadn't actually started any work, I was beginning to feel like I needed a break.

Being in the centre of the City, by far the most common people outside were office workers. From where I stood, they all looked the same, but every now and then, there would be a standout, someone strolling along lost in thought and oblivious to the world around them. Today was no different, as I spotted a young man in a light brown suit, with a rucksack on his back and thick glasses perched under a long droopy fringe. He was reading a book as he walked, and he seemed unaware of the mayhem around him. It was clear that his slow pace was annoying the other commuters and I decided that I liked him for that. Though too far away for me to make out what he was reading, he was clearly enjoying it, smiling to himself as he quickly turned the pages. When he reached a junction, he turned right and disappeared and was immediately replaced by a middle aged man in pinstripes, with an umbrella tucked under his arm. It was hot outside, even though it was early morning, and I wondered why the man needed an umbrella. He must have thought it looked impressive, but to me, he looked like a fool. Everyone was so busy creating an appearance. They weren't real people anymore, just caricatures of how they wished to be perceived.

I was about to go back to my desk when there was a knock at the door. Thinking it to be Mary, I quickly sat down and tried to look busy. But when the door opened, it was Henry and James who scuttled in. Although I invited them to sit down, they refused, bumbling out apologies for their conduct on Saturday night. I laughed and told them to forget about it. I didn't adhere to the belief that a person's true character came out when they were drunk. I thought they knew that. They'd seen me in a similar state on more than one occasion in the past. They both smiled, and Henry asked where Mary was. He received the same answer as I was given, and I was surprised to see what looked like a pout. It made his bottom lip look huge and bloated, and I wanted him to stop.

'Are you pouting Henry?' I asked, and James turned to look at him.

'Yes,' he replied simply.

'Oh, right,' I said, surprised by his admission. 'Well, can you stop? It looks weird.'

'Yes, please stop Henry,' implored James.

He smiled, and it was a relief when his regular face reappeared.

I asked them if they wanted to go for a coffee in the canteen. James refused, saying that he had too much work to do, which we both knew was a lie, but Henry said that he would. Taking my jacket off the back of my chair, I picked up my wallet, and we left.

As we passed a nearby bank of desks, I noticed Henry picking up a small pile of papers, which had been placed in a plastic tray for disposal. I asked him what he was doing, and he replied that having documents with us would make it look like we were discussing work-related matters, which made me laugh out loud. It also made me a little envious that I hadn't thought of something like that too. He'd always been better at playing the game than I had.

The canteen was a huge place by City standards. I recall how impressed I'd been on my first day, as I was shown around from one cuisine to the next. At the entrance to the sizeable marble-floored area was a sandwich bar, and next to that, a kiosk selling all kinds of salad. Further in was a circular booth making omelettes, while around the outside were concessions for Chinese and Indian food, burgers and wraps. If I were to be critical, I'd say that the choice was too much for me, and I often steered clear of it for that very reason. Just past the food area was a coffee stand, behind which stood Opi and Orlando, the baristas. They'd been there for as long as I could remember, and the good humour with which they carried out their roles put the rest of us to shame. Orlando had often joked to me that despite having no money, he was the most successful person in the building. He was happy, had a wonderful wife and two beautiful children. What more could he want? It was hard to disagree with him.

'Large coffee, please Opi,' I said as we reached the front of the queue.

'Free coffee day?' he asked with a chuckle.

'Oh, yes,' I replied, handing over my coffee card, complete with its full quota of stamps. We received a stamp on the card each time we bought a drink, and on the tenth, the drink would be free. I always purchased a medium-sized coffee, as that was enough for me, but on the free drink day, I felt obliged to ask for the largest available, even though it was too much. Henry had always mocked me for it, and today was no different.

'Tight-arse!' he said as he ordered his drink. I winked at Opi, and he smiled. Henry never used a coffee card, deeming it beneath him.

'Spit in his drink please Orlando!' I said, to which he nodded and made a gurgling noise, causing Henry to snatch his drink away quickly. As he did so, he managed to spill a small amount onto his hand, and I recalled my own coffee incident earlier that morning. I smiled and asked him if everything was all right, but he didn't reply.

Next to the coffee stand was a carpeted area, furnished with small round tables and large comfortable armchairs. Despite that fact that it was still relatively early, most of the tables were taken, so Henry and I wandered over to the far side, by the windows, and sat down. Outside, I could see it was going to be another hot day, the cloudless sky so bright that it was hard to look at. We were on the nineteenth floor, and the people on the streets below looked like tiny black ants, scurrying around in every direction. I watched them for a while as Henry shuffled the papers he'd brought with him, like someone preparing for an important meeting. At last, he put them down on the table and looked at me.

'Is everything all right, Thomas?' he said. He looked somewhere between concerned and confused. 'You were a bit quiet at Potter's do, and you didn't get half as plastered as normal. Is there something you want to talk about?'

I found it funny that my lack of drunkenness would be a cause for concern. Nevertheless, I told him that everything was fine. He was having none of it.

'Is it something to do with the conversation you had with the Walkers? I know that can be a bit heavy at times.'

It was clear that he had no recollection of our conversation on the night in question. I decided to tell him again anyway. And as I spoke, recounting to him how I'd been 'specially chosen' to babysit our American colleague, I realised just how irritated the whole thing still made me feel. It really wasn't that bad. I'd done worse jobs in the past, much worse, but for some reason this one seemed to annoy me more. I could see from Henry's face that he too didn't think it a big deal and when I finished, he just shrugged.

'That's it?' he asked. 'That's what's bothering you?' Of course, that wasn't all that was bothering me, but it had been the final straw. As always, Henry's solution was straightforward.

'Just get your own back,' he said. 'You're not a bad-looking chap. Not up to my standard, of course.' He actually believed what he was saying. 'When you get the chance, flirt a bit with his wife. From what I've heard, he won't be happy, but he's not going to sack you.' He paused for a moment to take a sip from his coffee. 'It might take your mind off things too.'

I could see that he was smiling and I could tell that he was pleased with himself. 'And you never know, this American might turn out to be better than you think.' He considered it for a while, then added: 'Probably not, though.'

It was such a ridiculously simplistic solution. But both Henry and I had now had the same idea. And maybe it would work. I thanked him and said that I'd think about it. At the very least, it would mean me taking a risk for once. Of sorts.

We finished our drinks and went back to the office, Henry nearly forgetting to pick up the papers he'd left on the table. The rest of the morning was uneventful, and I struggled to keep my mind on the mounds of work in front of me. By eleven o'clock, Mary still hadn't turned up, so I went to the door for the eighth or ninth time to see if she'd arrived. As with each of my earlier checks, her desk was empty. I was a little angry, as I didn't know where half the things I needed were kept, but my anger was more directed at myself than Mary. I should have been more knowledgeable about where everything was located in my own office. We never fully appreciate someone until we're about to lose them. Suddenly the phone rang, and I answered it. It was Yasmine Walker.

'Thomas,' she said. 'I've been trying to get in touch with your secretary all morning, but there's been no answer.'

'She's not in yet,' I answered, and I wondered why she was calling me.

'It's gone eleven. You should get rid of her,' she laughed.

It turned out the reason for her call was to give me directions to her house for the following day. I noted them down and said that I was looking forward to it, even though in reality, I wasn't. Company meals tended to be very dull affairs, with everyone trying to score points off each other. I'd never been into that sort of thing.

'I'm glad you can make it, Thomas,' she said after a while. 'Try not to be late.' I reassured her that I wouldn't, and with that, she hung up.

At two o'clock, Mary arrived, and she immediately came to see me. After apologising for being late, she stood in silence, so I offered her a seat, which she politely declined. At that moment, she looked so different from the woman who had confidently chatted at Potter's party, deftly handling her myriad of admirers. She was blushing slightly, and at her waist, her fingers fidgeted with a sheet of paper she was carrying. My earlier irritation disappeared, and I could see that I'd lost her. I couldn't think of anything to say, and she seemed to notice.

She smiled. 'You look like you could do with a coffee.'

'Thanks,' I replied. 'You can tell me about your meeting when you come back.'

'I will,' she said and left.

It wasn't long before Mary returned and closing the door behind her, she walked over and sat down, getting straight to the point.

'As you've probably guessed from my meeting this morning, I've been to see personnel. Well, it's today.' I was surprised by this, as I'd expected at least a week before she left. She must have seen my confusion. 'Don't worry,' she said with a smile, 'Jane, my replacement, will be in tomorrow. She knows how everything works.' Admittedly, this was a relief. At least the change-over would be smooth. However, I would still have preferred Mary to stay.

'Thank you for the coffee,' I said. It was, of course, not the right thing to say under the circumstances, but once again, I could think of nothing better. But she was used to my awkwardness, and I think she understood how I was feeling.

'I'd better go and start sorting my things out,' she said. 'There's a lot to do before I leave.' I nodded and thanked her again.

Now that I knew what was happening, I found it easier to concentrate on my work, and by six o'clock, everything had been cleared up. Picking up my jacket, I straightened my tie and left the room. Mary was still working at her desk.

'I don't go in for goodbyes much,' I said, and she smiled, understanding completely how I was feeling. We looked at each other for a moment, then she walked over and gave me a hug. I didn't expect to see her again.

'Goodbye, Mary,' I said at last.

'Goodbye, Thomas.'

And that was that.

There was a stiff breeze as I left the building, blowing directly into my face and pushing me backwards. It took much longer than usual to get to the station, but by the time I arrived, the wind had completely died away. I'm not sure how best to describe my feelings at that point in time. I'd been thinking about my situation for much of the afternoon, and I felt as though I'd come to a decision. But I didn't know what that decision was. Things were going to change, but I had no idea how.

My tube journey was the usual mix of unpleasant odour and stifling heat, and it was a relief when the doors finally opened at my station, the mass of commuters sweeping me out, like a piece of driftwood caught in the tide. A man wearing a light blue linen jacket and silver headphones bumped into me, apologised, then disappeared into the crowd. I instinctively checked my pocket for my wallet and finding it still there, I was saddened at how untrusting a decade in the capital had made me. I then checked my other pocket for my keys.

It was a five-minute walk from the station to my flat, but as it was a lovely evening, I chose to take a more roundabout route. There wasn't much waiting for me at home, so I decided to kill some time in the local music shop. It had been part of a large national chain until recently, when the parent company had gone bust. The majority of their shops had closed down, but this one had remained open, due to its location and relative profitability. Whether or not it was now running as an independent, I didn't know. Whatever had happened, the staff members were the same, a red-headed man in his twenties, with short-cropped hair and dark glasses, and a middle-aged woman who wore dark brown lipstick and thick eyeliner. She was very attractive and was one of the reasons I had far too many records and CDs in my flat.

As I entered the shop, only the man was there. He looked up from whatever he was doing and nodded to me politely. He was always polite. There were several people in one of the aisles by his desk, showing each other CDs and laughing as they chatted. I noticed that two of them were the teenagers I'd seen recently, walking down my street, with their huge headphones and bobbing heads. One of them glanced up for a moment, then went back to what she was doing, totally oblivious to my arrival.

The furthest aisle was home to all sorts of music, stacked alphabetically, though not by genre, as far as I could make out. I liked this area, as you could often find albums you hadn't thought about for a while and didn't even remember liking until you saw the cover. It was also home to a small shelf of vinyl records, many of them long since out of print. I'd started collecting them a couple of years ago, chiefly because I thought it was cool, but after realising I rarely played them, I'd gone back to CDs, which were easier. I thought they sounded better too, though I imagined the attractive woman would disagree.

I don't really remember much of what happened next, but I do recall reaching for a CD and putting it into my bag. It was a copy of Aladdin Sane, by David Bowie, which I already had at home. Apart from a pornographic magazine and a chocolate bar, which I'd stolen as a child, this was the closest I'd come to breaking the law. I hadn't even got a speeding ticket. I'm not even sure why I did it, but with that simple movement, my heart began to race, and I could feel myself starting to sweat. A lot. A minute later, I was walking out of the shop, bag clutched firmly in my right hand. One, two, three steps and I was outside, the warm air embracing me as I loosened the collar of my shirt. I waited for a few moments, then reached into my bag and pulled out the CD. There was David Bowie, his eyes closed, as if he couldn't bring himself to look at me.

As I stood there on the pavement, my breathing began to calm, and I looked back at the shop. The CD felt like a huge weight in my hand. What had got into me? I knew I was looking for excitement, but this? Half of me wanted to return it to the shop, hoping that no one would notice, but the other half was euphoric. I was feeling emotions, both good and bad, that I hadn't experienced for a very long time, if ever. And it felt great.

In the end, the decision was made for me.

'Excuse me, sir! Excuse me!' Running in my direction was the shop assistant. Euphoria gave way to nausea.

'Can I help you?' I said, trying to sound nonchalant. The assistant reached me, slightly out of breath and with a look of irritation on his face.

'I'm sorry, sir, but you seem to have left without paying for that CD.' I tried to look puzzled. 'In your right hand, sir,' he said helpfully. I slowly dropped my gaze, raising an eyebrow in surprise as it alighted upon the disc.

'Good lord!' I said. 'I'm so sorry. I had no idea.'

'It's okay,' smiled the young man. 'I often do that too. Here, I'll take it back.' I nodded apologetically, then frowned and handed it to him, at which point he returned to the shop. He was shaking his head as he left, though he was also smiling, as if he'd saved me from my stupidity. But he was too late.

Looking back, I can only assume that the assistant had believed my story. Otherwise, I would have been in a lot of trouble. This time at least, fortune was on my side. But I really should have thought it through before acting so impulsively. After all, that's what I always did.

I was still feeling ecstatic fifteen minutes later, as I stood at my front door fumbling to get my key into the lock. On the way back, the sky had become dark and cloudy, and I'd thought it was going to rain. But it hadn't rained, it had stayed dry, and very soon the clouds were gone, leaving the streets to bask in the late evening sunshine. And I felt alive. For the first time in years, I'd taken a risk, a real risk. And it felt good.

That night, as I lay on my bed, I replayed the scenario over and over in my mind. It was as though I was thinking of another person. Like when you see yourself in an old photograph, and you know that person is you, but it seems like a ghost. Only this time, it wasn't a ghost, it was me. The me who I wanted to be.

Chapter 5

I decided to take the next day off. I'd been working pretty much non-stop over the last few months, so had a large part of my annual holiday allowance still to take. It was late notice, but no one would complain, except perhaps Henry.

It was nine o'clock when I woke up and ten-thirty by the time I got out of bed. I was still thinking about the events of the day before as I headed into the kitchen to make myself a late breakfast. Or was it an early lunch? I had the whole day ahead of me, with very little to do, except make sure that my dinner suit was clean and my shirt ironed. I needed to be at the Walkers' party for around eight o'clock, so I would need to get a taxi at seven. It wouldn't take more than an hour to get to their house, leaving me plenty of time to do nothing.

The first thing I needed to do after breakfast was to take a shower. I'd perspired so much at the music store that I'd practically peeled the shirt off my back when I got home. The rest of the evening had gone by in a blur, and by the time I'd thought about getting a shower, it was already late, so I'd decided to wait.

During the shower, I planned my day ahead, soon realising that I was at a bit of a loss as to what to do. That often happened when I took a day off. With the whole day ahead of me, I could never think of anything to do. Today was just the same. I finished my shower and got dried, then as I was making a coffee, I decided that I'd listen to some music. Back in the living room, I smiled to myself as I searched through my catalogue of David Bowie albums. Aladdin Sane was the first one I came to. My music system whirred, and the CD drawer slowly opened. I skipped the first couple of tracks, then sat back to listen to 'Drive-In Saturday', one of my favourite songs, and my foot tapped against the coffee table, as I hummed contentedly into my coffee. I then listened to the rest of the album while my drink slowly got cold, quietly singing the lyrics to myself, or as close to the correct ones as I could remember. And when at last the album finished, and the room fell silent, I went over to the bookcase, and I searched the rest of my CDs, eventually returning with two more: Scary Monsters, which contained some of my favourite songs, and Diamond Dogs, which was absolutely my favourite album. Ever.

And that's how I passed several hours that day, happily listening to one album after another, remembering when and where I'd purchased them, and with whom, as I consumed vast amounts of coffee and very little food. Midday turned into two o'clock, then finally three, and as the last refrains of 'We Are the Dead' drifted off into the distance, I stood up and stretched. Now I was ready for anything.

It was at that moment, as I ambled aimlessly around my flat, searching for something to do, that I made the decision to do something I hadn't done for quite some time. Go to the gym. I had an ongoing membership at a gym less than five minutes from my flat, leaving me very few excuses for not going, but as time had passed, my membership had become increasingly less used, to the point where I was now not even sure where my gym kit was. Although I was by no means out of shape, a quick look at the photographs on my wall showed me there was perhaps some room for improvement.

The rucksack containing my gym kit was finally located under my bed, and as I pulled it out into the daylight, I was enveloped in a thick cloud of dust, causing me to cough. Carefully opening the bag, I peeked inside, hoping that I'd washed my kit after my last trip. Fortunately, and with some surprise, I found that I had. The protein bar lodged into one of my trainers didn't look good, so that would have to go. But apart from that, it was all neatly packed, with shirt and shorts folded and a clean towel rolled into a tube and wedged beneath the shoes. I found a lock in one of the pockets, and my membership card in another, and after a few moments of trying to convince myself that I'd forgotten something, I was finally ready to go.

Before leaving, I took a quick look in the fridge to see if there was anything to snack on, but finding nothing, I decided that I'd be fine. I could pick up something later.

Outside, unsurprisingly, it was still warm. The far side of the street, shrouded in shadows, was completely deserted, in stark contrast to my side, which bathed in sunshine. Small groups of people dotted the cracked grey pavement, strolling along in that lazy way we all do when it's hot, as though there is all the time in the world to get where we're going to. I'd only taken a few steps when I noticed my neighbour, Mr Jones, walking along the street towards me.

'Afternoon Mr Jones,' I said jovially as he approached, but Mr Jones was not a very friendly man, and he completely blanked me as he walked past. 'Miserable old sod,' I laughed, when I was sure he was out of earshot.

The entrance to the gym was surrounded by large plastic hoardings depicting groups of athletic people at various stages of exercise. Photographs of perspiring women in their tiny shorts and cropped tops were what had initially attracted me to the place. Those of muscular men, grinning as they lifted huge weights above their shoulders were what eventually put me off. The reality, of course, bore little resemblance to what was advertised.

Behind the desk, in what I supposed was the foyer, sat a tall man in a black T-shirt. Outwardly, at least, he epitomised the benefits of exercise and healthy living, but I'd seen him some weeks earlier, cigarette in hand, vomiting the remnants of a kebab and several pints of lager against the tube station wall. I smiled at him as I walked past, but he didn't look up.

Two large double doors opened automatically as I neared them, revealing a long passageway which led to the changing rooms. Thick carpet muffled my footsteps as I passed by a workout studio. In it was a large group of middle-aged men stretching and sweating in time to the instructions of a man wearing shorts which were far too small to be considered decent.

'Come on, guys!' he urged, clapping his hands loudly, and all around him, the group redoubled their efforts. I stopped and stared through the small glass window for a few moments, finding the whole thing strangely fascinating. One of the men, in a grey T-shirt too short to cover his belly, spotted me, and the look which passed between us left me in no doubt that my presence was not appreciated. I took that as my cue to leave.

Inside the changing room, I placed my rucksack on the furthest peg and began to decant my kit onto the wooden bench below. The large room was empty, though a strong smell of aftershave hung heavily in the air. Around the outside were dozens of lockers, many with small padlocks hanging from their handles, and across the floor were small patches of talcum powder. As I was about to get undressed, in walked Arno, a South African man in his early sixties, who I'd got talking to when I'd first joined. He was a pleasant guy, and despite living in London for over thirty years, had never lost his strong regional accent. Unfortunately, he had a habit of walking around the changing room naked, something which I wasn't comfortable with, his sagging flesh providing a glimpse into a future I wasn't ready to see.

Seeing me, Arno waved and said hello, after which he began to undress. More haste, less speed is the saying, but on this occasion, I combined both, and a few moments later I was making my way out of the changing room and down the glass staircase to the gym itself. I'd always found it odd that the staircase was made of glass, or perhaps some form of Perspex. The slightest amount of sweat, and it became slippery, almost dangerous. Carpet would have been better, or maybe wood.

It was half past four by the time I eventually got into the gym. Just standing there amongst the multitude of machines and treadmills, I was already beginning to feel fitter, so I made my way over to a treadmill and placed my rolled-up towel into the cup holder. I carefully checked that it wouldn't fall out as soon as I started running. There were two other men there, one on either side of me and in front was a broad carpeted pathway which led from the exercise mats to the free weights area. I estimated that there were about fifty people in the gym, which was a lot for that time of the day, and this meant that the treadmills were an excellent place from which to watch over the entire gym, helping to pass the time while I ran. Which was just as well, as I'd forgotten to bring any music with me.

I opted for a 'free run', mainly because I couldn't remember how to program any of the set runs into the treadmill's console. Then I set off. After twenty minutes, I was feeling very pleased with myself, and I toyed with the idea of increasing the pace to a more challenging level. But just then, a large door at the far side of the room opened, signalling the end of the afternoon spin class, and out poured a dozen or so women, their Lycra-clad bodies glistening with perspiration. Very soon, they were crossing the open area in front of the treadmills, chatting happily as they made their way to the exercise mats. Treadmill motors whirred as each of the runners, including myself, increased their speed, vainly attempting to look fitter than we were. And when two of the women stopped in front of us to exchange phone numbers, there followed an uncomfortable few minutes, as we rapidly began to tire. When they had finally passed, we slowed down, and the man next to me started to laugh.

'Pathetic, isn't it?' he said, turning to look at me. I saw that it was Arno, mercifully clothed, and I smiled back at him, too tired to talk.

The remainder of my run took place at a sedentary pace, and after a much shorter distance than I'd intended, I'd had enough. Arno had left by this stage, and the rest of the treadmills were fast becoming free. It was usually around this point that I would give up and go for a shower, but today I decided to try something else before I left. In the corner were a few stationary bikes, so I headed over and hung my towel on the handlebars of what looked like the newest one. I was surprised at how wobbly my legs were feeling, and I rubbed at my thighs. What that actually did, I had no idea, but I'd seen a few people doing it before, so I assumed it did something. Pretty soon, my forearms were aching too.

It took a few minutes to set up the bike, but in the end, I was ready to go. In this area, the music playing through the speakers was louder, and that felt much better. Without music, I'd always found the bikes to be very dull. I can't really say I pushed myself too hard that day, but at least after the treadmill, it was a good wind down. As I was about to finish, one of the personal trainers came over to ask me if I needed any help. I couldn't imagine what kind of advice I would need on a bike, but I politely told him that I was okay. I recognised him from my previous visits, and when he referred to me by my name, I tried to remember what he was called. It was either Ron or Roy, and it was frustrating that I couldn't recall which. He'd told me his name on numerous occasions before. In the end, I settled on Ron, and from his reaction, I knew that I'd made the right choice.

By six o'clock, I'd finished showering and was about to leave, when I suddenly remembered that I hadn't yet checked my dinner suit and shirt and hadn't even booked a taxi. So, stuffing my gym kit into my bag, I hurried out of the changing room and made my way back into the foyer. The tall man in the black T-shirt was still there, and as I passed him, I caught the faint whiff of cigarettes. That, in turn, made me think about kebabs, and suddenly I realised I was starving.

Back at my flat, I opened the sandwich I'd bought on my way back from the gym. It was cheese and ham, and it had been advertised as 'deep filled'. In reality, the deep filling only related to the bits which were visible through the packaging. Most of the sandwich was just bread. I ate it anyway.

It was now six-thirty, so I had to hurry if I was going to make sure everything was prepared for the evening. The first thing to do was to check my suit for any marks or splashes from Saturday night. It wouldn't be the first time I'd gone out in a suit showing stains from its last outing. Fortunately, this time, everything was fine, so I grabbed a shirt and made my way to the ironing board. Despite many years of practice, I'd never got the hang of ironing a shirt, and the finished item would usually be as creased as when I'd started. As one crease disappeared, another would take its place. Today was no different, and eventually, I gave it up as a bad job. It would be hidden under my suit jacket anyway.

Next, I ordered a taxi. One of the nice things about living where I did was that there were always lots of taxis on hand. I spent a lot of money on taxis. My local firm was called Roadrunner, and the lady who answered, Marjorie, recognised me by voice. She told me that they were very busy, but for me, she would get one as soon as possible. And though I knew she said that to everyone, I liked it when she said it to me. If only everyone was as polite as Marjorie. Derek would be with me at eight o'clock, she said, and I smiled. Derek sounded like a reliable sort of chap.

All that was left was to have a shave and get dressed. And those were two things I could do without any problems.

By eight o'clock, I was ready. By eight-thirty, I was chatting away to Derek. And by eight forty-five, I was on a long driveway approaching my destination. I'd be fifteen minutes late, but no one would mind. Judging by the length of the drive, it would take two or three minutes more before I got to the house. So that would be twenty minutes late.

As we drove, dense woodland surrounded us on either side, so dark that Derek had to turn his headlights on to full. The trees formed a huge natural tunnel, and I mentioned to Derek that it wouldn't be a good place to break down. He shook his head and warned me not to tempt fate. When I looked across at him, I could see that he was squinting, so I asked him if he should be wearing glasses.

'Yes,' he replied. 'I can hardly see a thing!'

Which didn't fill me with confidence.

Soon we were driving through gardens, their neat order a stark contrast to the randomness of the woods. And a little further ahead was the house, three rows of windows at the front, and in the centre, an enormous oak door. There were several large and expensive-looking cars parked in the gravelled area in front of the house, and Derek's poor banger looked sorely out of place. He muttered something, then gently patted the plastic steering wheel.

Getting out, I thanked Derek and handed him the fare, before making one last check of my appearance in the mirror. As I walked the last few metres to the door, the crunch of gravel underfoot sounded loud and harsh, and I looked down to see if any dust was getting onto my shoes. On reaching the house, I took a step back to look at the door. It was even bigger close-up, and I wondered how big the original occupants must have been, to have needed such a massive doorway. I rang the doorbell, then stood silently, waiting for an answer. Inside, I heard the sound of a gong, perhaps from the doorbell, though I couldn't be sure. I pictured the bare-chested Gongman from Rank films, and I started to giggle. No matter how hard I tried, I couldn't get the picture out of my head.

I wanted to press the doorbell again, just to make sure, but soon footsteps could be heard approaching the door, and the opportunity was gone. It opened, and a small, elderly looking gentleman appeared. He looked like a butler, but I wasn't sure if they were still a thing. When I announced that I'd come to see Sir Ian Walker, the old man smiled.

'Senior or Junior?' he asked.

'I beg your pardon?' I replied, and he beamed happily as I considered my answer.

'Senior,' I said, taking a guess.

'Well, that will be me,' he laughed.

And I didn't really know what to say.

It was something of a relief when a gentle hand took hold of his arm and directed him towards an old woman, standing at the top of the stairs.

'Come up here, Ian!' she laughed. 'And leave the young man alone.' Chuckling to himself, he went to join her, and as they disappeared into a room, I could hear them both laughing.

As it turned out, the gentle hand was accompanied by an equally gentle arm. Both of which were attached to a very beautiful Yasmine.

As I was apologising for my lateness, Yasmine started to smile. She shook her head, told me not to be silly and took hold of my arm.

'I was afraid you wouldn't make it,' she said. 'You're the last one to arrive. I should have guessed as much.'

We strolled through the entrance hall, its high ceilings and magnificent chandeliers looming overhead while she pointed out some of the paintings hanging on the walls. Portraits of Sir Ian's ancestors took pride of place. I nodded appreciatively, though they struck me as rather an ugly looking lot. Yasmine barely even looked at them. At the far end stood a strange-looking ornament, several feet tall and resembling a tree. She made no comment as we passed it, and I didn't ask.

The house was large enough for it to take several minutes to reach our destination.

'Well, they're all in here,' she said as we reached a dark wooden door, its handle polished so brightly that I could see my reflection in it. It made me look as though I had a huge head. I pointed it out to Yasmine, and she giggled.

'Stop stalling,' she laughed as she opened the door.

As we entered the room, there was a momentary hush, and I immediately noticed a few familiar faces. There were about a dozen people there, most of whom were my level at the company, though a couple of senior directors and, of course, the chairman were also present. Yasmine showed me to my seat, then joined her husband. Everyone was seated around a rectangular table, large enough that those at the end had to lean over to see their host. It was laid out ready for a meal, and I was pleased to find that I was sitting opposite Yasmine. Unfortunately, this also meant that I was opposite Sir Ian. Junior. Judging from the expressions as I had entered the room, several of the guests were surprised to be dining with me. Nor did they seem especially pleased. Next to Sir Ian was the only empty seat at the table. This was reserved for my American.

As for myself, I was placed next to Rodney Marshall, a good friend of mine, who was forthright in his opinions, and told things exactly how he saw them. I enjoyed his dry sense of humour, and we'd often shared a drink at the various company functions we'd been dragged into. I noticed he was looking at me.

'Nervous?' he asked, smiling.

'About what Rodney?' I replied, and he laughed.

'Your babysitting duties, of course. Pretty much everyone here's relieved it wasn't them chosen. And one or two seem pretty sure who it's going to be.'

He had my attention now.

'Well?' I asked.

'Slow down horse,' he laughed. 'You'll just have to wait and see.' He paused for a moment, for maximum effect, before continuing. 'Have you ever seen Mrs Doubtfire?'

'Oh, for Christ's sake!'

This was going to be a long evening.

Rodney chuckled, and he patted me on the back. 'Don't worry, they've no more idea than the rest of us. Do you think Walker lets anyone know what's happening, let alone us lot?'

So, there was still hope.

After a few minutes of idle chat, during which Rodney filled me in on some of the rumours going around, there was a call for silence, and Sir Ian stood up.

'You will have to excuse the wait, my friends, but we will also be joined by a colleague from the across the water this evening,' he announced.

A murmur went around the table, and several of the guests turned in my direction, smug smiles on their faces. I did my best to ignore them. The only thing I could think about was Robin Williams, dressed as an old woman. At that moment, I really didn't want to be there. 'As with most women,' he went on, 'she tends to spend rather longer than necessary getting ready.' Everyone laughed, apart from myself and Rodney.

Looking across the table, I noticed that Yasmine wasn't laughing either. Years of listening to such 'jokes' must have taken its toll, and I couldn't help feeling a little sorry for her. However, before I could think on it any further, a second bout of laughter signalled the passing of another joke from the chairman. I forced myself to pay attention to what was going on. It seemed that he was making small talk until the arrival of the American, reeling off anecdotes about people I'd never heard of and places I'd never been to. Of which there were a lot. It struck me that I was the youngest person in the room, by quite a margin, with the notable exception of Yasmine. I felt like I didn't belong there. I was an imposter, and a part of me wanted to run away.

Suddenly, Sir Ian stopped talking, and the door opened. Then, as everyone stood up, in she walked.

And from that moment, my life would never be the same

again.

Many years ago, my grandmother had told me not to stare, and despite my better judgement, I followed her advice. Instead, I looked around the table at the rapidly transformed expressions of my colleagues. Gone were the gleeful looks, the pleasurable anticipation of my impending adversity. Now I saw anger, and on one face something akin to nausea. The woman before us was no caricature of middle-aged decline, no butterball hellbent on making my working life hell. No, here was what I could only describe as a beautiful woman. It's a simple description, and in many ways it doesn't suffice, but as I sat there, finally giving in to my desire to stare, it was the word which struck me as the most appropriate—beautiful.

And as she moved to her place at the table, her blond hair brushing against the thin shoulder straps of her red dress, I felt a hand gently patting me on the back. It was Rodney.

'Lucky sod!' he laughed under his breath. 'Doubtfire my arse!'

With everyone finally seated, I found myself facing three quite different creatures. To the right sat Yasmine, elegant and refined and to the left was my American, stunning and cool. In between, sat Sir Ian, pompous and fat.

'Well, we may begin,' bellowed the host at last. All eyes moved to him. 'But first, let me introduce you to Ellen. I'm sure you'll all agree, we're lucky to have her.' The two women looked away, as the rest of the table murmured their agreement. And so, the introductions began, as one by one, Ellen was introduced to the guests. I glanced across at Yasmine. She was looking directly at me, and I wished I hadn't ogled with the rest of them. She smiled and shook her head, like a mother admonishing her child, and as I waited for her to look away, I heard my name mentioned. It was my turn.

'And this my dear, is Thomas, one of our younger managers.' Sir Ian halted for a moment before continuing. 'Thomas will be looking after you during your stay in England.'

'Hi, Thomas,' she smiled. 'It's nice to meet you at last.'

I smiled in reply. Henry was going to have a heart attack.

Half an hour later, we were about to start on dessert. The meal had been marvellous, and I sat there in a state of extreme contentment. Everyone seemed in agreement, and if I'd been alone, I would quite happily have taken a nap. The frantic conversations of earlier in the evening had given way to friendly chat, the gentleman two down from me going so far as to congratulate me on my forthcoming role with Ellen.

Unfortunately, our host had different ideas. I'd realised quite soon that he liked to play games with people, introducing topics, then sitting back to listen. He had very little interest in what we all thought. He just liked to see an argument. The subject of the homeless in London was introduced, and at once, everyone listened, eager to hear his opinion. They would make up their minds once he'd spoken. I was still drowsy after all the food, so I chose not to get involved.

'I think it's a regrettable situation,' declared Sir Ian, and everyone agreed. These were the same people who walked past the homeless every day, as if they didn't exist. And as profound statements flowed one after another, washing over me like a relaxing breeze, it was all I could do to stay awake. Someone mentioned charity, and the work we should all be doing to help out, but by this stage, I was no longer listening. It was just noise.

'And what about you, Thomas?' said Yasmine, snapping me back to attention. 'Do you have no opinions on the subject?'

It was the first time she'd spoken since the start of the meal. Had it been anybody else, I'd probably have shrugged and followed the consensus. But it was Yasmine, so I thought I'd try the truth for once.

'It doesn't really bother me, to be honest,' I said. 'I give money, but that's it. I don't think about it too much.'

A chorus of gasps rose from around the table, and I wished that I'd kept quiet. Apparently, honesty isn't always the best policy.

'But you must care, Thomas,' said Ellen, looking unimpressed, as though she was about to be tethered to a monster.

'I agree,' I said. 'I should care. I know I should. But I'm not going to lie to you.' The silence was uncomfortable, and I decided to shut up. Yasmine must have thought me a monster too. I looked over to her, but once again, I was surprised. She was looking at Ellen, and I could have sworn that they were smiling.

Or were they frowning? It was hard to tell. Either way, in future I would be less forthcoming with my honesty.

Conversation soon got back to normal, and as the table was being cleared, the guests were ushered into the living room, a room at least the size of my entire flat. Around the walls were more portraits and in the far corner yet another ornament, much like the tree-thing I'd seen earlier. I looked at it for a while, trying once more to figure out what it was, but in the end, I gave up. It was obviously meant for more sophisticated eyes than mine.

By this stage, everyone was in a good mood. Several of my colleagues came over to ask me what I had planned for my two months with Ellen. I replied honestly that I hadn't given it much thought. I'd been so preoccupied with feeling hard done by, that it hadn't occurred to me that I should plan something. But that was for another day. For now, I had to pretend to be interested in work. It was called networking apparently, and I wasn't very good at it. Neither was Rodney, as it turned out, so it wasn't long before we found ourselves together on the far side of the room, far away from the others. I asked him what he thought of the ornament.

'Pretentious,' he replied, and I laughed. He then asked me what I thought of the paintings.

'Ugly,' I said. We were both still laughing when Yasmine came over. Rodney wished me luck, then disappeared.

'He was in a hurry,' laughed Yasmine once we were alone. 'We're not monsters, you know.' I looked at her, with her long dark hair and exquisite features, and I thought that she looked sad. I was about to ask her if everything was okay, when suddenly she smiled. 'Your performance at dinner took my husband quite by surprise,' she said. 'He's not used to people refusing to play his games.'

'I'm not very good at playing games,' I said. 'I'd rather you hadn't asked me to join in.'

'I know,' she smiled. 'But you looked half asleep.'

I hadn't realised it was so obvious. Regardless, she didn't appear offended. I explained to her that I often felt sleepy after a meal, then immediately felt stupid for saying so. It wasn't the most interesting thing to say, and I hoped that for some reason she hadn't been listening. I assured her that it was nothing to do with the company.

'Well, I'd be disappointed if you had found the company interesting,' she said candidly. 'It's nice to hear people say what they really think once in a while.'

As we were talking, over strolled Sir Ian, accompanied by Ellen, and followed by the vast majority of the other guests.

'And what are you two planning?' he asked with a smile,

though it didn't look friendly. He placed his arm protectively around Yasmine's waist, as if I were contagious in some way.

'Lady Walker was just talking about your portrait collection in the hall,' I said calmly. 'I was very impressed with what I saw on the way in. It would be nice to see the rest of it.' Sir Ian was, without a doubt, an arrogant man, and arrogant men are invariably vain. Flattery was almost always the best approach. And it seemed to work.

'I'm glad you think so,' he said, his ego well massaged. At his side, Yasmine smiled at me approvingly. 'I'm sure my wife will show you the rest of it later.'

Before I had the chance to say anything further, I was reintroduced to Ellen. And as we chatted, Sir Ian suggested to his wife that she show the other guests around his portrait collection. It appeared his vanity was even greater than his jealousy.

'So,' he asked after a while, 'what do you have planned for our new arrival?'

I explained that I wasn't in the office the next day and that the day after, I was on business in Leeds until the weekend.

'So, I'm afraid everything may have to wait until next week,' I said.

'Nonsense,' he replied. 'I'm sure Ellen wouldn't mind accompanying you to Leeds.' Decision made. And I had no say in it. With that, he excused himself, leaving the two of us to get acquainted. Yasmine hung back for a moment, then turned to Ellen, with a smile.

'Apparently, Thomas often feels tired after a meal?' she said.

'Oh, really,' laughed Ellen. 'You must tell me about that sometime, Thomas.'

After Yasmine had disappeared to show the other guests around, Ellen and I were left on our own. Ordinarily I would find such a situation uncomfortable, but on this occasion it was fine. For the most part, Ellen talked, and I listened. I liked it that way.

'You don't mind me tagging along, do you?' she asked, after we'd talked for a few minutes. I replied that I didn't, though, in reality, I would have preferred to go alone. Ellen seemed nice, and plenty of fun, but I still didn't know her. First impressions are often deceptive. Regardless, there wasn't much I could do about it now.

I'd never really been one for small talk, so for want of something to say I asked Ellen if she wanted a drink. Alcohol is often my go-to in such situations.

'Yes, please,' she replied. 'I'll come with you.'

We moved over to the other side of the room, where the drinks table was located. It was quieter there, and that made it easier to talk.

'Do you think we can cut all the preliminary bullshit, Thomas?' asked Ellen as we reached the table. The way she said it was very matter of fact, and I quite liked that. I nodded and poured us both a drink. 'I'm sure you'd rather not have me trailing around after you,' she continued, 'but you never know, it might be fun.'

I smiled and offered a toast. To fun.

'I was afraid you'd be a bit of a taskmaster,' I admitted, and she laughed. It was a nice sound.

'Well, I've been called a lot of things in my time, but never a taskmaster!' she said, taking a sip from her drink. 'Maybe I'll give it a try.'

I asked her not to.

For a while, we chatted about nothing in particular. Ellen asked me what I did with myself when I wasn't at work, and I tried my best to make my life sound exciting. But my life wasn't exciting, so it was a hard sell. The most interesting thing I'd done recently was my failed attempt at shoplifting, but I decided not to mention that. To change the topic, I asked her if she knew the Walkers well, and she replied that she knew Yasmine very well. Sir Ian, not so much.

'What do you think of them?' she asked. It was a very direct question, and I wasn't too sure how to answer.

'They're okay,' I replied, which wasn't much of an answer at all.

'Sure,' laughed Ellen. 'That'll do. Well, if it's any help, I like Yasmine a lot. She's great. Very intelligent and kind.' She smiled at me from over the rim of her glass. 'I can see you're trying to flirt with her.' She let out a little giggle. 'You're not very good at it, by the way.'

I shrugged. There wasn't much to say to that.

'What about Sir Ian?' I asked.

She thought about it for a while, then shrugged. 'She's way too good for him. He's a dinosaur. And not one of the cute ones.'

I couldn't immediately think of any cute dinosaurs, but it was clear what she meant. I found her honesty quite refreshing. Maybe our two months wouldn't be such hard work after all.

As it transpired, Ellen would be renting a flat for her time in England. Or rather, the company would be renting it for her. It wasn't too far from where I lived, and I wasn't sure if that was a good or a bad thing. She'd be staying with the Walkers for a few days until it was ready.

'So, where should I pick you up on Thursday?' I asked. 'I'll be driving to Leeds. We've got Friday and Saturday there.'

'I suppose it'll have to be from here,' she said, a conspiratorial look on her face. 'That's a shame, isn't it!'

'Yes,' I replied.

Ellen and I talked together for a long time that evening,

and I soon discovered that she had a very dry sense of humour. It was very British in many respects, and she laughed at my jokes. It's always good when someone laughs at your jokes.

I'm not sure how long we talked for, but suddenly Yasmine appeared, having just finished another of her portrait tours. She didn't look very happy.

'Well Thomas, it looks like it's your turn,' she said with a smile, though it looked forced. Ellen left to talk to the other guests, and I could see a smile on her face too as she disappeared. That one didn't look forced.

'Yasmine, there's really no need to show me around,' I said. 'To be honest, I'm not that interested in your husband's pictures.'

'I know,' she said. 'But I want to show you.'

As we made our way through the house, Sir Ian's ancestors following our every step, I was happy, and that was something at least. The evening wasn't turning out to be anywhere near as bad as I'd expected. Ellen was fun, and I seemed to be getting on well with Yasmine. I may have been reading too much into it, but I got the impression she was enjoying my company. Perhaps I was wrong, but I didn't think so. For some reason, I thought of Henry and the advice he'd given me about being flirtatious. I'd made a start, and we all have to start somewhere.

The chairman's ancestors were a remarkable looking lot, almost identical apart from their clothes. I suspected something sinister but kept my thoughts to myself.

At last, we came to the end of a corridor, punctuated by a large oak door with a huge brass doorknob, the size of a fist. The door seemed out of place in its ornate surroundings, and I wanted to see what was behind it. I asked Yasmine if it was possible to go in, but she said that it was her own private room and not even her husband was allowed in. He'd be furious if he found out someone else had been inside.

'All the more reason for letting me in,' I laughed, at once wishing I'd kept my mouth shut. Not for the first time.

'Do you always get what you want?' she said playfully, at the same time sliding an old key into the lock. It rattled tunefully as she moved it first one way, then the other. Then click.

'Rarely,' I said, with absolute honesty. More often than not, I didn't get what I wanted, and when I did, it didn't turn out to be what I'd expected. And here was another such case. The door opened silently, and I was ushered inside. Next Yasmine shut the door and locked it with a sturdy-looking bolt. I wondered why she used a bolt, when she also had the key, but I guessed she had her reasons.

The room itself was a book lover's paradise. It was small, with a low ceiling and polished wooden floorboards. An old faded carpet lay before a large open fire, and above the fire hung a photograph. It showed a woman in her forties with a young child, and I knew at once who it was. Yasmine saw me looking at it, and she smiled, but said nothing. In the centre of the room was a writing desk with a reading lamp perched on the edge, and all around, bookcases clung to the walls like ivy. At no place in the room was there anything relating to her husband. In that room, Sir Ian didn't exist.

'So, you like to read?' I asked, adding to my growing list of awkward statements.

'Whenever I can,' she replied quickly, perhaps sensing my embarrassment. 'Do you?'

I told her that I did, which was true, but that I rarely found the time, which was a lie.

'We never seem to have time to do the things we really enjoy,' she said wistfully, an observation to herself, rather than for my benefit.

'So, your husband doesn't share your passion for literature?' I asked, gently prying into their relationship. She let out a sigh, replying that if it didn't involve money, then Sir Ian wasn't interested. She may have made peace with that fact, but I could see that it pained her.

Walking over to the desk, I noticed a large leather-bound book lying open on a small table beside the fire. Its pages had yellowed with age, but I recognised the text immediately.

'You're a fan of Catullus?' I said, finally finding a reason to be happy about my Latin lessons at school.

'There are a lot of things you don't know about me, Thomas,' she replied simply. 'I've liked Catullus for a long time.'

I wordlessly thanked Dr Singleton, my old Latin teacher. Catullus had written of his love for an unattainable married woman, and I still remembered one of his poems.

'Odi et amo. Quare id faciam, fortasse requiris.' I was feeling very pleased with myself, as I quoted the poem from memory. At least until I realised that I'd forgotten the second part, which was a bit of a problem. But then Yasmine took over, and I was saved.

'Nescio, sed fieri sentio et excrucior.'

It was odd that I should remember that particular poem, even if it was only the first half.

The two of us looked at each other, and Yasmine smiled.

'We should be getting back,' she said at last. 'Or you really will be crucified.'

Back among the guests, things had changed little. The smaller groups of earlier in the evening had now formed into a larger one, with Sir Ian's booming voice at its centre. Seeing Yasmine and me return, he called us over, and the group surrounding him parted, like the jaws of a beast, ready to swallow us.

The jaws closed, and I stood there, conversations washing over me, like waves of white noise. I could sense Yasmine leave, rather than see her, the incessant laughter too much even for her. And so, I also drifted away. My body was still there, but my mind was far away. This was a game for other people, not me. And that was fine.

After several minutes, I felt a hand gently tugging on my arm. At first, I thought it was one of my colleagues, but the pulling became more insistent. When I turned around, I was happy to see that it was Ellen, and the smile on her face was radiant.

'You looked like you needed rescuing,' she uttered quietly as we moved to the far side of the room. I thanked her and told her that I did. 'Not really for you, this kind of thing, is it?' she said. It wasn't a question.

I told her that it never had been, and she laughed.

'Well, you've chosen the wrong profession, if that's the case!'

There wasn't much doubt about that.

We made small talk for quite a while, during which she asked me again if I minded her going to Leeds with me. The fact was, I minded it less now than I had earlier, and I reassured her that it was fine. She wanted to know why we were driving rather than catching the train, and I couldn't think of an answer. The truth was that when I'd initially planned the trip, I hadn't expected anyone else to be there. I'd looked forward to being alone, listening to music and stopping at the motorway service stations. I asked her if she had a preference, and she said not. I then warned her that I wasn't great company on long car journeys, and she laughed and told me not to worry. She would do most of the talking anyway.

Just then, there was an explosion of laughter, and we looked over to the group around Sir Ian. Yasmine was back, and she signalled for Ellen and me to join her. I would have preferred to stay where I was, but that wasn't an option, so reluctantly I followed Ellen over. And for the first time, I saw how easy this was for her, how effortlessly she spoke to people and how quickly she put them at ease. I felt awkward in comparison.

An hour or so later, at just gone twelve o'clock, I'd had enough. Although I wasn't in the office the next day, I wanted to go home, to my bed. I thanked everyone for a pleasant evening, and Ellen and Yasmine said that they would see me to the door. Before I left, Rodney came over and shook my hand. He wished me luck, before adding that I wouldn't need it. It was a nice gesture. Finally, accompanied by Yasmine and Ellen, I made my way to the front door. It had been raining outside. A taxi was waiting on the gravelled driveway, so I said goodbye and thanked them both for their company.

'I hope we'll see you again soon,' said Yasmine.

'Sooner than you think!' grinned Ellen. When Yasmine asked what she meant, I explained that the two of us were going to Leeds together and that I'd be there at nine o'clock on Thursday morning to pick Ellen up.

'Well, I'll see you then,' she smiled and kissed me on the cheek.

I was quite looking forward to it.

Chapter 6

It was late morning by the time I awoke the next day. Not being in the mood to make any breakfast, I decided that, once again, I would head off to the local cafe. I felt like a cooked breakfast, something I didn't often eat. Following a quick wash and a protracted search for clean clothes, I grabbed my wallet and set off. About halfway between my house and the shopping precinct, I bumped into, and was ignored by, Mr Jones, out on his daily walk. I could have sworn he was smiling as he walked off.

I picked up a paper at the newsagents. Mr Sanders, the owner, asked me how I was, and I told him that I was well. And as I left the shop and headed down the small path to the precinct, I realised that I was whistling. Which was not like me at all.

As usual, the shopping area was busy, and the locals were out in force. To the right as I entered, a youngish man was making his way unsteadily from shopper to shopper, wishing them all a good day, then swearing at them as they turned away. Further away, in a dark grey pinstripe suit, an elderly gentleman was attempting to sell funeral plans for the over fifties. He seemed to be having limited success. No one wants to think about death when they're out shopping.

Having no desire for conversation, I mingled as much as possible, until finally, I arrived at the cafe, the glass door squeaking as it opened, causing the lady behind the counter to look up. She smiled at me and mouthed the word 'hello', as if she didn't wish to disturb the other customers. Her name was Sheena, and she'd been working there for as long as I could remember, though I'd never seen her outside of the cafe, making me think that she didn't live locally. Sheena stopped whatever it was she was doing and picked up a small paper notepad, then patiently waited for me to arrive.

'Do you want to see a menu, Thomas?' she asked, as I reached the counter.

'No thanks, Sheena,' I said. 'I know what I'm having.' She tilted her head slightly, her ballpoint pen hovering expectantly above the paper. 'The big breakfast, please.' She smiled and nodded her head, as though I'd made the right choice. 'The big breakfast' was no more substantial than any other one I'd eaten in the past, and I found the name a bit misleading. Especially as it was the only breakfast they made. However, it wasn't Sheena's doing, so I said nothing. As I looked around, it was clear that today was a slow day in the cafe, with most of the tables empty, except for two in the far corner, where a small group of people sat, talking loudly as they munched on bacon sandwiches. I walked over to the window, as far from the other people as possible and placed my newspaper on the small wooden table. It would be a while before my food arrived, leaving me ample time to catch up on what was happening in the world. Scandal in the government, plane crash in the Middle East, unemployment up, civil war in

Africa, et cetera, et cetera. The usual stuff, depressingly commonplace.

There was usually a funny story in there somewhere, buried amongst the tragedy, and I flicked through the pages until I found it, located between a picture of a dog and an article about a postman who was refusing to deliver his letters. The story revolved around a book that had just come out, detailing weird and unusual records, some of which were printed there by way of example: world's longest fingernails—six and a half feet; hottest chilli pepper—the Carolina Reaper; the world's shortest commercial flight—fifty-seven seconds. The last entry detailed the longest ever turd, measuring an impressive twenty-six feet. I read it again, just to make sure.

My average-sized breakfast soon arrived, and despite what I'd just read, I set about it with enthusiasm. The food in the cafe was always cooked exactly how I liked it, well done, with no grease. I used the accompanying bread to make a sandwich with the bacon, and it felt like two meals for the price of one. Which was always a good thing. By the time I'd finished, the plate was clean, and I sat back feeling satisfied, if a little too full. Inevitably, I was soon feeling tired.

As I was stretching, I heard a noise nearby.

'Are you leaving?' asked a heavily accented voice.

I looked up and there in front of me was a middle-aged man in worn, dirty clothing and with a face weathered by too many nights spent outdoors. He smiled at me, and I recognised him as the person who'd been swearing at passers-by. I'd assumed him to be drunk, but as he stood there, it was clear to me that he was quite sober. He asked me again if I was leaving, adding that he'd seen me finish my breakfast, and thought that perhaps I was about to leave. This was the table he always used. I looked up at him from my chair, and I noticed the most beautiful blue eyes, bright and intelligent, and I thought that with a haircut and a wash, he'd be very handsome. I wondered how things had turned out this way for him, and for some reason, I asked him if he needed anything. I'd never done that before. He smiled and shook his head.

'I'm fine, thank you,' he said. 'I have everything I need.'

And with that, I stood up, gesturing for him to sit down. I brushed myself with a napkin, sending several stray breadcrumbs tumbling to the floor, then placed my empty cup on the plate and used the napkin again to wipe the table.

'Are you taking the newspaper with you?' he asked, and I shook my head. He thanked me, then sat down. I left him reading a story about a tornado in Japan.

It was busy outside, with people milling around in the warm midday sun. As I turned to leave, I noticed something lying on the floor under a nearby table. Moving closer, I saw that it was a wallet, so I picked it up and took a look inside. It contained sixty pounds, a few shop receipts and one or two photographs, but very little by way of identification. The man I'd just spoken to must have seen it too.

'I found this by the table,' I said to Sheena as I handed the wallet to her. She seemed surprised but smiled at me and thanked me for my honesty.

'You know, most people would have taken it,' she said, as she placed the wallet carefully beside the till. But for once, I wasn't so sure.

The walk along the pathway from the shopping precinct to my street took me past a dwindling number of people. The crowds always thinned out in the early afternoon, as people went home for lunch, and by the time I reached my road, I was the only person around. I looked up at the rows of whitewashed houses and flats, and I wondered what their occupants were doing right now, whether they were at work or, like me, killing time until something else came up. Behind one of the curtains in a window high up to my right, I caught sight of a man looking down at me, and I stared back at him, until the curtain closed and he was gone.

In my absence, back at the flat, my letterbox had been crammed full of leaflets, though no letters. They were advertising everything from takeaway foods to foreign holidays, but amongst all the rubbish, one flyer, in particular, caught my attention. It was an advert for a film about the life of Leonardo da Vinci. I'd seen it on a recent business trip to America, where I'd spent my nights in my hotel room watching films, rather than 'networking' with colleagues. The film had been terrible, but had reminded me of an article I'd read at university, many years earlier. In his time da Vinci had been the world's most accomplished man in a vast number of subjects. I remembered art, sculpture, physiology, physics, invention, meteorology, geology, engineering, general science, architecture, mechanics, anatomy, and aviation. But there were many more. I had a good memory for lists. He could also compose ballads when thrown any stringed instrument. So quite how such a mediocre film could be made about him was beyond me. I would recommend it to Henry.

The rest of the afternoon was taken up with washing and packing for my trip, and by the time I'd finished, it was already late evening. All that remained was to double-check I had everything, then have a shower and finally get a good night's sleep. Usually, when driving a long distance, I would wear some old, comfortable clothes, such as tracksuit trousers and a T-shirt. But tomorrow was different. Not only would I be travelling with Ellen, but I'd also be meeting Yasmine again. I wanted to make the right impression, so I carefully ironed a shirt and pressed a pair of trousers. When, at last, all preparations were complete, and I was sure nothing had been forgotten, I turned off the lights and went to bed.

Outside, it was windy, and a heavy rain beat against my bedroom window. It had been so long since I'd seen real rain, that I got out of bed and went for a look. Peering from behind my curtain, I noticed that several of the streetlights had failed to light up, and all along the road, large puddles had formed. It was pouring down, and the rain bounced off the pavements like bullets in a war film. In the distance, I saw Mr Jones, probably on his way back from the pub. He was holding a bag above his head, and he looked absolutely drenched.

Across the street, someone was standing at a window. I saw that it was the painting lady, and when she noticed me, she waved, then pointed to Mr Jones. She started to laugh, and that made me laugh too. As he got closer, she waved again, then closed her curtain. But I continued to watch. He hadn't even got a coat on. I imagined he would sleep very poorly that night.

It didn't take long to arrive at the Walkers' house the next morning. The roads were beginning to dry out and, for once, there was relatively little traffic to slow me down. As a result, I pulled up nearly half an hour earlier than planned. Getting out of the car, I caught sight of old Sir Ian (Senior) ambling around the gardens, so I headed for the door as stealthily as possible, hoping he wouldn't notice me. Before I managed to ring the bell, the door opened, and Yasmine appeared, radiant in the morning air.

'I saw you sneaking up,' she said, and I could see that she was smiling. 'Don't worry, he'd never spot you at this distance.'

'I'm sorry to be so early,' I said. 'The roads weren't as busy as I'd expected.'

'It's fine,' she replied. 'I wasn't doing anything anyway.'

Suddenly, I heard a noise behind me, so I turned around. Old Sir Ian was running across the lawn, and he was heading in my direction. I was amazed at how quickly he was moving. Yasmine took hold of my arm, then pulled me inside the house, quickly closing the door behind us.

'He must have his new glasses on,' she laughed.

Ellen was upstairs getting ready, and Sir Ian (Junior) had set off early that morning for a business appointment in the City. This was the first time that Yasmine and I had been together, without her husband somewhere close by, and it was nice. I hoped Ellen was in no hurry to come down.

Yasmine offered me some breakfast, and I thanked her but said that a coffee would be fine. As she filled up the kettle, I noticed a coffee making machine next to her, so I asked her why she didn't use that.

'Style over substance,' she said simply. 'It looks nice, but it's not really up to the job.'

She handed me the coffee, and we sat down.

'I've got a small present for you, Thomas,' she said after a while. 'It's nothing much, but I thought you might like it.'

I had no idea what to say. Was I expected to bring something too? She handed me a small package, neatly wrapped in plain paper, and I thanked her, before carefully removing the paper. Inside was an old, leather-bound copy of Catullus's poetry. It was beautiful.

'You shouldn't have,' I said, though I was delighted that she had.

'I know,' she replied. Then she started to laugh. 'Maybe it will help you to remember the whole poem next time!'

At nine o'clock, Ellen came downstairs. She was dressed casually, in jeans and a T-shirt, in stark contrast to my own attire, and she looked fantastic. I looked forward to seeing the expression on Henry's face when they met.

'You're nice and early,' she said, grinning at me over a slice of toast. I was about to explain about the traffic but decided there was little point.

'We'd better head off soon,' I said. I was sure that if we stayed too long, Ellen would try to embarrass me.

'You're welcome to stay here until you're ready,' said Yasmine quickly. 'You've a long journey ahead, so you might as well have something to eat before you go.' Though most of her face was concealed behind the toast, I could see Ellen's grin becoming bigger and bigger. But just then, she seemed to notice something, and I turned to see what she was looking at. On the top of my bag, was the book.

'A fan of Catullus are you, Thomas?' she asked. 'Suddenly.'

I looked at Yasmine, and she shrugged. The two women smiled at each other, and I wondered what they'd been talking about the last day or so.

'That's a coincidence. So are you, aren't you Yasmine?' continued Ellen. She was enjoying herself.

'I think it's time you two set off after all,' laughed Yasmine.

Out at the car, Ellen tried her best to make a nuisance of herself, and in the end, I had to force her through the door. Yasmine, on the other hand, was the epitome of calm and after her customary kiss on the cheek, she wished us both a pleasant journey. A minute later, we were halfway down the drive, the house in the distance and Ellen next to me, smirking like a mischievous child.

By the time we were out of London, the sun had come out. The car heated up quickly, and I was forced to turn on the air conditioning. The sprawling suburbs of the capital gradually gave way to countryside, and soon we were surrounded by lush green fields and gently rolling hills. Ellen stared out of the window, and I thought to myself how happy she looked, her gaze jumping from one thing to the next.

'Have you never seen fields before?' I laughed.

'Sure,' she replied, 'but not such small ones!' She started laughing too.

'Oh, yes, I'd forgotten that everything's bigger in America!' I teased her.

'That's right.'

'Like your heads.'

Then she hit me.

We'd been driving for two hours, and I was hungry. I wished I'd eaten at Yasmine's. To take my mind off things, I asked Ellen which parts of England she liked the most, and she reluctantly admitted that during her many visits, she'd never been outside of London. I told her I found that strange, but when she replied that she'd stayed with Sir Ian each time, I began to understand. He didn't like the North. He'd advised her not to talk to anyone, unless it was an emergency, to keep her money safely concealed and never to stay outdoors after dark. I sighed. I'd heard all that from Henry. Experts in places they barely knew. I told her that she'd be meeting some of the nicest people she could hope to meet, but she didn't look convinced.

After a few hours of driving, the scenery changed dramatically. Gone were the fields and undulating hills. In their place were coarse rocky hillsides and scree-strewn slopes. To make the trip more interesting for Ellen, I'd left the motorway to finish the journey along the smaller, more scenic roads. As we entered Yorkshire, the smooth green farmland of the Midlands disappeared. Ahead lay the North and the vast wilderness of the Moors.

While I drove, Ellen pressed her face against the window, and I joked with her that she'd break it. Every so often she'd wrench her gaze from the sea of bracken and turn to me with a huge smile. 'Look at that, Thomas! It's amazing!'. It was endearing the way she found everything so exciting, and I wondered if I'd have been the same had I been in her shoes. The cheery, almost childlike, tone with which she described what she saw made me smile, and I found that I was actually enjoying myself. The journey started to fly by. She'd now spent over three hours in my car and not once had I wished I were alone. Now that was amazing.

Half an hour later, as we drove along a particularly narrow and winding stretch of road, I recognised a small stone cottage. I'd driven past it many times over the years, and as I watched smoke drift lazily from the chimney, I remembered a story my father had told me when I was a boy. I mentioned this to Ellen, and she asked me to tell it.

'Many years ago,' I began, 'a young couple had moved into the cottage, newly-weds, he a writer, she the daughter of a local landowner. As a sign of their devotion to each other, they'd withdrawn from the world and vowed to remain alone. This they did, and as the years went by, the only people to see them were occasional passers-by. But even they couldn't be sure of what they saw, a beautiful girl in tattered clothes with a young man, hand in hand, alone on the Moors.

'One night, they'd heard a noise outside, and the husband had left the house to see what it was. His wife waited indoors, preparing a meal for when her husband returned. But he never did.

'For many years, she waited, but she never saw him again. The last person to pass that way spoke of a frail old woman sitting by a fire, staring into the flames and waiting. Waiting for someone who fifty years earlier had said he would return.

She knew he would come. There'd been a noise outside, and he'd gone to see what it was.

'But that was years ago,' I said. 'Nowadays, no one remembers the tale of the old woman who waits by the fire.'

'Really!' cried Ellen. 'That's so sad!' There was a pause before she added: 'Complete bullshit, of course,' and I laughed out loud.

The Moors suddenly stopped, and we entered a small village, almost entirely composed of a single street. Down each side ran rows of terraced houses and towards the end stood a post office, a general store and, most importantly, a pub.

'Let's stop here for a quick drink,' said Ellen. She looked keen to explore. And if anything was going to be explored, the pub was an excellent place to start. So I pulled up the car. It was already mid-afternoon, and the journey was taking longer than I'd expected.

The pub, quaintly named the 'Slaughtered Pig', looked extremely small. Inside it was even smaller. I had to bend down as I walked through the dark wooden door. To either side of me, heavy coats and large umbrellas formed a narrow passageway into the bar area itself.

The room was quiet as we entered, though I'd heard plenty of noise before we walked in. As we made our way to the bar, a dozen sets of eyes followed us, some furtively, others more openly. Ellen reached out and took hold of my hand. I turned and asked her if she was okay, and with a nervous smile, she replied that she was.

'What can I do for you, sir?' said the barman with a grin. His thick accent rendered the question almost unintelligible. Ellen frowned. She had no idea what he'd just said.

'A pint and a half of bitter, please,' I replied.

'Aye, and what about the lady?' he said, his face now completely deadpan. Nearby, an old man chuckled into his beer.

'That is for the lady,' I replied, and the broad smile reappeared on the barman's face.

'Do I detect a northerner in there somewhere?' he asked. I told him that I'd been brought up in Lancashire.

'Ooh, very nice!' he said. 'Lancashire, eh? We don't get too many of you lot over here.'

'We don't get too many of the likes of her, either!' shouted a man from the corner, and everyone burst out laughing.

'Come over here and sit down, love!' shouted another. The noise I'd heard before we entered was back, and as the laughter got louder, Ellen's grip tightened on my hand.

'Take no notice love,' winked the barman. 'We're just not used to seeing pretty girls around here.' He was a plump man, in his sixties, with a balding head and an extremely red face. Ellen smiled and thanked him, her composure quickly returning. When he heard her voice, he smiled, revealing a toothless set of gums.

'And I'm not used to a lovely accent like that,' he said. 'Enjoy your drinks!'

We found a small seat in the corner, next to a large open fire. A few feet away slept a huge dog, about the size of a donkey, and beside it, a small man, perched on top of a stool. Though completely bald, a grey, wiry beard cascaded to his waist. In his right hand, he held a glass of beer, and in his left a shot of whisky. As I watched, he drank alternately from each glass, wiped his sleeve across his mouth and burped. He then apologised to the dog, before repeating the process once more.

At the other side of the fire sat an old man and woman, deep in argument over sandwich fillings.

'What do mean we've no corned beef left?' said the man. 'There was some in the fridge this morning.' He was extraordinarily thin, with quick, darting eyes and a gaunt face. His clothing was almost entirely knitted, of varying shades of grey, with brown leather patches at the elbows and knees.

'I put it in the sandwiches we had for tea!' shouted the woman in front of him. I presumed this to be his wife. 'I put it in the sandwiches we had for tea!' she repeated, making sure there could be no mistake as to what had happened to the corned beef. In contrast to her husband, the woman was enormously fat, with huge pendulous breasts and thick arms. She wore a green knitted dress and on her head perched an enormous hat, a mass of feathers and baubles, like a peacock crushed beneath a basket of fruit. The argument went back and forth, with no resolution, until at last, the man stood up a left, slamming the pub door behind him. When he was safely through the door, the woman picked up her husband's drink and drank it in one huge slurp. Next, she drank her own and then ordered another. Finally, she straightened her hat as though nothing had happened.

Ellen and I looked at each other in silence. She seemed confused. After a moment, she opened her mouth.

'What's corned beef?' she asked. I tried to explain, but I wasn't too sure myself. We settled at 'some form of meat'.

Throughout all of this, Ellen hadn't tried any of her drink. When at last she did, she looked as though she'd bitten into a lemon.

'Why did you buy me this, Thomas?' she asked, her expression dark, as though I was somehow trying to poison her.

'Take a look around,' I replied. Behind the small oak bar, there were six beer pumps, all of which supplied bitter. The optics further back consisted of two bottles of whisky and one of rum. High up on a shelf, surrounded by packets of crisps and jars of pork scratchings, was a small box of continental lager. It was unopened. Had I asked for the lager, I imagined I'd be leaving the pub a great deal swifter than I'd entered. This was bitter drinking country.

'I'll put it down to one of the northern oddities Sir Ian warned me about,' moaned Ellen, her smile slowly returning. 'I'm sure it won't be the last.'

At this point, several more locals entered the pub, and very soon it was beginning to fill up. As the tables around us became more and more crowded, we decided to it was time to leave, Ellen receiving enthusiastic waves as she left, though I received none. Walking across the grey gravelled car park to our car, I spotted the thin man from earlier, storming up the road in our direction. He passed by, muttering something about there being no bread, and when was gone, Ellen and I turned to each other and started to laugh. She looked at me questioningly, but I just smiled and shrugged. I didn't know where to start.

Once we were in the car, Ellen turned and thanked me. I asked her what for. For a new experience, she replied. It had been a nice introduction to the mysteries of the North.

'You know, I was named after a bar,' she said as I started the car. 'It was called Ellen's Bar, in New York. It's where my mother met my father.'

'Well, that's the name of your first child sorted,' I replied. 'Slaughtered Pig. It's got a ring to it.'

She shook her head happily, and her smile lit up the car. 'I'll have to think about that!'

As we set off down the road, I wondered what Yasmine would have made of it. I honestly had no idea.

It wasn't long before we arrived at the hotel. The Queen's

Hotel was one of the city's best-known establishments, a large brick building with an imposing facade, found near to the railway station. As a student, I'd spent several nights there, for one reason or another, and since leaving the university, I'd stayed there on business, spending most of my evenings watching television and depleting the minibar. My visits were infrequent now, and though I remembered one or two of the staff, none seemed to remember me. Ellen found it hilarious that I couldn't find the room reservations, but after several minutes of rummaging around in my bag, I finally located them—right at the bottom. She insisted on taking the reservations to the reception desk herself while I repacked the contents of my bag, and after a lengthy discussion between her and the hotel receptionist, she turned to me and smiled. We were all set. An elderly porter came over to collect our bags, and at last, we were shown to our rooms.

When the room reservations had been made several days earlier, I'd asked for two doubles. And when the confirmations had come through, we'd been given a small double and an executive suite. This was important because it meant that one room would have a small shower cubicle, and the other a large bath. Ellen had only found out about this on the journey up, when I'd informed her, not altogether honestly, that the larger room had automatically been allocated to me, as the person who'd made the bookings. I assured her that no matter how much I'd argued, the hotel had refused to swap them. It was a shame, but there was nothing I could do about it. I was pretty sure she didn't believe me.

Arriving at my door, I thanked the porter, and he handed me a shiny brass key. It was attached to a large wooden key fob, making it difficult to fit into my pocket. I decided that once in the room, I'd separate the key and leave the fob by my bed. The key turned in the lock, and a small green light flashed by the handle, followed by a buzzing sound and a click. I smiled to myself. The standard rooms probably didn't get this, so I was looking forward to teasing Ellen about it later.

The room itself was nice enough, though a little smaller than I would have expected. But, given the amount of time I was planning to spend there, all that I needed was a bed and a desk. And a minibar. Placing my bag on a chair, I went over to the window. I slipped off my shoes, feeling the thick carpet like a cushion beneath my feet. I was delighted to find that the room overlooked the main square, with its old stone statues and mottled wooden benches. It was a beautiful view. I imagined that Ellen's room overlooked the railway line.

On the bed was a white towel, folded into the shape of a swan, and next to it was a bathrobe, the name of the hotel embroidered onto its pocket. I'd planned on calling Ellen as soon as I'd unpacked, but seeing the towel, I decided to have a soak in the bath first. Over five hours in the car had left my muscles tired and aching.

As the bathroom door swung open, I was interrupted by the ringing of the telephone next to my bed. A small red light on the handset flashed insistently, demanding I pick it up. It was Ellen. And as she spoke, the bathroom door stopped opening, and the automatic light turned on. There in front of me, to my horror, and no bigger than a telephone box, was a shower cubicle. My towel fell silently to the floor.

'What the hell!' I said down the phone, and I could hear Ellen giggling at the other end.

'Sorry Thomas,' she said, 'I can tell that you're busy. I'll call you again in a bit.' There was a pause. 'Once I've finished my soak in the bath!'

Her earlier conversation with the receptionist came

surging back to me.

'Ellen, wait!' I shouted, but she was already gone.

Often, when we look forward to something, only for a substitute to arrive, we are left disappointed. My shower that afternoon ranked very high on my list of life's disappointments. Very high indeed. To make matters worse, the cubicle had been even smaller than I'd feared, and I'd hit my head on the door handle, bending down to pick up my shampoo. I now had a small bruise above my right eye.

It was just gone four o'clock, and I'd finished my shower, dried and got changed. The whole thing can't have taken much more than twenty minutes. I was feeling calmer by this stage, so I started to think about my schedule for the coming days. We'd only be in Leeds for two days, maybe three, depending on how things went. The schedule was pretty straightforward, but unforeseen problems were never too far away, so I'd booked the rooms for three nights. Tomorrow was Friday, and we had a full day of meetings. The Leeds office also worked on Saturdays, so we'd be there on Saturday too. I wasn't happy about that, but when I'd told Ellen, she'd looked at me as though working on a Saturday was quite reasonable. Which it wasn't.

As I stood there, looking out of the window at the streets below, I sighed to myself at the prospect of the many dull meetings coming our way. It wasn't going to be fun.

A little later, once I'd stopped feeling sorry for myself, I got to thinking about the rest of the day. I'd had the radio on in the background, and at one point an old song by David Bowie had come on—'An Occasional Dream', released in 1969. It reminded me of my recent trip to the record store, so I got to thinking, and very soon, my mind was made up. That's what I'd do.

The obvious problem, if problem was the right word, was Ellen. Or rather, how to get away from her for a few minutes. I couldn't really steal something with her stood right next to me. She'd take it in completely the wrong way.

Then it struck me—why not elicit her help? She wouldn't know she was helping me, of course, but she would certainly be a distraction. She always attracted attention, I'd seen that much already. It was perfect. And so, after a quick shave, I unpacked my bags and changed into my casual clothes. There was no time like the present.

The door to Ellen's room looked bigger than mine. I knew I was being ridiculous, but after the palaver earlier, I was expecting everything about her room to be that little bit grander and more imposing than mine. I knocked at the door. It was a relief to see a green light flashing on the door handle, not some rainbow coloured affair. A moment later, the lock buzzed, and I went in.

'It's still early, Ellen,' I said as soon as I was inside. 'How about we go out and have a look around the town before the shops close?'

'Great,' she replied. 'I'll get changed later.'

She'd walked into the room from a side door, and I wondered what was behind it, as my room didn't have an extra door like that. I was going to ask her but decided against it. She was probably dying to tease me about the rooms.

'Aren't you going to be a bit hot dressed like that?' she asked, looking me up and down, with a puzzled look on her face.

Admittedly, I was feeling rather hot. I was wearing a coat, and it was far too warm for this kind of weather. However, it was the only one I had with large pockets. And I was going to need those large pockets.

'I'll be fine,' I said. 'I'll take it off if I get too hot.' She eyed me suspiciously, and I smiled reassuringly, then told her to hurry up.

Outside, the streets were busy, as workers and shoppers mingled, each hurrying from one place to the next. A steady flow of commuters made their way to the railway station, shuffling along like a colourful snake, and Ellen and I had to wait several minutes before we could pass. We wandered around the city centre for a good half hour, with Ellen dragging me into all kinds of shops, selling everything from painted jewellery to handmade candles. Finally, we arrived at somewhere suitable. From the outside, it was little more than a large door, the name 'Gerard' displayed proudly above in gold-coloured letters. But inside, it was perfect. A treasure trove of clothing and accessories for the more discerning gentleman. Or so it said on a sign behind the counter. As soon as we entered, I could feel my heart racing. The two young assistants took no time in noticing Ellen, and as their eyes followed her all over the shop, I was left free to roam. For about ten minutes, I looked at everything, from expensive suits to hand-stitched hats, designer jeans to hooded tops. There were no security cameras, as far as I could see. Ellen came over to ask what I was looking for. She was holding a tie.

'Who's that for?' I asked.

'My dad,' she replied. 'He collects ties.'

'How odd.'

'Says the man in the winter coat!' she laughed. 'You must be boiling. You're starting to sweat.'

'Then maybe you can find me another one,' I replied, and she clapped her hands excitedly, before disappearing to investigate the coat section. She was right, I was starting to sweat. And my heart felt like it was going to explode.

I'd taken long enough, perhaps too long if I was going to

avoid suspicion. So I casually scooped up a pair of leather gloves and stuffed them into my coat pocket. Just in case I was being watched, I picked up another pair and pretended to argue with myself over whether to buy them or not. Putting the second pair back, I went to find Ellen. She was standing at the cash desk buying the tie. On the face of it, it looked like any other tie, and I wondered what sort of collection her father was creating. It was made locally, so maybe that was it. The assistants, both young men in their twenties, took a long time to serve her, as they vied with each other for her attention. But, at last, she paid, and we could finally leave. I was so hot, I felt like I was on fire.

Outside the shop, I breathed in the cool air and brushed the back of my hand across my forehead. I was burning up. It seemed incredibly busy, as though every car in the city was driving by at that moment, and I wanted to sit down. I suggested to Ellen that we go and grab a drink, and as we walked along the pavement, she said nothing to me. I could tell that something was wrong.

'Is everything okay?' I asked.

'I can see now why you wore the coat!' she snapped. I tried to look puzzled, but she was having none of it. 'The gloves, you asshole!' she hissed, and the accusation in her eyes made me want to look away. The gloves. No security cameras, but one very observant Ellen. This wasn't good.

'What about them?' I replied, trying my best to sound casual, though failing badly.

'What about them?' she rasped. 'You're joking, right?'

I've never been good in a pressure situation and had spent most of my career pretending that I was. I'd fooled most of my colleagues to that point, but it wasn't going to work with Ellen. I could see that quite clearly. At a complete loss as to what to say, I was hoping that something profound would spring to mind. But of course, it didn't. In the end, I said the first thing that came into my head.

'Look, there's an American diner over there. Let's go and get some food.'

Not the best choice, given the circumstances.

Ellen said nothing. She just stood there with her mouth open, a weird gurgling noise coming out. I didn't really know what that meant. I assumed that it wasn't good. So, rather than risk her attacking me in the middle of the street, I took hold of her arm and pulled her across the road.

Once inside the diner, the situation didn't improve. I ordered some food and a drink, and we found a small table in the corner, its white plastic surface dotted with coffee stains. Ellen sat in silence, a thunderous look on her face, and at that moment, all I could think of was how angry she looked. How was I going to make her understand? Was there anything to understand? I reached into my pocket. Humour is often the best approach.

'Look what I got!' I said with a grin and showed her my new gloves. It didn't work.

Amidst the outrage, I could also see disappointment, and it was that which stung the most.

'I know,' she snapped. 'I saw you steal them. Asshole!' That was the second time she'd called me that.

I thought about explaining to her how it wasn't really stealing, it was just a way to inject some excitement into my life. But I knew that wouldn't work, nor indeed should it. So, once again, I said nothing. And I'm not sure how long it stayed that way. But it was quite a while. I was hoping that the silence would dilute her anger, or even wash it away so that we could be happy again.

But she was hoping for something else. An explanation perhaps.

Nevertheless, as the minutes ticked by, I gradually saw a softening in her expression. Outrage and disappointment changed to annoyance and this in turn became puzzlement. She opened her mouth to speak, then closed it again, as if unsure of what to say. But at least she looked at me.

'You've got a bloody cheek,' she said, and I could sense the emotion in her voice. 'Why the hell did you take those gloves?'

Where to start? I wasn't even sure that I wanted to start. What had begun as something personal, had now affected someone else. And that hadn't been my intention. I wondered how to explain things without sounding crazy. What explanation would seem feasible? And how could I make this bad situation just a little bit better? In the end, I couldn't think of anything. There was nothing. So I decided on the only course of action available to me, and that was honesty. Perhaps that would work.

I started at the beginning: my life at work—the same day, every day; my social life—same people, same places; and my love life—the same scenario, only the faces changing. And once I'd started, I was unable to stop. I didn't want to stop. I talked to her of anything that came into my head, good and bad, relevant or not. My broken dreams, and the hopes I'd lost. I told her how I disliked London because it scared me, but I was too scared to leave. I disliked my job. It was dull, and I could do so much more. But I didn't have the willpower. And I disliked my lack of willpower.

'In short,' I concluded, 'I don't like any of it. That's why I took the gloves.'

And this was my attempt to come across as not crazy. By rights, Ellen should have been running away. But she didn't run; she listened.

'Is there anything you do like, Thomas?' she asked at last.

'I like this table,' I replied. 'And sitting at it, talking to you.'

Then she smiled. And at that moment, I knew it would be all right.

She spent the next few minutes admonishing me once more about stealing the gloves. But I could see that her heart wasn't in it, so I didn't really listen. Finally, she sighed.

'I can't see how your life can be that boring, Thomas,' she said. 'You're very successful.' She paused for a moment, then grinned. 'Well, quite successful.'

'Success?' I said, looking away. 'I've a decent job and enough money, but that's about it. The guy who cleans the toilets at work is always smiling and laughing to himself. Am I more successful than him?'

'Well that's not a good example,' said Ellen. 'I actually think he's crazy.'

She smiled reassuringly at me before continuing. 'But perhaps,' she shrugged. 'Perhaps not. Why should you have to compare? You speak as though you're in some sort of personal prison. And you're not.'

'Most prisons are of our own making,' I replied, immediately thinking how pretentious that sounded. Ellen shook her head and told me to stop feeling sorry for myself, her candour just what I needed at the time. She told me how fortunate I was compared to many people in the world, and it reminded me of the sermons my parents used to give me. I nodded quietly, just as I had done all those years ago.

'My life may not be the most interesting in the world, either,' she said finally. 'But it's enough for me.'

'Really?' I replied.

'Well, it doesn't make me go around stealing things!'

And that was that.

The rest of the evening was somewhat quieter than the earlier part had been. We chatted about our lives and generally did what most people do when they find themselves stuck together on work trips—we drank, we talked, we drank some more. I was surprised how easily she forgot, or at least appeared to, the events which had earlier been so important. In fact, as the evening progressed, she seemed to withdraw into herself in a way I hadn't seen before. Perhaps that was how she was. We'd known each other for such a short time, and there was so much I didn't know about her. In an odd way, I liked that. It was more interesting that way.

In the end, the conversation and the alcohol dried up, and it was time for bed. We had a busy day ahead of us.

At breakfast the next morning, things weren't quite back to normal. Ellen was still quieter than usual, and I was afraid that I'd permanently damaged our relationship. I asked her about it, but she assured me that everything was fine. Finally, however, she admitted that the discussions of the previous night had posed some questions about her own life choices. It made her uncomfortable, as she'd always been so sure of things.

I apologised, but she just smiled and told me not to be silly.

'Anyway,' she said, standing up. 'We'd better get a move on.'

It was nine o'clock, and we were going to be late.

At the Leeds office, the day passed by in a blur of meetings and presentations, each more tedious than the last. I was acutely aware of how tired I felt but was comforted to see that Ellen was faring worse. Neither of us had slept well. We got through the morning, then picked at some lunch in the canteen. Next, it was a presentation entitled 'Profitability and the challenges of shrinking markets.' There was little chance of me sweating with excitement that afternoon.

The thin man at the front of the room pointed from one presentation slide to the next while I fought resolutely to stay awake. At the end of it, he asked the audience if they had any questions. Unsurprisingly, there was silence. I looked across at Ellen, who was staring blankly ahead, and I wondered how she was feeling. Apart from the thirty minutes of lunch, I'd spent very little time with her that day, and we'd barely exchanged more than a few words. I was finding it all a bit uncomfortable, and I hoped things would get back to normal soon.

Everything was wrapped up by five o'clock, so I went looking for Ellen. I found her in conversation with a very tall lady, whose name I couldn't remember. She'd chaired one of the morning sessions. She wore a dark blue trouser suit and had bright red hair, pulled back tightly into a ponytail, and though Ellen was by no means short, she peered down at her like a school governess.

'Ah, there you are Thomas,' said the woman, as I approached. 'How have you enjoyed your day?' I replied that it had been educational, which seemed to make her happy. 'Ellen tells me that you're going to show her around Leeds tonight.'

'I am?' I asked. I looked across at Ellen, who smiled back at me and nodded. 'Yes, it would appear that I am.'

'Greta and I met when she was over in the States a year or so ago,' said Ellen, helpfully stressing the woman's name, knowing full well that I'd forgotten it. 'Apparently, there's an excellent play on at the theatre tonight.'

'You really should try it,' added Greta. 'It's terrific.'

I thanked Greta for the suggestion, though I'd no intention of going.

It was time for us to head back to the hotel. The two women hugged, and I received a firm handshake.

'What are we actually doing this evening?' Ellen asked casually as we headed out of the building. 'I quite fancy a drink.'

'Okay,' I said, pleased with the turn of events. 'We can go into Headingley. I know a few places there.'

As we walked, Ellen seemed to be in a much better mood. I wanted to ask her if everything was now good between us, but I was worried about the answer, so I didn't. I'd ask her later.

On our way back to the hotel, we came across a pharmacy, and I suddenly remembered that I needed a few things. Ellen looked at me suspiciously, so I assured her it would be nothing more than a regular spot of shopping. She smiled, then said that she'd come with me anyway.

The pharmacy itself was a pokey little shop, but it took me a long time to find what I was looking for—a toothbrush and some soap. The soap at the hotel was fine, but it smelled funny. Ellen kept a close eye on me, but she was soon bored, so she went off on her own. In total, we were there a little over ten minutes. Products purchased, nothing stolen and out.

Back on the street, the weather had changed dramatically. Gone was the balmy heat of a few minutes earlier, replaced by a chill breeze and thunderous looking clouds. It quickly became colder, and as we made our way into the hotel, I felt a drop or two of rain splash onto my head. There was no one in the foyer, and I took off my coat. It was much warmer inside, but the sudden drop in temperature had left me feeling unusually cold. Ellen must have been frozen. All she had on was a light summer coat and a thin blouse. I suddenly realised that she'd not said a word since the pharmacy, and I turned to her to see if everything was okay. To my surprise, she had a broad grin on her face, and although she was shivering, I could see at once that something wasn't right. Taking a step closer, it suddenly hit me—she was sweating!

Without a sound, her hand slowly withdrew from her pocket. She gazed at me as I stood there open-mouthed.

'Ta-Da!' she said and started to laugh. And as she danced around the foyer like a delighted child, a bottle of perfume somersaulted through the air and fell to the floor. And then it was quiet.

I watched her for a while longer, captivated by her odd dance. A few moments later, she walked over to me and took hold of my arm.

'Well?' she giggled and kissed me on the cheek. I could smell the floral scent of her perfume, subtle and understated. Unlike that in the bottle which now lay on the thick carpet of the hotel floor.

'Unbelievable!' I replied. And it was. Quite unbelievable. She had completely and utterly played me, and I was shocked at just how gullible I'd been. I laughed, both at my own naivety and at the memory of Ellen's peculiar dance. And it was perhaps the first time in months that I'd really laughed.

The New Inn was a small pub in Headingley. It had been a long time since I'd been there, but things had changed very little. Ellen seemed to like it, and it wasn't long before she was used to the taste of the beer. It was very much a student pub, with most of the customers a fair bit younger than us. But despite that, it was fun, and no one bothered us. That was the important thing. Every so often, when I went to the bar, someone would stroll over to Ellen and offer to buy her a drink, but as soon as I returned, they would disappear again, and we would be left alone.

'It's true what you say, Thomas,' said Ellen, after another sip of her beer. 'That really was quite exciting!' It had been a couple of hours since Ellen had taken the perfume, and she was in a very chatty mood. She probed me about my personal life, life at work, and the things I liked to do in my spare time. Much more deeply than she had on the previous evening, and when I mentioned my recent trip to the record shop and my discussion with Henry about flirting with Yasmine, she listened intently. I wondered if I'd in fact said too much. But I was starting to feel drunk, so I didn't really care.

'You know, perhaps you should be a bit careful with Yasmine,' said Ellen after a while. 'You won't be the first person to flirt with her.' Then she laughed. 'Why do men always think a woman will drop everything for a handsome face and a bit of attention?' She had a point. I told her that it was nothing serious, and she shrugged, as though it wasn't her concern. She'd given me my warning, and that was all she could do.

As it turned out, Ellen and Yasmine were better friends than I'd thought. They'd known each other for a few years, ever since Yasmine had made a trip to New York, accompanying Sir Ian on a tour of the US offices. Ellen spoke very fondly of her and described her as an intelligent woman, caring and an excellent counterbalance to the more ruthless character of Sir Ian. In short, Yasmine cared about people, while her husband cared about money.

By the time last orders rang, we'd both drunk far too much, especially as we still had another day in the Leeds office tomorrow. We ordered a taxi and to the apparent disappointment of a group of young men at a table nearby, we made our way back to the hotel.

During the course of the journey, Ellen's manner became less and less subtle, until at last, we were standing outside the door to her room. I don't know if it was the amount of alcohol we'd consumed or just the fact that we were two adults, alone and to some extent lonely, but we did as many people had done in that situation, when finding themselves in unfamiliar surroundings, with little to do.

'Would you like to come in for a nightcap?' she asked, taking me by the hand before I had the chance to answer.

Yes, I thought, I'd like that very much.

Chapter 7

The next morning, it took a monumental effort to get out of bed. Ellen was in the shower, and the temptation for me to curl up and go back to sleep was strong. It had been a long evening. If I was going to survive the tenure of my appointment as Ellen's baby-sitter, I'd have to avoid going shopping with her on too regular a basis.

'Come on lazy,' she said as she came out of the bathroom. 'We'll be late for work.'

'I don't feel well,' I protested. 'Maybe I'm catching a cold.' It was a pitiful attempt.

'I don't think so,' she smiled. 'You're just a little tired, that's all.'

She looked so fresh. I wondered how she managed it, what with work, shoplifting and drinks. I suddenly felt very old.

I slowly got out of bed, affecting every ailment I could muster, but to no avail. Ellen was totally unsympathetic. After a quick shower and a shave, I got dressed, and together we headed for the office.

The weather was mild outside, though still cool enough for a coat to be worn without looking out of place. I noticed that Ellen had on a coat too and I hoped she had no plans to go shopping with me that day. I told her that if she stole anything while I was around, without first telling me, I'd inform security.

'You're a hypocrite,' she laughed as we walked into the office.

'And you're a thief,' I said with a smile, receiving a punch on the arm for my trouble.

Back in the office, I'd expected to wait around all morning for the papers I required, as was usually the case on my trips to Leeds. However, today Ellen had spoken to the office manager, and sure enough, when I got to my desk, everything she'd asked for was already there, neatly piled and awaiting my attention. It was irritating when I thought of how many hours I'd wasted in the past, waiting for papers, when obviously they were much easier to locate than I'd been told. Then I smiled to myself, realising I would have done precisely the same, had someone come in from Head Office and demanded to see my work. It was petty, but at the same time, entirely understandable. We're all a bit petty at times.

After what felt to me like a hard morning's work, everything was finished, thus leaving the afternoon free. We'd been given a room for the duration of our stay, and Ellen had been in and out of it all morning. I got the impression that she didn't like flowcharts and company reports. As I finished stacking the last of the papers, she asked me if they were all okay, and before I had a chance to answer, she stretched and let out a huge yawn. Of course, that made me yawn too. I laughed and asked her why she was so tired, given that she'd done no work at all that morning.

'Just because you don't see what I'm doing,' she said, 'it doesn't mean that I'm not doing anything.'

So I asked her what she'd been doing.

'Things!' she laughed, and I knew that was as much information as I would get.

Just as we were considering what to do for food, in walked Dudley Jones, the regional manager. He immediately invited us both out to lunch. This came as something of a surprise to me, seeing that he'd never asked me to lunch on my previous visits. I smiled at Ellen, and she returned the smile, fully aware of what I was thinking.

Dudley, or Dud as Ellen insisted on calling him, was a well-known face in the office, a man whose love affair with the expense account was almost as legendary as Henry's. He was a sharp dresser, but where his waistline had expanded with age, his clothing had struggled to keep pace. The stretched white fabric of his shirt provided glimpses of a hairless body beneath, and I could see Ellen trying not to stare. She was obviously not keen on his company, so I considered letting the two of them go to lunch alone. However, there were two reasons why I chose not to: firstly, Ellen would kill me; and secondly, I was hungry.

I wasn't very involved in the discussions over lunch, with Dudley dominating the conversation, most of which was directed towards Ellen anyway. That was fine by me, and it was fun to watch her trying to be polite when she so obviously didn't want to be there. Whenever possible, I made an excuse to leave the table, inventing urgent phone calls or reasons to speak to the waiter. By the time the meal was nearly over, I'd left the table over half a dozen times.

'What the hell's wrong with you?' snapped Ellen as Dudley disappeared to the bathroom. 'Stop leaving me alone with him all the time.' I apologised and explained to her that I wasn't particularly enjoying the meal.

'I can't say it's a bundle of laughs for me, either,' she said irritably. 'Every time you go, his eyes are all over me.' At that point, she paused for a moment, and it was clear that she'd had an idea. 'Just try to divert his attention for a minute,' she said. 'I'm going to teach him a lesson!'

Before long Dudley had returned and my chance to get further details about the plan was gone. He sat down, inappropriately close to Ellen, and when I said nothing, she coughed to remind me of my role as her decoy. I had no idea what she was planning, but if I didn't start talking soon, I was going to be in trouble.

'I hear there's a possibility of your office being upgraded, Dudley,' I said. This wasn't strictly true, but it did the trick. Ellen nodded appreciatively.

For several minutes while I invented information regarding the upgrade, Ellen didn't so much as bat an eyelid. I must have talked for around ten minutes by the time I looked at her again. This time there was a marked difference. Though I was horrified to see that she'd started to perspire, what was even more alarming was the fact that her right hand had somehow made its way into Dudley's jacket pocket. As I watched his wallet slowly reveal itself, I began to hatch increasingly outlandish plans for his office. And just as I was running out of things to say, Ellen coughed. My job was done.

As I glared at her, sitting there like a fraudulent saint, I wondered how she could appear so innocent while at the same time stealing a man's wallet. I had to admit that it was an impressive skill. The bill came over, and Dudley thanked me heartily for the information. Kissing Ellen's hand, he insisted on paying for the whole meal himself, a shake of the head at once silencing our protestations. As a rule, I don't enjoy seeing people making fools of themselves. In fact, I tend to get embarrassed on their behalf. So, as Dudley frantically searched through his pockets, vainly attempting to locate his wallet, I would have expected to feel sorry for him. But once again, I was to surprise myself. It was actually quite enjoyable. At first, as he put his hand into his inside jacket pocket, a slight expression of surprise registered on his face. No doubt, he thought he'd put it into another pocket. But, as each subsequent pocket turned out to be empty, the look of surprise disappeared. Very soon, there was puzzlement. Puzzlement turned to irritation, and finally, irritation became embarrassment. It was a sorry sight. Ellen, for her part, did her best to look concerned, and if it weren't for her stoicism, I'm sure I would have given the game away. As it was, we both sat quietly, waiting for him to give up his search.

And at last, he did just that. As he looked up, I noticed his face had turned a deep shade of crimson. It's hard to describe exactly how he looked. A bit like someone who was being strangled.

'I...I don't know what to say!' he stuttered. 'I can't seem to find my wallet.'

There was a pause as Ellen patted his hand sympathetically. 'Don't worry Dud,' she said, 'we'll get this one.'

As we left the restaurant, Dudley still apologising about what had just happened, I looked back at the table. There on the chair, where moments before Dudley had been squirming, was his wallet. I looked at Ellen, and she smiled. I was glad that she'd left it behind. The restaurant would call him in a day or so, and everything would be all right. Somehow, it would have been wrong to have taken it.

Back at the office, we gathered our work together, and I

decided to go back to the hotel for a sleep. The previous night, coupled with my mental exertions over lunch, had left me feeling exhausted. At that moment in time, there was nothing I wanted more than to take a hot bath and to curl up in bed.

If my room had had a bath, that is.

I'd be ready for dinner, but until then, everything else could be put on hold. Ellen said that she was tired too, so once we were back at the hotel, we went straight up the stairs, said our goodbyes and disappeared into our respective rooms.

There's nothing quite like getting into a clean, freshly made bed. It's even better when you've just had a shower. I could finally see the funny side of Ellen's last-minute switch, but it still irked me that I didn't have a bath. That would have been even better. The feeling of sinking down, enveloped by the hot water, had always made me feel safe. Perhaps because it reminded me of my childhood. My house didn't have a shower, only a bath. My father had always wanted to buy one, but for some reason, he never did. I was glad about that.

I showered for a long time that afternoon. As a result, when I eventually made my way out of the bathroom, my skin looked wrinkly. I dried myself quickly and frowned at my fingertips. I had the hands of an old man. I shuddered and covered them with the towel.

A few feet away, the bed beckoned to me, and as I slowly slid between mattress and quilt, the scent of fresh linen wafted into the air. I embraced the pillow like a long-lost friend, and moments later, I was asleep.

When I awoke, it was seven o'clock. I was surprised, though not unhappy, to find Ellen's head resting on my chest, the rhythm of her breathing indicating that she was asleep. She was wearing black tracksuit bottoms and an old white T-shirt, and her hair moved softly with each breath. I thought that I'd locked the door behind me when I came in but obviously not. It felt good to have her here beside me. Strangely natural. And as she pressed against me in her sleep, I put my arm around her shoulder. I'd wake her in a while. But not just yet.

We remained like that for some time, until in the end, my arm began to ache. I'd been careful not to move, but as all sensation slowly left my arm, I knew it was time to get up. I was hungry, and we both needed some food. It had been hours since we'd eaten and if we waited much longer, the hotel restaurant would be closed.

'Wake up, Ellen,' I said softly. Too softly. She didn't move. I tried it again, with the same result. It took me several tries, with gradually increasing volume, before she finally stirred. The first thing she did was look at the clock.

'You're joking!' she groaned. 'It feels like minutes since I dropped off.'

I smiled and told her that we should go for some food. She said sleepily that she didn't feel hungry but would come along anyway. It would have been so easy to stay there, in the warmth, ignoring my stomach, but in the end, common sense prevailed, and I jumped out of bed, nearly tripping over Ellen's discarded shoes. I could hear her giggling from the bed as I stumbled around. In the end, she sat up to watch me.

'You can be a bit disorganised at times,' she laughed. 'Why didn't you just put everything away in the drawers?'

'Wait, we have drawers?' I laughed. Then I shrugged. 'The chair was closer.'

That made her smile, and she finally got out of bed. In comparison to her, I really did appear disorganised. She'd brought a change of clothing with her, folded neatly on top of the bedside table, while mine lay creased across the back of the chair. I asked her if they were perhaps a bit too creased, but she assured me that they were fine, and a few minutes later, we were changed and ready to leave. It was eight o'clock.

We decided to walk down the stairs. Our rooms were on the fourth floor of the hotel, and it didn't take long for us to realise that we were lost. At the end of a corridor, we arrived at a fire door, and as far as I could see, there was no other exit. Across the middle of the door was a long metal bar, with the word 'PUSH' printed above it.

'Don't touch that bar!' warned Ellen.

'But it's telling me to,' I replied with a grin.

'And I'm telling you not to! Do you want to set off the alarms?'

I didn't push the bar.

The narrow corridors were like a maze, and it took us much longer than it should have to find our way to the reception. We both agreed that in future it would be better to take the lift. Although Ellen insisted that it was called an elevator.

It wasn't until halfway through the starter that we were both fully awake. The sleep had worked wonders, and we decided that, as this was our last night, we'd go to a club for a dance. Or rather, that's what Ellen decided. I wasn't really a club man. I told her that I hadn't been to a club for nearly ten years and she teased me, saying that I needed to loosen up. She asked me if I still called them discos and with a straight face, I said yes. She looked relieved when I told her that I was joking. I was a poor dancer, and for some reason, I didn't want her to see that.

During the meal, Ellen was very quiet, and though that didn't bother me particularly, I wondered what was on her mind. When asked, she replied that it was nothing, but I persisted, and finally she gave in, telling me that she was worried things might get out of hand. I asked her what she meant, and she replied that while it had been thrilling taking the bottle of perfume, she was concerned that we needed to keep things under control. She'd felt that way since first taking it, but now that she'd followed it up with the wallet, she was alarmed at how easy it was. It would become problematic at some stage, perhaps very soon. I agreed with her. In fact, it was something that had been playing on my mind too. We'd have to be careful, as it was a fine line between taking risks and being foolhardy. We talked about it at length, at last coming to the conclusion that we should mix things up. We could still have fun, but it didn't always have to be illegal. Besides, doing the same thing all the time would be self-defeating. Wasn't that what we were trying to get away from in the first place?

But what to do? I suggested using some form of points system to grade each risk, and very soon, Ellen was crying with laughter, tears streaming down her face as she playfully christened me Mr Numbers or Captain Accountancy. She joked that perhaps I should set up some form of spreadsheet to monitor our undertakings. I'd actually thought about that, but looking at her tear-streaked face, I thought it best to keep it to myself. It would only be further ammunition. When finally she quietened down, we were still at the same point. Ellen suggested that we play it by ear, to see what came up. Having no better ideas myself, or at least none that I wished to share, I reluctantly agreed.

The nightclub was ten minutes' walk from the hotel, next to an old circular building that had once served as a market, selling everything from corn to fabrics. By the time we arrived, Ellen was in high spirits and repeatedly told me how much fun we were going to have 'dancing the night away'. I'd eaten too much, so wasn't sure that dancing was a good idea. But seeing her excitement, and the way she radiated as we made our way through the doors and down the wooden stairs to the bar, I couldn't help but smile.

The club itself was busy and reminded me of a warehouse that someone had decided to polish. Enormous dancefloors pulsed with bright lights, flashing in time to the music, and everywhere I looked there was chrome. Chrome bars, chrome pillars, even chrome tables. It looked so ridiculous that I wanted to laugh. I turned to Ellen, and she smiled, then pointed to the bar. I took hold of her hand, and we made our way through the crowd, closely followed by our gleaming reflections.

At the bar, I ordered a lager and Ellen said that she'd have the same, though in a smaller glass. It reminded me of my mother, who'd always ordered two halves to my father's pint. Ellen looked at me and asked what I was smiling about. I told her it was nothing, though in truth it was far from it.

She attracted a good deal of attention as we stood there, but I was getting used to that. One person after another came over, then disappeared as they realised she wasn't alone. It was clear from their faces that I wasn't particularly welcome. But I was used to that too. I think she must have noticed because she moved close to me and placed her arm gently around my waist. I saw a couple looking over at us from a shining pillar nearby, the woman far too beautiful for the awkward man by her side. I smiled and pointed them out to Ellen, and she laughed, our reflections copying us as they pointed and laughed in reply.

When we finally got our drinks, we disappeared, away from the other people and into the shadows. We found a seat up some steps, above the dancefloor, and Ellen informed me straight away that she wanted to dance. I told her that I'd join her soon, and she left, throwing me a pout as she went. Moments later, she was swallowed up by the crowd.

For the next few minutes, I sipped at my drink and looked at the dancefloor, trying in vain to see where Ellen had got to. I wanted to see her dance and wondered if she could dance well. I was pretty sure that she could, at least when compared to me. It didn't take long before I heard movement behind me and I turned, expecting to see her.

'I've not seen you around here before,' said a woman, dressed in a short white dress and knee-length black boots. She was quite attractive, and as she smiled, I could see that she was drunk. In her right hand, she held a glass of white wine, and in her left, a half-finished cigarette.

'You from Leeds?' she asked as she sat down next to me, so close that her leg was touching mine. I shook my head, quickly looking to the dance floor, in the hope that Ellen would see me and come over. I hated small talk, and she knew that. But even if she did see me, she'd probably leave me to stew for a while. Either way, I couldn't see her, so all I could do was wait.

'Do you want a fag?' asked the woman. I'd been an occasional smoker for as long as I could remember and had been trying to give up. Sort of. But I'd been weak-willed for much longer than that, so I smiled and reached out my hand.

'Thanks,' I said, helping myself from the outstretched packet. She lit the cigarette, and I took a deep drag. As the smoke filled my lungs, my head became light. The club wasn't so bad after all.

'What do you do for a living?' she asked.

'Nothing illegal,' I replied, and she started to laugh. I took another drag on my cigarette, and she began to talk about herself, though by this stage, I was only half listening.

'Do you mind sweetie?' said a familiar voice after a few

minutes. 'This one's taken.' The woman looked up, then immediately left. Ellen sat down.

'I can't take you anywhere,' she laughed.

I asked her about her dance, and she shook her head, mentioning something about a cattle market. By all accounts, she'd spent most of the time removing hands off her behind, so hadn't danced much at all. I grinned and told her that it was a fine behind, and though I didn't catch her reply, I could tell that it wasn't very ladylike.

'I didn't know you smoked,' she said after a while. I told her that I didn't, and she rolled her eyes. 'You should have said. I really don't mind.'

For the next hour, we talked about nothing in particular, until suddenly, she got up and went to the bar. Moments later, she returned with a couple of drinks. And a packet of cigarettes. She lit one and passed it to me, then took out one for herself.

'I didn't know you smoked,' I grinned.

'I don't,' she said and handed me the packet.

As we sat in the club, plumes of smoke rising into the air, I noticed a huge man prowling around in the darkness nearby. Though he barely looked at me, his eyes were glued onto Ellen. He was carefully watching her, and I quickly became uncomfortable. I asked her if she knew him and she shrugged, before telling me that he'd followed her onto the dancefloor earlier and had refused to leave her alone. She told me not to worry and once again invited me for a dance. I shook my head, though reassured her that I'd keep an eye on the dancefloor. If she had any problems, I'd go over to rescue her at once.

As soon as she'd gone, I caught sight of the big man moving onto the dance floor. He made straight for Ellen, and I smiled to myself as she turned away, leaving him to circle around several groups of dancers before he could face her again. Then I lost sight of them.

Cigarette once more dangling between my lips, I leaned back and surveyed the surroundings. It was quite dark so I couldn't really see too much. From what I could make out, the section above the dancefloor was set aside for couples. It had been constructed in such a way as to provide a dozen or so booths. In each of the booths there squeezed six to eight people, for the most part four women and four men, though this varied from booth to booth. I didn't want to look too closely, fearing I'd be mistaken for a voyeur, but every so often a flash of light from the dancefloor would illuminate the area, revealing a bared breast or exposed thigh. I stared ahead, my focus fixed on my drink, wondering how long it would be until Ellen came back.

Not long, as it turned out.

'Right, let's go!' she said irritably as she returned to the table. Though I was relieved to see her, she did look very angry. 'If I have to put up with that asshole for a second longer, I swear I'll kill him!'

I wanted to ask who she was talking about, but I had a pretty good idea. Fearing another flash of light from the dancefloor, I grabbed our coats and quickly took Ellen's arm. When we got to the exit, I realised that I'd forgotten the cigarettes, so I turned to go back for them. Ellen said that she'd meet me outside, and I promised her that I'd be quick as I headed back up the stairs. I was only gone for a minute, but when I got outside, to where we were meeting, I couldn't see her anywhere. I looked around, wondering if she'd decided to go back without me. But I knew that she wouldn't do that. Besides, she had my wallet.

Just as I was considering what to do, I caught sight of a couple a few metres down the road. They seemed to be arguing, and I knew at once that it was Ellen. The other person towered over her, and I recognised him as the big man from the club. Ellen looked furious, and as she caught sight of me, she stormed up the road in my direction, the big man following at a distance. He didn't look happy to see me.

'Thomas, do something!' she said through gritted teeth. 'He just won't leave me alone.'

When I asked her exactly what she expected me to do, she shrugged, before dragging me off in the direction of a nearby taxi rank. We hadn't gone far when a large hand landed on my shoulder, deftly spinning me around. I looked up to see the big man, his eyes full of drunken aggression. He was bigger than I'd imagined. Much bigger.

Behind me, I could hear Ellen giggling.

'I'll give you five points if you kick his ass,' she whispered, and I thought it an odd time to make fun of my earlier suggestion. I felt a shove in my chest, powerful enough to send me staggering backwards. 'Call that ten!' she said, randomly plucking numbers out of the air. I felt another shove.

It's at times like these when we hope for inspiration, some recollection of past glories, when we overcame insurmountable odds, to emerge victorious. Or at least survived with some dignity intact. I tried to think back to the last time I'd been involved in a fight, but alarmingly, I drew a blank. I could only assume that the man now snarling in front of me had no such problem. I did have one advantage, however—he was roaringly drunk. His movements were laboured, to the point of slow motion, and as I ducked under his punches, I suddenly became confident. Just as I was about to embark upon a series of attacks, which I knew deep down I was wholly incapable of, I felt a thudding pain in my cheek. And then I fell backwards to the concrete. Out of the corner of my eye, I could see a huge figure lumbering towards me, fists clenched like two large kettlebells.

I'm not sure what happened next, as I think I'd closed my eyes, but suddenly his hands shot between his legs, and he let out a groan. Behind him stood Ellen, steadying herself as she prepared to kick him a second time. I raised my hand to stop her.

'Don't worry,' I said, sitting up and blinking at the whimpering figure before me. 'I think I've taken care of things.' She burst out laughing.

Helping me to my feet, Ellen gently kissed my injured cheek. As she inspected me for damage, I prodded my face, checking my fingers to make sure there was no blood. When we were both satisfied, we hurried away from the club, not stopping until we were nearly back at the hotel. Sitting on a cold wooden bench in the main city square, I rubbed my cheek, as Ellen inspected her shoe. Behind us, the sound of a police siren punctuated the silence.

'What was that all about?' I asked her at last.

'You did say you wanted a bit of excitement, didn't you?' she replied. 'Well, wasn't that exciting?'

I think we had differing ideas about excitement.

She stroked her hand across my injured cheek. 'Does it hurt?' she asked. I assured her it was fine, and she smiled. 'Maybe I should be a bit less impulsive in future.'

I told her that was a good idea, then added jokingly that I was ahead on points anyway. Her smile broadened.

'My own Jake LaMotta!' she laughed.

I had no idea who she was talking about.

The next morning, we slept in until late. Ellen had stayed in my room again, on the pretence of keeping an eye on my injury, but she'd fallen asleep almost as soon as her head had touched the pillow. Despite my own fatigue, I hadn't slept well. I'd spent a large part of the night staring at the ceiling, thinking about all that had happened in the two short days since we'd left London. I told myself that everything would be fine, but I still felt uneasy. My original idea of the odd piece of shoplifting had now changed into something different. At the beginning of the week, when I'd first taken the CD, it had all seemed so simple. Trivial and inconsequential. I was looking for some excitement, and I'd found it. It was the same with the gloves. A bit of fun, nothing else. But now things were different. It was no longer just me, and I wasn't in control. I needed to be in control. I never relied on other people because other people were unreliable. I'd reassess over the next couple of days, once we were back in London. Ellen would no longer be with me, and I'd be alone again.

We were returning to London that afternoon, and I was in no hurry to start packing, so we threw on some clothes and headed down to the hotel restaurant. Ellen asked me to order for her, and before long, we were sitting before two large cooked breakfasts. She looked at me suspiciously. 'What's this?' she asked, pointing her fork at the black pudding.

'Black pudding,' I replied.

'What's black pudding?'

'Pig's blood and fat.'

She pushed the black pudding to the side of her plate.

'I don't think I'll bother.'

The offending item found its way onto my fork, and I grinned at her as it disappeared whole into my mouth. She watched on in horror, shaking her head, then made a point of not looking at me for the remainder of breakfast.

After we'd finished eating, Ellen went for a shower. She'd

left most of her breakfast, complaining that it was too oily, though I had a feeling it was more down to her having a hangover. I stayed at the table to have another coffee. I was feeling fine. Perhaps my hangover had been punched out of me the night before. I'd checked my cheek in the mirror that morning and had been pleased to see that there was no bruising. Some tenderness perhaps, but that aside, I'd escaped pretty much unscathed.

The waiter came over and asked if I wanted anything else, so I ordered a coffee.

'Do you know who Jake LaMotta is?' I asked when he returned with the coffee pot.

'I've no idea, sir,' he replied simply. 'A singer?'

I'd never heard any of his songs.

Looking out of the window, I saw that it was cloudy. According to the radio, London was still in a heatwave. Apparently, it would continue for at least another week. I didn't trust meteorologists. I'd lost confidence in them during a disastrous school trip to Paris. They'd promised good weather, so my mother had packed me light clothing and a thin jacket. We'd then spent the whole week cowering under umbrellas and running from storms so that when I'd returned to England, I'd spent the next week in bed with a cold.

So now it was going to be hot? I already knew that. It had been hot for weeks.

Once back in the room, I found Ellen standing there, already dressed and ready to go. She had somehow relocated into my room during the trip, and I wasn't entirely sure how that had occurred. Like most things, it had just happened. If I'd thought about it, it would have been more logical for me to move into her room. At least there would have been a bath.

And I would have found out what was behind that extra

door.

She asked what time we were planning to set off, to which I replied that I hadn't given it much thought. 'I don't know,' I shrugged. 'Mid-afternoon, maybe.'

'Then that gives us time to buy presents,' she announced. It had never occurred to me to buy presents. Perhaps because there was no one to buy presents for. I mentioned this to her, and she looked surprised.

'What about Yasmine?' she said.

'What about Yasmine?' I asked. For a moment, I thought she was joking. The look on her face convinced me otherwise. 'Don't you think that's a bit forward?' I said. 'After all, I've only met her three times.'

'Then I suppose you think the Catullus book was forward?' she said. She had a point.

I had no idea what to buy Yasmine. I thought of asking Ellen, but immediately decided against it. Knowing her sense of humour, I would probably have ended up with something wholly inappropriate.

As we wandered around the streets, the sun came out, and the temperature rose quickly. Ellen handed me her coat and asked me to be careful, her purse was in the pocket. I thanked her, adding that it was just what I needed—a hot day and two coats.

'You're welcome,' she replied, before trying to give me her bag.

We wandered around for half an hour, seemingly without purpose, before finally stopping at an old bookshop. Ellen pulled me inside.

'A book?' I said sarcastically. 'Not exactly the most original gift.'

She looked at me and started to laugh. 'No, it's perfect,' she said. 'I don't know why I didn't think of it earlier.'

The shop smelled musty and looked as though it hadn't been dusted in years. I half expected to see candles, but dotted about the ceiling were dozens and dozens of small spotlights. I looked at them and small stars shined at the back of my eyes. When I looked away, I could still see them shining, and I felt a little dizzy.

I was surrounded by bookcases. Row upon row of them, tightly packed with all manner of books, from travel guides to novels. Their placement seemed random, and I wondered how anyone found anything. But perhaps that was the point. A random choice to see what you got.

The books themselves were all hardbacks, most of which looked like they'd been there for years. I casually picked one up, a collection of short stories by yet another person I'd never heard of, and as I leafed through its yellowing pages, I became increasingly aware that I had no idea what I was looking for. And the more I looked, the more unsure of Ellen's idea I became. Just as I was on the verge of giving up, Ellen danced over and told me that she'd found it, the ideal gift. At first sight, it wasn't exactly what I'd have chosen, a set of poems. But before I could say anything, she opened the book and read a passage out loud. I still wasn't convinced, but seeing the look in her eyes, I nodded and told her it would be perfect.

As we made our way to the cashier, I looked over at Ellen. Her thoughts were elsewhere. I asked her if everything was all right, and she smiled. But it was a sad kind of smile.

'It's nothing really,' she said. 'Yasmine will love the book, Thomas. I just don't want to see you get hurt.'

I didn't know what she was talking about. When I asked her what she meant, she just shrugged. That was as much as I was going to get.

We linked arms as we made our way back to the hotel, and

I'm sure passers-by would have thought we were a couple. On the way, I asked Ellen to name me a song by Jake LaMotta, and she laughed, squeezing my arm. She asked why a boxer would record a song. I replied that someone had told me, and she smiled and leaned her head against my shoulder.

So, he was a boxer? Well, that made more sense.

The drive back to London took less time than I'd expected. It was only eight o'clock by the time we arrived back at the Walkers'. Yasmine and Sir Ian were out, and Ellen invited me in for a coffee. The journey had made me quite drowsy, and I wanted to get back to my flat. When I told her that I was going, she looked sad, so I decided to stay for the coffee after all. And then she looked happy.

We chatted for an hour, and at just gone nine o'clock I decided to leave. Ellen came over and gave me the most enormous hug, then kissed me repeatedly as I tried to escape. She thanked me again for taking her to Leeds, even though I'd had little choice. I thanked her in return and told her it had been fun. And in truth, it had.

As I turned to go, I noticed a book, lying on top of one of her bags. I hadn't seen it before.

'Where did you get that?' I asked.

'Oh, I picked it up at the bookshop this afternoon,' she replied.

That was strange—I'd been looking after her purse.

Chapter 8

The following Monday, Ellen's arrival at the office caused quite a stir. James and Henry, in particular, looked shaken.

In reality, it turned out to be just what the office needed, and from that day on, everyone turned up in their best suits, with neatly combed hair and highly polished shoes. I moved her desk into my office, and over the next few weeks, our relationship blossomed. Ellen spent a few days each week at my flat, and again, I wasn't entirely sure when this had happened. But I was happy that it had. Despite its diminutive size, we got by easily enough. It was a good time.

There had been no more 'incidents' to talk of, bar the odd theft here and there, and nothing of any real expense.

At around the same time as Ellen's arrival, my new assistant arrived too. Of course, James fell madly in love with her, but being James, he was too shy to reveal his feelings. He told Ellen and me, but we swore not to say anything, although on several occasions the temptation was strong. He'd mumble incoherently whenever he talked to her, and several times I had to stop Ellen from helping him. At least her own brand of help. A promise was a promise after all.

About a week after our return, Ellen started to receive mysterious gifts through the internal mail. At first flowers, then later, chocolates and perfume. They were accompanied by letters, and it didn't take long to work out that they were from Henry. This was confirmed when his expense bill came through, with its numerous claims for 'miscellaneous expenses'. Out of interest, I had the accounts department send up his receipts. Ellen laughed so much, I thought she was going to pass out. I decided to spread a rumour that she was keen on the classics, and by the end of the week, Henry was walking around with a copy of the Odyssey conspicuously tucked under his arm.

As for myself, things were going okay. I'd spoken to Yasmine a few times, though when I did, it was usually over the phone and prompted by Ellen. I'd never been one for telephone conversations, but by and large, they went well, with silences kept to a minimum. It wasn't really flirting, but that was fine.

Then there was Ellen herself. Many times, I told her she should find herself a proper boyfriend, but every time she refused. She was happy with how things were, or so she said. As it turned out, one day she admitted to having a boyfriend back in New York. Apparently, they planned to get married when she returned. I was sad after that. And Ellen never made me feel sad. I didn't say anything, and it didn't last long. Just having her around made me happy, and it wasn't long before we were back to joking and messing around. She was good at that.

And as all this went on, London was enjoying a heatwave. For once, the weathermen had been right.

One Friday afternoon, James invited Ellen and me to his house for the weekend. I had no other plans, so accepted, as did Ellen. Henry overheard the conversation and invited himself along too. Though he was invited anyway. Ellen suggested to James that he should ask Jane, my new assistant, and though we all knew that he wanted to, he said that he couldn't.

'Nonsense,' I said and shouted over to Jane. 'You'll come along to James's house for the weekend, won't you?'

'If that's all right,' she laughed. We assured her that it was, and James whispered his thanks. He was as red as a beetroot. James had prepared a map, in some detail, which he handed to each of us while I teased him about how busy he must have been at work. He laughed and told me to mind my own business, which made Ellen and Henry laugh too. I was the only one who wasn't laughing.

Ellen had moved into her new flat, conveniently close to mine, so we departed together. Before she left, however, she took James aside and whispered something into his ear. As we walked along the road, she gave the impression of being very pleased with herself, and though I quizzed her non-stop, she refused to reveal what the conversation had been about. By the time we got to the Underground, I'd stopped asking. She was infuriatingly good at keeping secrets. We stopped off for a quick drink at a bar near my flat, and Ellen asked if she could spend the night with me. I pretended to look in my diary, to see if any other women were due round that night, and she punched me playfully on the arm. It turned out that I was free, so after picking up some wine, we made our way back.

I was feeling hot when we arrived, the result of spending a full day in a suit, so the first thing I did was jump into the shower. Ellen made a couple of phone calls. The shower was too hot, so I turned down the temperature, at which point it became too cold. No matter how hard I tried, I couldn't get the temperature right, and that was precisely why I preferred baths. In the end, I got out and dried myself on the large white towel I'd taken from the hotel in Leeds.

By the time I got back into the living room, Ellen had finished her phone calls and was sitting patiently on the sofa, her shoes neatly placed by the door and two glasses of wine waiting on the coffee table. We turned on the television and flicked channels, finding nothing of interest. At least nothing that appealed to both of us. I reminded her that it was my TV, so I should choose. She replied that as she was the guest, it was up to her what we watched. First, we watched a few minutes of an American comedy, which I didn't really understand. It wasn't funny, and I couldn't see why Ellen found it so hilarious. When she saw that I wasn't laughing, she looked at me and shook her head. We then watched a British comedy. Now that was funny. It was about a man who ran a working men's club in the north of England, and I laughed from start to finish. Ellen decided that I needed psychiatric help.

At last, the late film came on. It was one of my favourites, and as luck would have it, it was one of Ellen's too. This time, we both laughed. Laughing with someone else is so much better than laughing alone.

We arrived at James's just before lunch. We were later than expected because of a detour to Ellen's, to pick up a few things for the weekend. 'A few things' seemed to have a different meaning in America. My bag could best be described as a medium-sized holdall, but compared to Ellen's, it resembled a small purse. Being a gentleman, I offered to carry her bag, and being Ellen, she let me.

'Well, here you are!' said James as he opened the door. His house was a large modern affair, and it had taken us a few minutes to find our way from the car to his front door. As far as I could see, there were no other houses nearby. However, it was surrounded by a woodland, so I could quite easily have been mistaken. All manner of things could have been hiding in there. He showed us into the house, wincing noticeably as I handed him Ellen's bag.

'Henry's already here,' he said. 'I've invited along a few others too.'

'And Jane?' asked Ellen. He blushed and nodded his head.

'I hope you've brought your swimming costumes,' he added. I hadn't but, of course, Ellen had. Her bag contained just about every item of clothing imaginable. Probably a set of aqualungs too. James smiled and told me not to worry.

'You can borrow a pair of mine,' he said as Ellen giggled behind me. I wasn't sure if he was joking or not, though I hoped that he was.

The house was magnificent and very 'James'. The design was open plan and extremely spacious. In the corner was a huge television and by each chair was an electronic console and several small gadgets. I asked James what they were all for, and he admitted that he didn't know. Some of them he recognised, but others he couldn't even remember buying. In the centre was the dining area and to the left, in a small dip, was the lounge. Bedrooms were located at the end of wide passageways and at the far wall, an enormous window looked out over a pool. We were obviously paying him too much.

Ellen and I looked around, pressing buttons and peering behind curtains. Before long, James returned with a pair of swimming trunks.

'Here you are,' he said. 'Are these okay?' They looked more like a G-string than a pair of swimming trunks. Ellen was grinning, and she begged me to put them on.

'Do you have something a little more conservative, James?' I asked. He shrugged his shoulders and went off to look. While no one was looking, Ellen gave me a kiss.

'I'd have died if you'd worn them!' she laughed. 'Why not wear shorts? I've got a pair in my bag.' Of course, she had.

When James returned, I told him I'd found some shorts, and he took back the trunks. He then showed us to a room where we could change. The room was almost as big as my flat, and Ellen squeezed my arm sympathetically.

'Your place is much more homely,' she said with a smile.

Once I was ready, I told Ellen I'd meet her in the kitchen. I wanted to find some beer before going to the pool. She stayed behind in the room, but promised not to be long. I was still searching for the beer when she came out. She was wearing a black swimsuit and looked stunning. Henry was going to have a fit.

'Do you think it's okay?' she asked. I told her it was fine. Compared to the trunks James was wearing, her swimsuit was positively Victorian. At last, I found the beer, and we headed for the pool.

Outside it was beautiful. The midday sun was piercingly bright, allowing little by way of shade. We were standing in a large paved area, and at its centre was the pool, with perhaps thirty people around it, relaxing on sun loungers and wooden chairs. One or two people were already splashing around, and tiny drops of water, like liquid silver, flew through the air.

Compared to most of the guests, Ellen and I were conservatively dressed. There was far too much flesh on show for my liking. Seeing my colleagues dressed in tiny swimming costumes was downright uncomfortable, and it didn't take long for Ellen to notice my discomfort.

'Everything all right, Thomas?' she asked with a grin.

'There's still time to take James up on his offer of the trunks?' I assured her I was fine.

I recognised everyone there. At least their faces, if not their names. To the left were some people from accounts, two women and a man. They sat on the same floor as me, though around the corner. Next to them were some of James's friends, all hair gel and pimples. I couldn't recall their names, though I had a feeling that one of them was called Darius. Or perhaps Marius, I wasn't sure. To the right were three faces I recognised instantly.

'Oh, my God!' gasped Ellen. 'Look at Henry!' He was sitting next to Jane and James, wearing the smallest swimming trunks I'd ever seen. It didn't take long for him to spot us, and he immediately began waving. Despite my best efforts to pretend that I hadn't seen him, he continued to wave, and soon he was shouting my name. In the end, we had little choice but to join him. As we walked over, I pointed out to Ellen his copy of the Odyssey, lying inches from his pale, hairless legs, and she screwed up her face, trying hard not to laugh.

'Help me, Thomas!' she whispered, though I feared there was little I could do.

'Hello, you two,' smiled Henry as we arrived. 'It's good to see you.'

'Hi, Henry,' I said. 'Nice trunks.' Ellen ran back into the house. When she returned a few minutes later, it looked like she'd been crying. The tears must have affected her vision, as she immediately stood on my foot.

James invited us to sit down, so I took the seat between him and Henry. The cold wood of the chair felt soothing against my legs, and I was relieved to find myself under the shade of a large parasol. Ellen looked at me and smiled, then announced that she was going for a swim. Henry said that he'd join her. For one wonderful moment, a look of horror crossed her face, and she quickly asked me if I'd go too. I replied that I was fine where I was.

For the next few minutes, James and I watched in fascination as Henry pursued her around the pool, his half-naked buttocks quivering beneath the surface of the water. The whole thing was strangely enthralling, though I'm sure Ellen didn't think so. She was so cross when she got out of the pool that I started to laugh. And that made her even worse.

'I'll get you for that,' she hissed. I had no doubt that she would.

Once Henry returned, the five of us chatted idly. The kind of conversation that's forgotten as soon as it's said. Like a soothing white noise. I stretched out and could quite easily have fallen asleep, were it not for Ellen poking me and pouring cold water onto my stomach. She must have thought it would annoy me. But it was actually quite pleasant.

When James announced that lunch was ready, everyone moved to the dining room. Stuck to the large glass window was a seating plan, and I was pleased to find that I was between Ellen and Henry. I didn't know the others well enough for casual conversation. Ellen seemed happy, as well. She smiled at Jane, who was sitting next to James, and Jane smiled back. The seating plan was not so random after all.

The food was delicious and beautifully presented. Jane, no doubt, had a hand in that too. I congratulated James, and Jane blushed. Then he thanked her, thinking that no one could hear.

All throughout the meal, Henry quizzed Ellen on various aspects of classical literature. She was very well-read, which took Henry completely by surprise, and it was good to see him so clearly out of his depth.

As the meal was finishing, there was a knock at the door. James and Ellen smiled to one another and Ellen went to answer it. When she returned, she was accompanied by Yasmine. So this was what they'd been planning at the office. Yasmine took a seat next to James, and Ellen poured her a drink. The rest of the guests looked as though they'd seen a ghost and I wondered if they were regretting their choice of swimwear.

Despite Yasmine's arrival, it didn't take long for everyone to relax, and by the time James invited us back out to the pool, conversation had once more returned to the trivialities of earlier. As I left, I caught sight of Ellen and Henry in animated discussion, and I smiled to myself. Henry had wrapped himself in a large beach towel. Reluctant to be seen by Yasmine in such disgraceful swimming trunks, he'd wrapped himself so tightly that his torso looked contorted. Like a balloon being squeezed in the middle. It took Ellen some time to persuade him to lose his modesty, but when he finally did, he strutted around the pool like an overweight peacock. I waved to Ellen, and she beamed back at me, thrilled with her powers of persuasion. Behind her I could see Yasmine, looking on over the top of her sunglasses. I'm unable to describe the look on her face.

And for the first time that afternoon, I decided to go for a swim.

I'd never been the greatest of swimmers. With me, it was style over substance. At school, it had frustrated me that no matter how good my technique, the speed was never there. A friend once described it as elegant drowning. And it was a fair description.

And so, as I splashed around the pool, it didn't take long for me to tire. I was about to get out when in jumped Henry, and before long, the pool was teeming with bodies. James suggested a game of water polo and sides were chosen. Ellen, Yasmine and Jane indicated that they wouldn't be joining us. I was placed on a different team to Henry, so I decided to dunk him for as long as possible, without actually killing him. Whether or not he sensed my plan, I'm not sure, but he steered well clear of me as the ball flew across the water. More than once, I was pushed beneath the surface, and more than once, I returned the favour. I had no idea who was the assailant or who was the victim, but it was good fun. And when we finally left the pool, my team was declared the winner, and I smiled at Henry, who looked disproportionately annoyed. It was a double victory.

'You looked like you were having a few problems in there,' laughed Yasmine as I pulled up a seat, wrapping myself in the nearest towel. And while the three women poked fun at me, comparing me unfavourably to various swimmers I'd never heard of, I sat back in the sun and opened a beer.

By the middle of the afternoon, it was starting to get cooler. The gardens of the house were ridiculously large, and I decided to go for a walk. Yasmine said that she'd join me, though Ellen decided to stay by the pool, gossiping with Jane. Before we went, Ellen told me to look in my bag. She'd brought something along for me. I wandered off to the house to see what it was, and when I got to the room we'd changed in earlier, I located the bag. In it was the book I'd bought in Leeds. She must have slipped it in that morning.

'Did you find it?' asked Ellen when I got back to the pool. I told her that I had and thanked her for packing it. She smiled and told me to have fun. But it was that sad smile again.

When we were at a safe distance from the house, I gave the book to Yasmine.

'I didn't know that you liked poetry, Thomas,' said

Yasmine, smiling as she turned the book over in her hands.

'I don't really,' I admitted. 'To be honest, it was more Ellen's idea than mine.'

That made Yasmine laugh. 'I thought it might be,' she said. 'It's a very nice gift anyway.'

I thanked her, though I wasn't sure what for.

We walked a little further and eventually arrived at a small grove. A few metres away in a clearing, there was an old stone bench, and we strolled over to it to sit down. After a day in the sun, it felt cold to the touch, and my skin prickled, as though a thousand tiny ants were crawling along my legs. A sudden breeze started to blow, and above us the branches of the trees creaked, shaking droplets of water onto our heads. Yasmine laughed, and it sounded melodic against the silence of the woods. It had been so warm over recent weeks that I found myself wondering how there could still be water in the trees. But there it was. And as the water fell, Yasmine continued to laugh, and I thought how much she reminded me of Ellen, the innocent joy in her laughter, so carefree and happy.

Finally, the water stopped, and I brushed at my legs with my hands. I looked across at Yasmine. There were small beads of water sparkling in her hair, like tiny diamonds. Then moments later they were gone, and it was as if they'd never been there at all.

At that moment, I realised I didn't know what I was doing. In my desire to spice things up while at the same time annoying Sir Ian, I'd embarked upon a course of action so childish it now seemed absurd. The whole idea of flirting with Yasmine was ridiculous, and I wondered why I'd listened to Henry in the first place. I often wondered why I listened to Henry. Yasmine was a good person, someone I actually liked, and there were precious few of those. I was in danger of making a complete fool of myself.

'What are you thinking about, Thomas?' she asked, after I'd been quiet for some time. I didn't know how to answer.

'Oh, work I suppose,' I said.

'Then I must be very dull!' she said with a smile, and I immediately apologised. I seemed to spend a lot of time apologising.

Then we talked. Yasmine asked me about my work, and I told her that it was okay, though perhaps not what I'd hoped to be doing. She nodded.

'We rarely end up at the destination we'd hoped for, Thomas,' she said.

It felt like she'd shared a confidence, so I pushed my luck and asked her about Sir Ian.

'Ian does what he wants,' she shrugged. 'He asks for my advice, but he's already made up his mind.' I wasn't entirely sure what she meant but decided not to press her further.

It was Yasmine's turn to fall deep into thought, and I was afraid that I'd upset her somehow.

'Let's head back,' I said, more to break the silence than because I wanted to go. 'People will probably be wondering where we are.'

We stood up, and Yasmine brushed a leaf off her leg. She was smiling again, and she thanked me for the walk.

In my mind, our chat had clarified a few things, and as we strolled back to the house, I felt a lightness, an unburdening that I hadn't felt for quite some time. And that felt good.

Halfway along James's gravelled driveway, I could see that the pool was deserted. There was music coming from inside the house. As we walked towards the front door, Yasmine stopped me and said that unfortunately she had to go. Sir Ian would be coming home soon, and he would wonder where she was. She asked me to pass on her apologies to Ellen and

James. I walked her to her car, and in the fading light, we said goodbye.

Rather than go straight back into the house, I decided to stay outside for a while. The heat of the afternoon had been replaced by a pleasant warmth, and for some reason, I thought of my childhood. I pictured my mother and father sitting in the sun by the back door, drinking with friends while I played nearby. They'd had so many friends, and it was odd that I had so few. Of course, the weather hadn't always been warm, but that's the way I liked to remember it. Laughter and warmth. I refused to recall it in any other way.

I must have been gone for a while, because when I got back, Ellen was waiting for me. By the look on her face, it was clear that something had happened. Taking me by the hand, she led me to a small group of people over by the kitchen. James was there, as was Henry and Jane. It looked like Jane had been crying.

When I arrived, everyone started talking at the same time, and I had to ask them to slow down. It was Henry who took control. It appeared that one of James's neighbours had been round, complaining about the noise. An argument had ensued, during which he had hit James in the face. I looked over to James, and he smiled, but I could see that he was shaken. When Jane had tried to stop him, the neighbour had hit her too. It didn't really bother me that James had been hit, he should have learned to take care of himself, but Jane was different. I was responsible for her being there, at least partly, so in a way it was my fault she'd been hit. And that annoyed me.

'Someone should teach him a lesson,' I said, and Ellen looked at me. I could see straight away what she was thinking. But I didn't feel like getting beaten up again. We'd have to think of something else.

While the other three continued to replay what had happened, Ellen took me to one side and whispered into my ear.

'Do you think we should pay him a visit?'

That evening, we found ourselves crawling through thick bushes. It was damp underfoot, and once again, I wondered how that could be the case. In front of us, across a broad expanse of lawn, was the house. I'd spoken to Ellen at some length, and she'd finally promised to behave. We were going to break a few things, but that was as far as it went. She'd tried to remind me how 'exciting' things had been during the fight in Leeds, but I'd assured her that was not my recollection of events. And while her promise was reassuring, I wasn't sure I fully believed her.

The house itself was predictably large, about the same size as James's, though perhaps more traditional. There was a light on in one of the windows, but apart from that, it looked deserted. Ellen and I were dressed in dark tracksuits, with matching hooded tops, and again, I found myself marvelling at the number of things she'd managed to pack. Ellen's clothes fitted her perfectly, of course, while mine were far too tight, something which seemed to amuse her a great deal.

The grass was damp. It was cut short, like a putting green, and its size provided little by way of cover as we crept from the bushes. Every few feet, Ellen would make a disgusted noise, as if she'd trodden in something, and I smiled to myself as she swore under her breath. The closer we got to the house, the more conscious I became of the noise, so I told her to quieten down.

'God, you can be an asshole!' she retorted, making me smile again.

'It's arsehole actually,' I said, knowing that would wind her up even more.

But she laughed.

'What do you mean arsehole?' she asked. 'That sounds stupid!'

And then we both started to giggle. We must have looked ridiculous.

Just as we were discussing what to do, someone came out of the house and headed for a large car parked on the driveway. I saw straight away that it was a man. He looked worryingly big, and I was glad of Ellen's earlier promise. I looked at her, crouched down on the grass next to me, and she grinned, then threw a few punches in my direction. The car started. It was a shame, I'd quite fancied scratching it. But at least the house was now empty.

'How about taking a look around the house?' said Ellen, wiping something off her hands onto my back. 'It looks like no one's in.'

The light in the window had gone out, so it seemed we were safe. And with that safety came a surge in confidence.

'Sure,' I replied. 'Let's go around the back.'

Scampering across the remainder of the lawn, we circumnavigated the house and, at last, found the back door. It was made of wood, but above the door handle was a large pane of glass, which looked easy enough to break. I told Ellen to stand back. I'd break the glass and open it from the inside, very much like I'd seen on TV. It seemed easy enough. I explained the plan to Ellen, and though she looked unconvinced, she handed me a cloth. I asked her why she had a cloth with her, but she just shrugged, as though it was a natural thing to be carrying. I then asked her if she was carrying a brick too, but she shook her head.

'Why on earth would I be carrying a brick?' she asked. She looked genuinely puzzled.

Picking up a nearby stone, I wrapped it in the cloth and then swung it at the glass. I'd expected the cloth to dampen the sound, but in reality, there was an almighty crash, and small shards of glass shot through the air. I looked over to Ellen to see if she was okay. She checked herself over, then burst out laughing, complimenting me on the smoothness of the operation. I told her it was the fault of the cloth and advised her to bring a thicker one next time.

Then, slipping my hand through the enormous hole I'd created, I found the lock and slowly gave it a twist. It was already unlocked.

Inside, it was a real mess, with glass everywhere. It would take ages to clear it all up. As we walked down the hall, I became increasingly angry with James's neighbour. I felt as though he'd made a fool of me, even though he hadn't been there.

'What are we going to do?' asked Ellen after a while.

'I don't know,' I replied. 'Smash it up?'

'Don't you think that's a bit severe?' she said.

'Probably.'

The first place we entered was the living room. There was no need for lights, as the curtains were open, and the moonlight illuminated the room. Everything was so clear. It felt unreal, like we were in an old black and white film. Noticing a large porcelain vase in the corner, I went over to it and picked it up. Ellen called to me, and I threw it to her, then watched as it slipped smoothly through her fingers and smashed on the floor.

'Oops, butterfingers!' she laughed, though it wasn't clear whether she'd tried to catch it or not. By the time we left the room, the floor was littered with pottery. Next, we went upstairs. It took us no time to find his bedroom. It was such a large room that I was unsure where to start. Too much choice is not always a good thing. At the far end was a stone fireplace, above which hung an oil painting.

'That's him!' cried Ellen as I took down the picture, carefully laying it on the bed so that I could see it more closely. She handed me a pen, and I added a moustache and a pair of spectacles. By the time I'd finished, he was barely recognisable.

'Much better,' said Ellen, and she planted a kiss on my cheek.

As we were leaving the bedroom, the sound of a car door closing could be heard, swiftly followed by the jangle of keys in the front door. Not much later, there was a great deal of swearing, then footsteps rapidly making their way up the stairs. Ellen looked at me startled, and I told her to hide. No sooner had I jumped into a wardrobe, than the bedroom door opened and in stormed a very annoyed looking man. Despite the lack of spectacles and moustache, I recognised him at once.

He was much bigger close up.

Unfortunately for Ellen, she hadn't reacted as quickly as me. She was still in the middle of the room when he entered, and she didn't move. A rabbit caught in headlights is perhaps the best description, frozen in place and defenceless. I watched as her expression changed from shock to horror, then quickly to panic. Thinking back to that time in Leeds, I wondered if she was finding this scenario exciting. It certainly didn't look like it from where I was standing.

In truth, I'd expected him to call the police, but it was soon apparent that he had other intentions. Grabbing her by the shoulders, he shook her, and a stream of profanities spewed from his mouth. I didn't recognise many of the words, and I wondered if he was making them up. It's odd what comes into my mind at times. And as I peered from the wardrobe, he slapped her across the face, and she fell to the floor. Enough was enough.

'I think you should stop there,' I said calmly, stepping out from the wardrobe. I'm not sure how it came out like that, as calmness was certainly not my overriding emotion. Anger perhaps, fear definitely. But not calmness. A look of relief passed over Ellen's face. I think she'd expected my intervention a little earlier.

She propped herself up on one elbow and smiled at me.

'You've got a tie stuck to your shoulder,' she said.

I looked and saw that she was right. It was green, with a small shield in the middle. I used to have a similar one myself, but that one had been blue.

The man turned to me and shouted. So now it was my turn for some treatment.

Another expletive, another word I didn't recognise, and then he was moving. In my mind, I pictured an oil tanker, powerful yet incredibly slow. As he came towards me, moonlight streamed through the windows, painting the scene with an unearthly glow, as though at any moment the lights would turn on and everything would disappear. But the lights didn't come on. And we couldn't disappear.

My immediate future didn't look bright. Behind him, Ellen was back on her feet, and I could see her smiling at me, as she threw some more of those weird shadow punches. If it weren't for the man bearing down on me, I would have told her just how completely unhelpful she was being.

For a moment, I thought back to the previous fight, and wondered if that experience might help in my current predicament. Nothing immediately came to mind, and as I stood there bracing myself for the inevitable, I noticed Ellen pointing to something behind me. She'd stopped her boxing and was now urging me to turn around. Against my better judgement, I did just that, and I immediately found myself staring at a metal poker, no more than six inches from my right hand. Moments later, I was wafting it around, doing my best to look menacing. And when Ellen started to laugh, I wasn't sure who I wanted to hit first. It was too close to call.

At last, the man had reached me. I swung the poker at him, and I missed. He swung a punch at me, and he hit. It was all so predictable. Just once I would have liked to find myself on the right side of the equation. It was, however, a surprisingly weak punch, and his lunge seemed to have thrown him off balance. He hit me on the shoulder, more of a glancing blow than the knockout punch he'd intended. I looked at him in surprise, and as I was doing so, I heard an almighty crash, closely followed by the sight of pottery flying through the air. The man groaned and bent forwards, revealing Ellen behind him with the remnants of a large porcelain pot in her hands, the topmost portion of which had completely disappeared. She looked surprised, as though she didn't understand where it had gone.

Then she looked at me, her eyebrows raised, as if to ask what we should do. So I hit him with the poker.

And then for what seemed like an eternity, we watched as the man, now staring blankly, toppled to the floor. It reminded me of a controlled explosion, where at first the building doesn't move, then moments later it starts to fall, picking up speed until it crashes to the ground. Or in this case, the edge of the stone fireplace. A small pool of blood spread out across the carpet while Ellen and I stared at each other, neither of us knowing what to say. Finally, it was Ellen who broke the silence.

'I think we've killed him.'

When we arrived back at the party, we headed straight for

the food. With a chicken leg in one hand and a can of beer in the other, I thought to myself about what had just happened. I was surprised by how little I felt. There had been adrenalin, of course, but as for soul searching and questions of morality, there was nothing. Also, it had been easy, much easier than I would have expected. We have such exaggerated ideas about things we know little about.

Things had moved on since my compact disc days.

As soon as we returned, Ellen and I went to the changing room and removed our tracksuits. We stuffed the dirty clothes into two carrier bags, then washed and got dressed into something clean. Ellen had packed a pair of jeans and a green polo shirt for me, while she opted for trousers and a T-shirt. Walking to the door, she noticed a small piece of pottery in my hair, so she removed it and put it into her bag. We were good to go.

Very soon, James came over to see us. We chatted for a while, and it was immediately evident that he had no idea we'd gone out. He lurched unsteadily from one foot to the other, and I could see that he was drunk. He was at that point where time had no meaning, so I handed him a beer to blur things further.

In our absence, many of the people had started to leave. Those that remained looked tired. Or more likely drunk. I noticed Henry in the far corner deep in conversation with one of the women from our HR department and by the look of things, they'd treated themselves to a little too much of James's wine. I wondered if anything was going to happen between them, and when I pointed them out to Ellen, she shook her head.

'You don't think they're going to do anything, do you?' she said, looking slightly appalled.

'I'm not sure they're in a fit state,' I replied.

But I was wrong.

The police arrived early the next morning. Everyone was still in bed, and it was a very rough sounding James who went to answer the door. Ellen and I were awake immediately, listening to the conversation from the safety of our bed.

'For such an expensive house, there isn't much by way of sound-proofing,' observed Ellen. I listened more closely, and sure enough, I could hear every word.

'You're right,' I said. 'That would really annoy me.'

James and the policemen spoke together for around thirty minutes, and when they finally left, Ellen and I lay back in the bed, waiting for James. It wasn't long before the bedroom door opened. The conversation had obviously sobered him up, and he was in a very excited mood.

'You'll never guess what happened last night?' he said.

'Henry got lucky,' I replied. Behind me, I could hear Ellen giggling.

'No, even worse than that,' continued James. 'My neighbour got murdered.'

Ellen and I gasped.

'Yes, really!' he continued. 'Apparently he caught some burglars in his house. He must have tried to take the law into his own hands and ended up getting himself killed.'

I shook my head in disbelief. 'That's terrible,' I said. 'We're not even safe in our own homes.'

'Anyway, I told the police we were all here last night, so they won't be bothering us again.' That was good to hear. A house full of drunks is always a good alibi.

As he left the room, he turned to us and smiled.

'And yes, Henry did get lucky!'

Ellen pretended to be sick, and from the look on James's face, she wasn't the only one feeling queasy at the thought. I asked them if they thought Henry might have worn his skimpy swimming trunks, and Ellen shoved me playfully.

'Don't even joke about it!' she laughed.

At breakfast, Henry was looking extremely pleased with himself. He clearly wanted to tell me about his evening, so I made a point of staying as far away from him as possible. I tried to push Ellen towards him, but she didn't find it funny, so I stopped after the fourth attempt.

News of the incident with James's neighbour did little to dampen the spirits, and as we munched through fresh croissants and strawberry jam, it soon became apparent that no one had any recollection of our absence, not even Henry. Speculation was rife as to who the killer might be, but in the end, it was decided the police were correct, and it was probably burglars. Ellen and I agreed, and finishing our food, we went out to sit by the pool.

It was hot again outside, and the sun sparkled on the water. The wooden chairs and sun loungers were out, but today there were fewer people, perhaps twelve or thirteen, so we could choose where to sit. Someone had tidied up from the previous evening, and I thought of Jane. It was very much something she would do.

Very soon, the rest of the guests came out to join us. I noted that James's friends were still there, though I couldn't see Darius. Or Marius. James and Jane sat next to us. Even I could see that something was going on. It was nice to see the two of them, like loved-up teenagers, and I caught Ellen smiling, as she watched them from over the top of a magazine.

As with the day before, I was the only man in shorts, the others opting for their earlier attire. Ellen still found it amusing and was in such a playful mood that I didn't get a moment's peace right up until lunchtime.

I ate lunch quickly, as in all honesty, I was still feeling full from the breakfast. There was so much food on the table that I found it somewhat off-putting. Not that the others seemed to mind, and I watched in astonishment as Ellen ate sandwich after sandwich. In the words of my parents, she must have had hollow legs. When she caught sight of me staring at her, she smiled then shrugged. Her eyes never left me as she shoved into her mouth the most enormous piece of cake she could find.

'You're going to burst,' I said.

She started to laugh, and small pieces of cake tumbled from her mouth.

'Burst with happiness!' she laughed.

After lunch, I decided to go for a short walk. Too much lazing around had put me in a restless mood. I asked Ellen if she wanted to come, and she said that she'd love to. While the rest of the guests went back outside to the pool, we set off, and as we walked across the lawn, I could see James's grinning face in the distance.

The temperature had been rising steadily since mid-morning, and it was with no small relief that we eventually reached the sanctuary of the woods. I quickly located the stone bench I'd sat on with Yasmine, and this time I sat there with Ellen. Once again, it was cold to the touch, and I soon felt the familiar prickling sensation on my skin. If anything, it was hotter than yesterday, and I asked Ellen if she'd brought a bottle of water with her.

'What?' she asked. 'You mean you haven't brought one with you?'

Oh, here we go, I thought to myself. I could see that she had a bottle tucked away in the mesh pouch of her bag.

'No, Ellen,' I said slowly. 'I must have forgotten.'

'Beg me!' she said with a grin. I told her that I wouldn't. I wasn't a particularly proud person, but even I had my limits.

'Very well,' she shrugged.

And with that, she opened her bottle and proceeded to drink the lot. Several drops of water fell onto the stone bench below, and seeing them there, so near and yet so far away, I was aware of just how thirsty I was. Without thinking, I reached out and touched them.

'A desperate man should be more careful what he says,' she said.

Just then I noticed another bottle, poking seductively from the top of her bag. Whether or not she'd placed it like that for my benefit wasn't clear, but I smiled and asked her if the bottle was for me.

'You're so bloody stubborn,' she said, by way of reply. 'You could have at least played along with me!'

I laughed. 'Please Ellen. May I have some of that water. Please!'

'That actually sounded creepy,' she said with a smile and handed me the bottle. 'Just drink the water!'

The temperature had finally levelled off, any hotter and it would have been unbearable. Sitting there, shaded by the trees, I looked around and thought how different the place felt compared to the previous day. Gone was the humidity, replaced by a dryness which scratched at my throat. Above me, the branches still creaked, but this time no water came down, only dry leaves, carpeting the ground around me. It was the same place, but in a different world.

'Do you think we've done anything wrong, Thomas?' said Ellen, after a while. I sighed to myself. It had to be asked.

'No,' I replied, though we both knew we'd done something very wrong. 'It was unavoidable Ellen. Self-defence.'

Even to me, it sounded unconvincing.

'I'm sure the police wouldn't see it like that.'

'Probably not. But if you can justify it to yourself, what does it matter what other people think?' She thought about it for a while, then took hold of my hand.

'Yeah, why not,' she said. 'Let's go with that.'

The look of sadness in her eyes nearly broke my heart.

In future years, I did manage to convince myself. If we repeat something enough, it finally becomes reality. It's impressive really. I did think of it as self-defence. We were being attacked, and we defended ourselves. And I forgot about the poker, and how he was probably unconscious even before I'd hit him. I didn't want to think about that.

'Try to forget it, Ellen,' I said. And in time, she would too.

After a while, the conversation changed to other topics, notably that of Henry and his escapades of the night before. Ellen could often be brash and impulsive, but there was also a more sensitive and romantic side to her. She genuinely wanted Henry to be happy, and I could see that, despite all of our joking, she had an honest affection for him. As one of his closest friends, she asked me about his past, what he did in his spare time, and if he had a family. It came as something of a shock to her, and to me too, that I had no idea. I got the distinct feeling that she wasn't impressed.

We sat on the bench for a long time that day. We were in no hurry to get back to the house, so decided it would be fun to explore further into the woods. It wasn't long before the undergrowth began to change, as dried leaves gave way to small shrubs and bunches of stinging nettles. It got to the point where it was difficult to see ahead, and just as we were considering turning back, Ellen spotted something in the distance, through a mass of ferns and overgrown bushes. We held hands as we walked, eventually coming up against an old stone wall. Dark green moss clung to the surface, and in places it was starting to crumble. It was too high to see over, so I lifted Ellen onto my shoulders and slowly eased her up until her head disappeared out of sight. The next thing I knew, she was calling down to me. There was something on the other side, and she wanted me to join her. I climbed carefully up the wall, and very soon, I was sitting next to her. Down below, perfectly hidden amidst all of the trees, was a deserted old garden.

My initial impression was one of neglect, with most of what I could see overgrown. Thick brambles and large mossy trees were everywhere, and if something had been grown there, it was now long gone. We sat there for several minutes, just staring, and without saying a word. Suddenly, Ellen noticed something and pointed to a place, far to our right, where I saw flower beds and a small strip of land for growing vegetables. It was such a contrast to the rest of the garden that I wondered how I'd missed it. To the side was an old stone fountain, surrounded by rough wooden benches, and it looked so idyllic that we decided to take a look.

Ellen went first, carefully lowering herself until her feet touched the ground, and I followed, taking great care not to slip. I jumped the last couple of feet, and my landing was softened by a large pile of leaves. Standing next to each other, we took a few moments to look around. There was something about this place which was beautiful, and at the same time a little sad. Ellen smiled, then led me to the fountain.

There were twelve benches in total, old and discoloured, forming a large circle around the fountain. In its day, the fountain would have been a grand affair, but now it was broken, covered in moss and beginning to merge with the rest of the garden. The intricate carvings that had once travelled its length were fading, and very soon they'd be gone. Just like the rest of the garden.

I reached out to touch it, and where my fingers made contact, the stone crumbled and fell like sand onto the leaves below.

'You must be gentle,' said Ellen. 'Some things need to be handled with care.' She was smiling, and though I knew it wasn't her intention, I felt guilty, and I wished I'd left it alone. And as the shadows moved slowly across the garden towards me, I heard a voice nearby.

'She speaks the truth.'

Standing a few feet away, with a small cloth bag in his hand, was an old man. His clothes were old and worn—a white shirt, unbuttoned at the neck, and grey baggy trousers. He was thin, and he looked tired, though his eyes were incredibly bright. It was odd the way he looked at us, as though we were animals in a zoo, and I noticed that he didn't blink. People who don't blink have always made me nervous.

'If you carry on like that, there'll be nothing left of this place!' he laughed.

Recovering from the initial shock of his appearance, I apologised, then asked him who he was. He shrugged and replied that he was nobody, just someone who looked after the garden with his wife. She'd been cooking, when they'd heard a noise outside, so he'd come to see what it was.

We apologised for disturbing them, and then Ellen asked him about the garden, how old it was and if anyone visited. The man replied that he knew very little about it. He'd come here years ago with his wife and had been looking after it ever since. Being so well hidden, no one ever visited. At least not until today. I asked him where he and his wife lived, and he pointed to an old wooden door at the far end of the garden. It must have been a tiny house, as we'd seen no sign of it on our way here, nor indeed from the top of the wall.

'It's a beautiful garden,' said Ellen to the old man, and he seemed pleased.

'I'm glad you think so,' he replied. 'Though I'm sure most people would disagree with you. It's a bit out of the way, you know. But to find the things most worth finding, we have to look that little bit harder.' He smiled at her before adding: 'Don't you agree?'

'I do,' she smiled. 'And sometimes they're right in front of us.'

The old man started to laugh.

We talked together for a while, until finally, it was time to go. As the old man disappeared, we climbed back over the wall. I looked everywhere for the house, but I couldn't see it. Ellen stopped and pointed. There, about fifty metres away, in a gap between two old trees, was a small cottage. The door was open, and through the window, I could see a fire burning. And as we stood there hand-in-hand, a small plume of smoke rose lazily from the chimney, then disappeared.

'Here you are!' said James. 'We thought we'd lost you!'

'You very nearly did,' I replied. It was five-thirty and time to eat again. Everyone rushed to grab a chair, but I wasn't hungry, so I took a drink and went to sit outside.

I was surprised that James had never spoken of the garden. Yes, these were huge houses, and I guessed their occupants rarely looked beyond their own fences, but it felt odd all the same. I thought about telling him, but it felt wrong to do so. Ellen and I had glimpsed something which most people didn't see, and I quite liked the idea. I'd leave him to his ignorance and the old couple to their privacy.

I don't know how long I sat outside, but when I finally went back to the house, the music had started up again, and everyone was laughing. It looked like they'd be staying for another night. The next day was a holiday, so no one had to bother about work. I'd completely forgotten about the holiday.

'Any idea where Ellen and Jane have got to?' asked a voice from behind. I turned around to find James, who for some reason, was wearing a moustache. It made him look weird, and I wanted to ask him to remove it. But it was his house.

'They're in the kitchen,' said a young man, wearing a fireman's helmet. I'd obviously missed something.

James thanked him, and we headed off to the kitchen.

'Fancy dress,' said James, seeing my confusion. Of course.

Sure enough, they were there. We were about to go in when I heard Ellen talking. I signalled for James to stay where he was, and he winked at me and grinned. And as he did so, his moustache fell down at one side.

'He thinks he's not sensitive,' said Ellen. 'But he is. And he says he's not passionate, but he's full of passion. There's nothing I wouldn't do for him.' I'd never heard her talk about her boyfriend before and the little I heard now was more than enough. Without saying anything to James, I turned and walked back to the party. By the time Ellen showed up, I was drunk.

I awoke the next morning with a raging headache and no idea how I'd got to bed. On a chair to my right, my clothes were neatly folded. I didn't know how that had happened either. Even sober, I rarely folded my clothes so carefully. The last thing I remembered about the night before was feeling extremely ill and at the same time incredibly tired. After that, things became a little hazy.

My mouth was dry, and I decided that I needed some water. Just as I was contemplating getting up, into the room came Ellen. She had a glass of water in her hand, and she looked exhausted.

'Here,' she said. 'I thought you could do with this.' I thanked her and asked her what had happened the night before. It turned out that it was her who'd put me to bed. Then, afraid I was going to be ill, she'd stayed up all night to watch over me. She hadn't slept. As a result, here she was now, completely worn out.

I felt terrible.

'Come over here,' I said and stretched out my arms. She smiled and walked over. Pulling back the sheets, she carefully slipped into bed next to me, and as soon as her head touched my chest, she fell asleep. I kissed the top of her head. Not many women would put up with me, I knew that much. I was pretty lucky if truth be told.

It was midday by the time she eventually woke up. James had been in a couple of hours earlier and had said that it was time for lunch. I'd told him that I didn't want to wake Ellen, so he'd left quietly, only to return with Jane two or three minutes later. They'd both made a great fuss, trying to push toast into my mouth while I lay motionless in the bed. Despite the odd teething problem, I'd managed to eat quite a lot in the end. I was now surrounded by crumbs. But at least I wasn't hungry.

For most of the time while she was asleep, I thought about Ellen and what she'd said to Jane in the kitchen. I realised that I was being unreasonable. We knew what we were getting into, and if it had been the other way around, I'm sure she would have understood. I'd often talked to her about Yasmine, even sought her advice on what to do. For me to get upset now would have been ridiculous, and in the end, I decided to forget about the whole thing. I wouldn't even mention it.

'What time is it, Thomas?' she said sleepily.

'About half past two,' I answered. She apologised for

staying asleep so long, and I told her there was nothing to apologise for. If anything, it was me who needed to apologise, and I thanked her for looking after me the previous night.

We talked for a while before deciding that it was time to get out of bed. I was starting to feel better, and Ellen said that she was too. In fact, she seemed completely refreshed. Due to my excesses, she'd drunk very little the previous night, so was now in high spirits. She teased me about my lack of self-control, and I hurried to get dressed. I was well aware of my own shortcomings, so I didn't need reminding. Once ready, we went into the lounge, where we met up with Henry, James and Jane. They all looked well too, and for some reason that irritated me. It's no fun being the only drunk.

Most of the other guests had left, though a few were planning to stay another night. Personally, I felt like getting home, and Ellen felt the same. Henry was staying, which made James smile. It was always going to be the case. We collected our bags from the room, and I shook James's hand. Ellen embraced Jane and thanked her for all that she'd done. She looked a little embarrassed and glanced across at James. He was beaming with pride.

'Well done, mate,' I said, and he knew what I meant.

'Thanks,' he replied.

There was a fresh breeze blowing outside, clearing away any lingering cobwebs of my hangover. I got the feeling that James would have liked all the other guests to leave too, but he was far too polite to say.

Hauling Ellen's huge travelling bag onto the back seat of my car, we got in and prepared to go. But the car wouldn't start.

'I think it's the battery leads,' said Ellen, as we peered under the bonnet. I knew nothing about cars, but she looked confident.

159

'How do you know so much about car engines?' I asked sceptically.

'My father fancied himself as a bit of a mechanic,' she said. 'I used to watch him a lot. I guess I just picked it up.'

We adjusted the leads and once again got back into the car. It started first time. Ellen looked amazingly pleased with herself, and I smiled at her. She never ceased to surprise me.

Half an hour later, we were back in the heart of London.

It had been a good weekend.

Chapter 9

Two weeks after our trip to James's, it turned out that somebody was blackmailing Henry over his dalliance at the party. It appeared that the lady from HR was married. I already knew this, of course, having spoken to her on many occasions, on many subjects. Henry, who was not in the habit of talking to 'the administrative staff', did not. One morning, he'd stormed into my office as I sat talking to Ellen and ranted for a good twenty minutes about the erosion of society and its general lack of morality.

'How could anybody blackmail me? he shrieked. 'Me of all people!' I asked him if he knew who it was, but he had no idea. It could have been anyone at the party, or even somebody who'd heard about it through the company grapevine. Henry hadn't exactly kept quiet on the subject himself, so the list of people wasn't short.

The sum of one thousand pounds was to be paid into a post office box, otherwise the full details of the weekend would be made open to her husband. The very thought of it was enough to send him into convulsions. He wondered if it was possible to charge it to expenses, then asked if James's party could be classed as a company function. I apologised and told him that it couldn't. Behind him, I could see Ellen shaking her head.

And on that note he left, leaving Ellen and myself to ponder what we were going to do with the money. I fancied a trip somewhere, but after some thought, Ellen came up with a much better idea.

Quite apart from Henry's misfortune, the two weeks also proved eventful for Ellen and me. I had lunch with Yasmine soon after returning from James's house, then a few days later, we went for a coffee. On both occasions, I could feel the hand of Ellen working away in the background as she did her best to look out for me even when she wasn't there. Yasmine turned out to be a surprisingly candid dinner date, and it didn't take me long for me to find out that she wasn't entirely happy at home. She refused to go into detail, so I was left to fill in the blanks, but it didn't come as a great surprise. I also learned that, for tax reasons, Yasmine was joint owner of the company. But that was as far as her influence went. Decisions were made by Sir Ian. Yasmine had many ideas of her own, though they were never acted upon. That was no surprise to me either.

Ellen, on the other hand, was busy making preparations for her return to America. Her time in England was coming to an end, and she was due to leave in a couple of weeks, though as yet the exact date hadn't been decided. I really didn't want her to go, and if it had been up to me, she'd have remained in England. But Sir Ian had other plans for her.

And while all this was going on, our little side-line continued. Local tradesmen complained of missing items, although the culprits were never found. Interestingly, neither of us sweated any more. We'd become comfortable in our wrongdoings, which was both a good thing and a bad one too. All in all, it was a good time, and if it weren't for Ellen's leaving, I would have said that it was perfect.

At last, by seven o'clock, the queue was beginning to move. Although dusk was settling on the village, it was still hot, and tempers were starting to fray. It was a great relief to everyone when the man finally announced that the doors were open. Due to the length of the wait—it had been at least an hour—the line had grown considerably, trailing back around the deserted houses like a gently meandering stream. It seemed like the whole community had turned up.

Near to the front of the queue, sandwiched between a middle-aged couple, was a small boy, smartly dressed in brown shorts, a clean white shirt and a brown corduroy jacket with leather patches at the elbows. The jacket hung loosely over his small frame, suggesting that it had been bought for somebody else. But he didn't care, this evening least of all.

By the time they reached the entrance to the huge tent, the press had become more urgent, and he felt the protective hands of his father on his shoulders, gently guiding him. His mother was saying something to his father, but he couldn't hear what it was, so he shuffled past the turnstile and made his way to the wooden seats by the side of the circus ring. Despite numerous splinters, he sat patiently, eyes wide and fixed upon the small opening at the side of the ring. At last, to the accompaniment of an out-of-tune trumpet, an elderly gentleman appeared and strode theatrically into the centre of the arena. He was greeted by cheers from the audience, though none were more vocal than the small boy. He shouted as loudly as his lungs would allow, despite some disappointment at the old man's lack of red jacket and amusing black hat.

Still cheering, he wrenched his gaze from the circle and looked around the crowd. The tent was full to overflowing, the people who'd been unable to find seats standing wherever there was space. Some of the more adventurous ones had even climbed onto the shoulders of their friends.

His mother and father were sitting next to him now, one on either side, and to his great embarrassment, neither of them were paying attention to what was happening. His father had removed a shoe and was inspecting a hole in his sock. His mother was watching, a look of mild exasperation on her face. The boy quickly glanced around to see if anyone was looking. To his relief, they weren't. And then, with a low sweeping bow, the old man disappeared. And it all began.

By the end of the evening, he'd decided to become a clown.

I smiled to myself as I looked at the photograph, gently faded in its wooden frame on my desk. I remember clearly the vibrant mass of people, enveloping me with their excitement. Now I was surrounded by reports. I never did get to be a clown. Another dream gone.

Everyone had left the office, but I'd stayed behind. I wasn't sure why. It had just happened. I couldn't really think of much else to do.

It was still early, so I decided to go for a walk along the Thames. Leaving the office, I said goodnight to Peter at the night desk. Peter the Porter. I chuckled to myself, wondering why I'd never thought of that before. He looked up at me from whatever he was doing and wished me a good evening.

It was cool outside, a pleasant change after all the recent heat, and I stopped to button up my coat, burying my hands deep into the pockets.

Many years earlier, I'd taken this same walk with Antonella, my Italian girlfriend. We were studying in Leeds at the time and had only known each other for a few weeks. One day, just after Christmas, we'd decided that it would be fun to go down to London for the weekend, so had packed our bags and set off. We'd arrived at about seven in the evening, and being winter, it was already dark. Following a short tube ride to Westminster, we'd strolled across the nearby bridge, stopping every few feet for Antonella to take a photograph. She'd made me pose in front of the Houses of Parliament and Big Ben, and I'd felt ridiculous, so she'd teased me by taking unnecessarily long over each picture. When I complained, she'd called me a typical conservative Englishman, which was probably not too far from the truth at that time.

Finally, she had enough photos, and we'd walked along the Thames, the weather turning suddenly cold. I remember how happy I was, with my arm around her shoulders and hers around my waist. But, with the first realisation of happiness, came the fear that I'd lose it. It became an obsession, and a month later, she was gone. I never saw her again.

After walking for twenty minutes, I came across a small pub. It was old, built entirely of stone, and I recognised it immediately. I'd last been there with Antonella, though I don't know why I hadn't been there since. It was a lovely pub and very close to the office. Memories perhaps. But tonight was a good time to put those memories to bed.

Inside it was quite full, and it took me a while to get to the bar. I expected to wait a long time to be served, but the barman came over at once, and several of the other customers started to grumble. Flashing me a friendly smile, he asked me what I wanted, and I ordered a lager. He told me that the barrel needed changing, so I'd have to wait, and I wished that I'd ordered something else. Just as I was about to ask him for a glass of wine instead, he disappeared, and I didn't see him again for five minutes, during which time everyone else got served.

At last, my drink arrived, and the barman apologised for the wait. I told him it was fine, then glass in hand, I carefully weaved my way through the bar towards a seat I'd spotted on the far side of the room. As soon as I was seated, I noticed a band getting ready to play some music in the corner. There were four of them, three musicians and a singer, and I didn't recognise the instruments they were holding. They looked to be homemade. Before too long, they were ready, so I settled back to listen.

The band wasn't good, not much better than mediocre, but it seemed popular, and all around me people started to dance and sing. Quite against my better judgement, I felt like joining them, but decided instead to tap my foot on the floor, in time to the beat. That was much more like me. I was soon drumming my fingers on the table too, in a way that had always embarrassed me when my parents had done it. The memory made me smile.

The pub itself was a strange shape, with numerous alcoves sprouting off from the main room. Massive wooden beams formed a web across the ceiling, and countless brass charms littered the walls. It was a homely sort of place, and after a while, I got talking to the gentleman sitting next to me. A big mistake, as it turned out. Apparently, this pub was his local, and there was nothing about it he didn't know. And so, for the next half hour, he educated me, filling in the gaps in my knowledge, of which there were many.

By the time he'd finished, I'd barely touched my drink, but at that point all I wanted to do was to get away from him. It annoyed me that I'd fallen so easily into his trap. It was a busy pub after all, and the fact that he was surrounded by so many free seats should have served as a warning to me. I would have to be more careful in future, but at least it had given me an idea.

Looking at my watch, I feigned surprise at the time, then hurriedly thanked him for the chat and left. Though not before casting one last glance at my half-full pint on the table.

Outside, it had started to rain, signalling an end to my stroll down memory lane. I walked for a few more minutes, the rain coming down more heavily now, soaking my jacket and plastering my hair slick against my head. Arriving at the main road, I signalled a taxi. The experience in the pub had drained me both physically and mentally, and I soon nodded off, not waking until the taxi was outside the door to my flat. As always, the fare had doubled while I was asleep.

The next morning, I got very little work done, and by the time it came to lunch, Ellen decided that I needed some fresh air and a bite to eat. It seemed like a good idea, so I put on my jacket, and we left the office. Once outside, we turned to walk over the bridge, and as we passed a young homeless man, Ellen gave him some change. He looked up and treated her to a huge smile.

'God bless you,' he said as we walked away.

Just then, she remembered that she wanted a magazine, so asked me to wait while she went to get one. There was a newspaper stand nearby, so I wouldn't have to wait long. When she had gone, I looked back at the homeless man, who'd already resumed his surveillance of the pavement. I glanced over to Ellen, to make sure she wasn't looking, then pulled a couple of pound coins from my trouser pocket. I walked back and gave them to him. He accepted them in silence, not even bothering to look up at me.

It was a pleasant day, so we decided to eat outside. I knew of a nice spot nearby, with views over the river, so we decided to buy a couple of sandwiches and to eat them there. Before that, however, we had a little business to take care of. Popping into the post office, I asked if there was anything for me. I was handed a large brown envelope and looking inside, I found a thousand pounds in used banknotes. Good old Henry! I asked Ellen if she wanted to look after the money, but she was happy for me to keep hold of it. We smiled at each other, like two kids who'd been naughty, but had somehow gotten away with it. Now all we had to do was think of an appropriate way to spend it.

I'd always been self-conscious about eating sandwiches, as they tended to fall apart in my hands. As a result, whenever I ate them, I covered my mouth with a napkin. For some reason, this amused Ellen, and she started to laugh at me. In my confusion, I let the napkin drop slightly and a piece of tomato splashed onto my leg. The sight of the tomato, mixed with the look of annoyance on my face, was too much for her, and she began to choke on her food. It was several minutes before she regained her composure, during which time I was showered with half-eaten mouthfuls of tuna sandwich. She apologised, though I doubted her apologies were sincere. Then she started to laugh again. It had been a bad idea to get sandwiches.

When we were finished, I was eager to get back to the office, not least to change my trousers. The tomato had caused a nasty stain, and I was hoping people wouldn't get the wrong idea. No doubt Ellen would embellish the story as well. I thought it best to avoid contact with colleagues, so we returned to the office via the many small back streets in the area.

As we were walking down a small cobbled road, flanked on either side by shops selling expensive shirts and designer suits, I suddenly heard a scream. Ellen and I turned around at once, and a short distance away, we saw a little boy wandering into the road. He was wobbling as he walked, and it made me think of those figurines people place on their car dashboards, the ones with a large head attached to the body by a spring. It was probably not what most people would have thought about at such a time, but I specifically recalled my neighbour's car, with its Elvis figure gyrating through the window as he drove along. It was actually quite funny, and I smiled despite myself.

'What are you smiling about?' asked Ellen calmly, and I wondered if perhaps she'd not seen the child.

'Oh, my neighbour had this Elvis figure in his car,' I began, but she immediately cut me off.

'That's very nice, Thomas,' she said, 'but don't be cruel. I believe there's a child at the end of the road!' She smiled, delighted with herself. I was impressed. Three Elvis songs in one sentence.

'It's now or never,' she added, and that made it four.

No one else seemed to be doing anything, so it was up to me. Normally, I'd have pretended that I hadn't seen anything, but as I was with Ellen, and as she'd made such a good stab at the Elvis songs, I felt as though I owed her.

I headed off at a trot, but as I did so, I noticed a large car turning out from one of the side roads. It was heading directly for the child. I went through the gears and very soon was running at full speed, impressing myself with how fast I felt and, at the same time, how not out of breath. Perhaps my recent trip to the gym had paid dividends after all.

I was soon passing the screaming woman. It was odd that she wasn't doing anything herself, just standing there shouting, as if she might blow the car away. I thought about telling her that she should actually try to save her own child, rather than relying on a stranger, but I didn't have the time. Nor, in fact, the inclination.

At last, I reached the little boy, and as the car sped towards us, I scooped him up and leapt for the pavement, stumbling as I did so and landing on my back. The mother had stopped screaming by this stage and came over to take the child.

'Stupid boy!' she said, though it was unclear who she was referring to.

And with that, she walked off, leaving me there, my suit jacket torn and as if nothing had happened.

Conscious that I was lying down on the pavement, I stood up and brushed myself off, just as Ellen came over. She kissed me on the cheek.

'Ungrateful cow,' I said, nodding my head in the direction of the rapidly disappearing mother. 'Not even a thank you.'

'Well, I think you're a hero,' said Ellen with a smile. 'My very own Captain America.'

My shoulder was killing me, and when I took off my jacket, I could see a large rip at the back. Ellen suggested that I looked like a tramp, and I bowed theatrically, thanking her for her concern. We both laughed at that, then hurried away, keen to be gone before anyone else saw us.

Back at the office, I changed into a clean suit. I always kept one handy, just in case I got run over. I asked Ellen not to mention to anyone what had happened, though she didn't understand why. I made her promise anyway, and she finally agreed. A couple of weeks ago, I'd taken a life; today, I'd saved one. Villain and hero. Not much difference really. And for some reason, I remembered a fancy-dress party I'd gone to at university. The theme had been good and evil, and my friend Yuri had gone as a pirate. I went as a clergyman.

By three o'clock, Ellen had finally shut up about the incident, and I was starting to get down to some work. Suddenly, there was a knock at the door and in walked Henry, clearly in an excellent mood. Seconds later, he was followed by James. For some reason, Henry was carrying a walking cane. I looked at him quizzically, as he bowed his head, like some sort of country lord greeting his serfs. James was wearing a bright bow tie and thick red braces. I looked across at Ellen, but she was trying her best not to catch my eye. Then I looked back at Henry and James. They appeared to be very happy about something, so I invited them to sit down. I knew from experience that they'd require little prompting, so I sat back waiting for one of them to talk. It was Henry who broke the silence.

'If there's one thing I've always said,' he started, 'it's that the French are the trickiest devils to do business with'.

As far as I was aware, he'd never said that.

'Unfortunately for them, today they've met their match.'

I waited, but that was it. He sat there smiling, looking back and forth between Ellen and myself, as though all should be clear. I racked my brain, and slowly it came to me.

'You've sorted out the contract?' I said at last.

'Over a drink or two last night,' he laughed. He was irritatingly proud of himself, though in truth he had good cause to be. The contract in question had been in negotiations for months and had encountered numerous setbacks. It was quite a coup. I was really pleased for him—the amount of time and effort he'd put in on the project had been prodigious. A huge weight had been lifted from his shoulders, and he looked like a new man. Well, almost.

'Seriously though,' he continued, 'they were the most

hard-headed, double-crossing, underhand swine I've ever done business with.' High praise indeed.

'I don't like the French,' blurted James, as if to himself. 'They're bigoted bastards.'

'The downside,' continued Henry unperturbed, 'is that the contract will have to be signed in the hinterland.' I took this to mean their office in Lancashire. For Henry, the North-South divide started just above London. Beyond that, lay a land of marauding barbarians, unintelligible vernacular and whippets.

'What have I done to deserve this?' he moaned.

'Well, this calls for a drink,' I said. Everyone agreed. All except Ellen, who still had some work to do.

As the two of them went for their jackets, I spoke briefly to Ellen, then left to join them. At just gone quarter to four, the three of us could be seen gingerly slipping out of the building and heading for the river.

As we walked along, I announced that I knew the perfect place for a drink, and five minutes later, we stopped at a small pub with live music coming from inside. I crossed my fingers, hoping that the local pub historian would be there. Inside, a familiar music floated through the air, and I looked around, searching the tables for the man I was looking for, eventually finding him in the same place as before. There were plenty of free seats around him. Giving Henry a conspiratorial nudge, I turned to James.

'I'll get these,' I said. 'Why don't you go and grab those seats over there, by that man?'

He wandered off innocently, and I immediately filled Henry in on what had happened the previous night, so that when the drinks arrived, we decided not to move. From the look on James's face, he'd realised quite quickly that he'd been set up. I told Henry that he'd now be at the point where the pub was flooded, over a hundred years ago. There or thereabouts, I hadn't listened too closely. There then followed twenty minutes of pleading glances and failed excuses before James eventually broke free and came storming across the pub to rejoin us. When he arrived, we dragged him around the corner.

'You look like you could do with a drink,' I laughed.

'Bastards!' he hissed. 'I almost died over there.' He seemed visibly shaken by the experience.

'Let that be a harsh lesson to you, my boy,' grinned Henry. 'When a northerner offers to buy the first round, something evil is afoot!' I patted James on the back, and he started to smile. He was never able to stay angry for long.

After a few drinks, it was universally accepted that nothing of importance would be achieved that day, so we decided to continue drinking. Not that any of us needed much persuading. By the time six o'clock came, the place had begun to fill up, so I decided to head back to the office to see if Ellen had finished her work. I said goodbye to Henry and James and told them I'd be back soon. James went to the bar for another drink.

I realised it was a mistake as soon as I got outside. The cool evening air hit me, and I immediately felt much more intoxicated than I actually was. I steadied myself against a wall, and it was a minute or so before I was okay to set off again. The streets were always busy at this time, and it took me longer than expected to get back, which in a way was a good thing, as I arrived feeling much more sober than when I'd set off. Peter the Porter was looking through some paperwork when I entered the building, and he didn't seem to notice me. I hurried past and was soon in the lift to my floor. Just about everyone had left, and with the lights turned off, it was difficult to negotiate the maze of opened drawers and randomly placed chairs. More than once, I stumbled, before finally arriving at my room. Ellen was still working.

'Having a bit of trouble?' she said as I entered.

'What's with the lights?' I replied. 'Are we on some sort of austerity drive?'

'There's a light switch by the elevator,' she laughed.

I walked over to my desk and pretended to look for something, as if trying to persuade her that I hadn't been drinking, even though she knew full well that I had.

'Are you all right?' she asked after a while, the look on her face making me think I looked much worse than I felt. I reassured her that all was well and asked her how much longer she was planning to be. A while yet, was all that she replied. Her work wasn't going well. I asked her if she needed any help, and she laughed, then said that she was fine. We talked together for a few more minutes, but it was starting to get dark outside. If I wanted to get back to the pub without seriously injuring myself, now was the time to go. Ellen smiled and said that she'd see me later. And with that I left, taking great care as I weaved my way once more to the lift.

Peter the Porter wasn't at his desk when I got to the ground floor. I wondered where he was, thinking that he'd get into trouble if he was caught. But just then, he came around the corner and from the smell I could tell that he'd been outside for a cigarette.

'I didn't know you smoked, Peter,' I said.

'I don't,' he smiled, and I laughed.

'None of us do, do we?' I said, but I don't think he heard me.

'You took your time,' laughed Henry on my reappearance. 'And you seem out of breath!' I knew what he was getting at, but in fact, I'd run the last hundred metres or so to escape from a sudden downpour of rain. I was out of breath though. Perhaps I wasn't as fit as I'd thought after all. I recalled the incident with the child, and at once pictured the Elvis figure in my neighbour's car.

'What are you smiling about?' asked James.

'Oh, nothing,' I replied.

Noticing that they'd switched tables, I quickly changed the topic and asked why they'd moved from where we'd been earlier. Peering over James's shoulder, the answer was clear.

'At least no one can say you're unpredictable, Henry,' I laughed as the three young women sitting at the next table talked amongst themselves. I should have known. If there were ever any women around, he would find them.

'Perish the thought!' he grinned.

Pretty soon, James was looking somewhat the worse for wear. His bow tie had become undone, and he'd unbuttoned the collar of his shirt, revealing the pale skin of his chest. It was the colour of uncooked chicken. I always liked James in this condition: firstly, because it made him come out with the most absurd comments; and secondly, because he insisted on buying the drinks.

Henry had noticed too, so smiling to each other, we mentioned that it was time for another drink, and as the two of us argued together, vying for the pleasure of buying the next round, James unsheathed his wallet.

'Don't be bloody stupid!' he said. 'I'll get these.' And before we had time to protest, he disappeared off to the bar, waving his wallet like a sword. Henry and I smiled at each other. The trick never failed. It was so predictable, you'd have thought we'd be bored by it. But we weren't.

It took James such a short time to get served, given how busy the pub had become, that when he returned, Henry and I quizzed him on how he'd managed it. Youthful good looks was his reply. So there was one of his absurd comments, right there.

As always seemed to happen when we went out, the more we drank, the hungrier we became. Pretty soon, it got to the point where we decided to abandon our drinks to go in search of something to eat. Miraculously, James seemed to be sobering up, and he mentioned that he knew of a good Thai restaurant nearby. Henry nodded and said that he'd like to try it, at which point I told them that I didn't like Thai food. A heated discussion ensued, during which Henry reminded me of all the occasions in the past when I'd insisted on eating Thai. I questioned his recollection of events, and when it became clear that I wasn't going to change my mind, we agreed on Italian, on the proviso that I pay for it. That was fine by me—I had a thousand pounds to spend.

Ten minutes later, we arrived at Casa Mancini, where we were greeted by the owner and shown to a table by the toilets. Another argument followed, with James adamant that he wanted to move, while Henry was delighted, adding that it was convenient for when we wanted to be sick. I wasn't bothered either way.

It was a restaurant I'd always liked, though I hadn't eaten there for months. It was well known in the area not only for its delicious food, but also for the owner's unfortunate habit of picking his nose and poking around in places where he really shouldn't be poking. He also doubled as the chef. As a result, it was seldom busy, though tonight it was heaving. I mentioned this to the owner when he came over, and his face lit up with a broad grin.

'I add a little something to the food,' he announced proudly. I didn't want to know what that little something was.

I decided upon the carbonara. I always had that. I would make a show of looking at everything on the menu, but in the end, it was always carbonara. I expected a sly comment from Henry, but when I looked at him, there was nothing. He was sitting there, staring into the distance, as though trying to work out something he couldn't quite understand. I asked him what he was looking at, and he pointed to an opening which led to the other side of the restaurant. The more expensive side.

'I didn't know there was another side to this place,' he said after a while.

'Of course, there is,' laughed James. 'Everyone knows that. It's nice, but you've got to book it in advance.' He paused for a moment. 'Why?'

'Oh, nothing,' smiled Henry. 'It's just that Ellen and Jane are in there, that's all.'

James made a noise, which sounded remarkably like a squeak. Henry and I looked at each other.

'Did you just squeak, James?' asked Henry.

'Yes,' answered James, 'I think I did.'

'Okay then,' replied Henry. 'I just wanted to know.'

After a short discussion as to the etiquette of disturbing the other table's meal, we decided to ask the owner if we could move. He shrugged—one of those 'how the hell should I know' kind of shrugs—then told a waiter to go and ask. When word came back that it was okay, three extra places were set at their table, and as we made our way through, Henry straightened the collar of his shirt while James redid his bow tie. They were new men by the time we arrived.

'Hello,' said Ellen, greeting me with a warm smile. 'This is a pleasant surprise.' When she was sure that no one could hear, she leaned over to me and whispered into my ear: 'I thought you'd be here half an hour ago.'

'I intended to be,' I said, 'but Henry and James took some persuading.'

'Have you still got the money?' she asked, and I replied that I had most of it. Next, Ellen gave formal introductions, as apart from herself and Jane, there was another woman at the table. Her name was Beth, and I was pretty sure that I'd never met her before. I guessed that she was in her mid-forties and her long red hair hung loosely at her shoulders. She was wearing a dark jacket and cream coloured blouse, unbuttoned to a scandalously low level. Henry immediately sat next to her. James positioned himself next to Jane.

We ordered the food, and it came within minutes. Beth and Jane remarked on its unusual smell, as Henry and James replied in unison that it was the chef's special flavouring. They nodded appreciatively, breathing in deeply and commenting on its earthy odour. Ellen, who was well aware of the rumours, pinched my leg under the table.

'Well, this is nice,' said Henry, ordering drinks for everyone—two bottles of red wine and two white. James announced that he would pay, and I reminded him of our earlier agreement. Everything was on me that evening, a celebration of Henry's coup with the French. I turned to Ellen, who was staring directly at me with a huge smile on her face.

'My, you're a generous man!' she said mischievously.

We then turned to Henry and watched in fascination as he stuffed his face, blissfully ignorant that he'd be paying for most of the evening himself. Small pleasures and all that.

'That must be why Ellen likes you so much!' laughed Henry as the final piece of bruschetta disappeared down his throat. And for a brief moment, Ellen and I were shocked. It was the first time anyone had stated so openly that there was something between us. There'd been no shortage of innuendo, of course, but this felt different and somehow strange. Yet there it was, out in the open, and the more I thought about it, the clearer things became. Ever since the weekend at James's, Henry hadn't really talked about Ellen. Not in a sexual way at least.

'It must be his good looks!' interrupted James, and Ellen started to laugh. I couldn't see what was so funny about that.

'But there are plenty of good-looking men around,' added Henry. 'And let's be honest, Ellen could probably take her pick.' Ellen shook her head modestly, and it was clear that Henry was enjoying my discomfort.

'True enough,' said Ellen. 'But there's more to a man than good looks.' She looked at me and smiled. 'To make him truly attractive, he must have a flaw.'

'Ah!' sighed Henry. It was as though a puzzle he'd never quite understood was being solved before his eyes. He nodded to himself and laughed.

'The Brontean beast!'

After the meal, we sat drinking, and the conversation moved onto other, less personal, topics. We discussed work for a while, then politics briefly, but it was when education came up that things started to get heated. Unsurprisingly, Henry felt that all children should go to public school, specifically the boarding variety. I'd heard this argument many times before, and an unfavourable comparison to the state school system was a guaranteed way to upset him. So that's exactly what I did.

'No! No!' he protested. 'A child who goes to public school has a much better chance of success in life.'

'Are you saying that from the age of eleven to eighteen, your child will be sent away to boarding school?' asked Ellen. She seemed disturbed by the idea. 'Those are some of the most formative years in a person's life. They shouldn't be spent away from the family.'

James explained that the child came back for a few weeks holiday each year, but she was still unimpressed.

'No wonder you Brits are such cold assholes,' she said.

'It's arsehole,' I interjected helpfully, immediately wishing I hadn't.

In the end, neither side was prepared to budge, so eventually we begged to differ. It's the sign of a good friendship that an argument can be heated, then immediately forgotten with no animosity held. And that's how it worked here, with Ellen and Henry soon joking together as though nothing had happened.

During the course of the meal, the seating arrangements had shifted slightly. We were still in the same order as before, but several of the chairs were now conspicuously closer together than they had been. As expected, James and Jane were practically in each other's laps, while Ellen had draped one of her legs over mine. But the couple I found the most amusing was Henry and Beth. They'd both become quite drunk, and I could no longer understand what they were saying. From what I could gather, they were talking about Bloomsbury, though it could just as easily have been Dewsbury. And as I watched them slowly swaying from side to side, I heard Ellen next to me talking to James.

'You can do just what you want, James,' she said. 'You're a free person.'

'I can't really,' he sighed, and he seemed to have sobered up completely. 'And I'm not even sure that I am free. I've been doing this job for so long, there's nothing else I can do. The job is me.'

'You'd be surprised,' she said. 'You can be anyone you want. Sometimes it's good to take a step back and think just who you might be. You're never too old to change.'

I wanted to kiss her.

The meal eventually finished at a little after eleven o'clock. Everyone thanked me once again for my generosity, and I smiled, assuring them that it was my pleasure. Ellen had her arm around me, and I noticed Jane in the background looking at us and smiling. Henry and Beth were leaning on each other as if they were about to fall over. We said our goodbyes and Mr Mancini came over to wish us a safe journey home. We were the last ones there, and I caught him looking at his watch as he ushered us through the door. Ellen came back with me, and as we turned and walked down the road, I watched the others disappearing into the darkness. James and Jane walked hand-in-hand, like two lovebirds, with Henry and Beth stumbling unsteadily behind.

Outside, the streets were still busy, and I could hear loud music coming from several of the pubs nearby. Even though I was tired, I asked Ellen whether she wanted to stay out. She stifled a yawn and said that she wanted to go back. Despite it being the weekend the next day, she wanted to get home. It was the first time she'd called my flat 'home', and it made me smile.

There was a chill in the air, and as we walked along the road to the taxi rank, the lights of St. Paul's cast shadows in front of us. It looked like it was going to rain. By the time we got to my flat, Ellen was nearly asleep.

I lay awake that night, listening to the rain, thinking about what I had and what I was soon to lose. And for the first time in months, I was unhappy.

Chapter 10

'Come on, Thomas. Let's go and get something to eat.'

It was ten o'clock, and I was exhausted. Though we must have been in bed for nearly ten hours, I hadn't slept well, and all I could think of doing was rolling over and going back to sleep. Ellen had different ideas.

'You can take me to that little cafe you told me about.'

That little cafe was my sanctuary. I'd never taken anyone there before. But before Ellen, I hadn't blackmailed or murdered either. If I was going to start breaking my own rules, she was the best person to do it with. I told her that I'd be up in five minutes, and then we could go. She clapped her hands excitedly, and with a smile, she rushed into the kitchen. A minute later, she was back with two cups of tea.

'What are your plans today, Thomas?' she asked. Steam from the tea floated into the air, and for a moment, her face was lost in the haze. She laughed and wafted at it theatrically, as if in doing so, she might also focus my thoughts.

'I don't have any,' I said. It sounded like a barbed

question, and I was afraid she was about to suggest something energetic. Or at least something which would involve us leaving the flat. Not for the first time, she proved me wrong.

'How about watching a movie, then maybe some TV?' she suggested.

That was precisely what I wanted to do. I made her promise not to make me watch any American comedies after the film, and she agreed. She then made me promise not to watch any British sitcoms, so we looked in the TV guide to see what else was on. Not much, as it turned out.

Finishing my tea, I got out of bed and slipped into a pair of old jeans and a cotton shirt. Ellen was already dressed, so picking up my wallet, we left the flat and went in search of breakfast. It was another warm day outside, and all traces of the night's rain had more or less disappeared. Above us, the sun shone brightly, searing shadows into the bleached concrete of the road.

The walk to the cafe was, for the most part, conducted in the shade, due to the large number of trees lining the street. Every so often, we were forced into the full heat of the sun before once again dipping back into the shadows. This process of slow leisurely strolls, followed by short bursts of activity, continued until we reached the shops. There the buildings had been cleverly arranged to provide no shade whatsoever. Blazing heat and torrential rain, it was all the same. As always, the place was packed, with the usual groups out in force. Ellen smiled and pointed to a flock of birds circling overhead, their dark wings tipped with gold. And on the ground, a small dog was making its rounds, tail wagging as it barked at passing strangers.

'What a cute dog!' laughed Ellen. It was heading in our direction.

'Don't touch it, Ellen,' I said, positioning myself behind

her. 'It's a beast!'

It was upon her in seconds, but rather than mauling her, it nuzzled its head into her outstretched hand, and its grey tail swished from side to side like an overexcited metronome.

'Don't be stupid, Thomas,' she said. 'It's just a puppy.' She looked up at me and smiled, then playfully invited me to stroke it. Much to my embarrassment, I found that I was nervous, so I declined.

'Come on,' I said, a little too hastily. 'Let's get to the cafe before it takes your arm off!'

There are thousands of cafes in London, so I had no idea why I liked this one so much. Most likely because I'm lazy and it was the nearest one to my flat. But it went further than that. It wasn't the decor, nor that there were any books or newspapers to read, and it certainly wasn't because of the food. No, I suppose what I really liked about this particular cafe was what it represented. It was a haven, my haven, a place where I could go and be on my own, to do and think what I liked and have nobody judge me for it. And that was a rare place indeed. I'd never thought of bringing anybody with me before. I'd end up resenting them for coming and would spend the whole time being uncomfortable and wishing they'd leave. But with Ellen, it was different. With her, I was comfortable. I spoke when I wanted to, and she didn't mind if I said nothing. We could spend hours talking together, and then pass a morning in complete silence. And both were fine.

'What's a 'Greasy B'?' she asked, menu in hand and with a puzzled look on her face. 'I think I'll have one of those.'

'I'm not sure you'll like it,' I said, before detailing the various fatty foods involved in its preparation. She decided to look for an alternative, finally plumping for brown toast and a cup of coffee. It was probably the safest choice, and I went for the same.

As we were talking, I noticed an elderly woman weaving her way through the crowds, heading in the direction of the cafe. Her name was Vera Stubbs, and I'd met her in the bookshop several months earlier. Quite apart from her other faults, she was an incorrigible chatterbox, and once she started talking, it was very difficult to stop her. She also harboured an irrational dislike for Americans. It was best that she didn't find me with Ellen.

Fortunately, she seemed not to have seen me, but just in case, I covered my face with a menu. Ellen asked me what I was doing. Still hiding, I told her all about Vera, how I'd met her and how she would talk and talk and talk. Ellen found it all very funny and accused me of exaggerating. When I mentioned the dislike of Americans, she laughed out loud.

'Now I know that you're lying,' she said. 'Everyone likes Americans!'

I wasn't sure if she was joking or not.

'She's gone anyway,' she announced. 'It's a shame. I'd like to have met her.'

Relieved, I slowly lowered the menu, and to Ellen's delight, was immediately spotted. And as Vera made her way to the door, I pleaded with Ellen to tone down her accent. She nodded obediently.

I should have known better.

'Hello, young Thomas,' said Vera. 'How are you?' She paused briefly to clean her spectacles on an old handkerchief. 'I haven't seen you for a long time.'

'No, I've been very busy recently,' I replied. 'Anyway, it's nice to see you again, Vera.'

I was hoping she would leave, or at least not stay too long. But as the seconds ticked away, she steadfastly refused to budge. I guessed that she was waiting for me to introduce her to Ellen. But that was the last thing I wanted to do. Ellen was far too unpredictable. There followed a long and uncomfortable silence, until finally I gave in. I made the introductions.

'Hello, young lady,' she said. 'It's nice to meet you.' She held out a hand, which Ellen shook vigorously.

'Howdy ma'am,' she replied, in the most absurd Texan drawl. 'It's mighty fine to meet y'all.'

I couldn't believe my ears. I was gripped by two contradictory urges: the first was to attack Ellen with the menu I still held in my hand; the second was to run from the cafe as quickly as possible. My own version of fight or flight. In the end, I did neither, and in an attempt to control the conversation, I mentioned to Ellen that Vera was from Dover, something I'd learned during our first marathon conversation.

'Where the cliffs are,' added Vera condescendingly.

'That's quaint!' exclaimed Ellen. I could see that she was enjoying herself. 'We've got some of those in the States. Except they're bigger!'

The colour of Vera's face was changing rapidly. What could once have been described as a pallid or pasty hue, was now the vibrant shade of a ripening tomato. She pursed her thin lips, dried out by years of smoking, and for a woman in her late seventies, she was actually quite menacing.

That didn't seem to bother Ellen. By now, she was in full flow. Their conversation continued while I sat there quietly, defeated and resigned to my fate. Listening to Ellen, I wondered if anyone from Texas actually spoke like that.

'Oh, so you're seeing each other then?' asked Vera at last. She looked surprised.

'Hell no!' shrieked Ellen. 'It's just sex.'

At that point, I think I groaned. It certainly sounded like it. If not, it was something very similar. I turned to Ellen, who was sitting there, grinning from ear to ear. Then I turned to Vera. But she'd already left.

'I'm not sure you'll be seeing much of her again,' said Ellen as we watched Vera disappearing through the crowds. I nodded. 'And it's probably best if you don't tell me how to speak in future.' I nodded again.

And then we both started to laugh.

It took a few minutes before we were able to talk again. Sheena was watching us from behind her till, and she smiled at me, then shook her head, as though I'd gone mad. She'd probably never seen me laugh before. As Ellen filled me in on the bits of the conversation I'd missed, I asked her about the accent. Like most accents, she said, it was accurate for some people, but not all. Not every Londoner spoke like Dick Van Dyke, she added, but undoubtedly there were some. I assured her that there weren't.

The remainder of the breakfast went by without incident, which was something of a relief. Sheena came over and asked us if we wanted another drink, but we both said no. I introduced her to Ellen, and Sheena shook her hand, then told her how beautiful her accent was. I smiled, as Ellen blushed, and I think it was the first time I'd seen her embarrassed. It was endearing, and as Sheena disappeared back to the kitchen, we decided to go.

It was hotter than ever when we left. A few hours in the sun had made the pavements hot, and I could feel the heat through the soles of my shoes as we walked. Once again, I dodged from shadow to shadow while Ellen did her best to drag me into the open. It wasn't long before we were both laughing, and I spotted an ice-cream van parked over by the gate. I bought two cones, one with a flake and one without, and for a while we stood there watching the people as our ice-creams melted and dripped onto our fingers. And for the briefest of moments, it felt like I was by the seaside again.

After wiping our hands on some paper towels, Ellen nudged me and pointed to something on the other side of the metal fence. A group of children from the local Catholic school were running in their sports gear, closely watched by a priest. They were sweating heavily, and several seemed close to exhaustion. It reminded me of my own school days. I looked at Ellen, and she was shaking her head. Perhaps it was a requirement for all children, not just those in this country.

We ambled along, slowly making our way to the flat. One of the boys had collapsed, and the rest were taking a breather while he lay on the ground drinking some water. The priest looked angry, and I wanted to shout at him, but Ellen told me not to, as it was like shouting at God.

A little further away, a group of people had gathered outside the health food shop, Human Nature. I'd always liked that name, as it reminded me of the Michael Jackson song. A close knot of perhaps twenty or thirty people were urgently chattering to each other, like a flock of geese arguing over bread. I'd never been a nosy person, but today, with little else to do, I took Ellen's hand, and we wandered over to see what was happening. Carving through the idly curious, followed by the moderately inquisitive, we finally got to the downright nosy at the front. And there, at last, was the source of the commotion—the unconscious figure of one of the local rough sleepers, with a small dog by his side. No one would touch him.

I looked across at Ellen, and I could see that she was shaken. From her expression, it was unclear if she was sad or angry.

'Why the hell is no one doing anything?' she hissed.

Angry then.

'You don't know what you'd catch!' said a man standing

next to her.

'Oh, for heaven's sake!' she shouted and pushed the man out of the way. Dragging me with her, she forced her way into the centre of the circle and crouched down by the unconscious man and his dog. We recognised the dog from earlier, and Ellen scratched behind its ear reassuringly, the dog's head pushing back against her hand. Loosening the man's shirt, she told me to look after the dog. I asked her if there was something else I could do.

'You can give this gentleman the kiss of like, if you'd prefer,' she said.

'I'll look after the dog,' I replied.

Ellen shouted for someone to call an ambulance, and then, with her ear to his chest, she listened for a few seconds. There was no heartbeat. She thought that his heart must have only just stopped, and I wanted to ask her how she knew that, but it probably wasn't the right time. I looked at her, then back at the man. At that moment, she gave me a smile, then without hesitation, she pinched the man's nose, supported his neck and took a couple of deep breaths.

Behind me, someone made a retching sound, but I didn't turn around, I just stood there watching Ellen. I watched her as she fought so hard to save the life of someone she'd never met before. And I admired her for it.

Several breaths, linked hands, pushes on the chest, several breaths, linked hands, pushes on the chest. After each, she checked for signs of life, but each time there were none.

'It's no good, Thomas,' she gasped. 'I'm not strong enough. You'll have to push.' So I joined her. I waited until she gave the signal, then pushed. The coarse hair on his chest felt greasy against my skin, and I wanted to pull back. I thought of Ellen and what she must have been going through, and suddenly my role didn't seem so bad. After five hard pushes, she leant forward and listened to his chest. Shaking her head, she went back to work.

It seemed a long time before there was any change. We didn't notice anything at first, but then, all of a sudden, the dog started barking. Ellen placed the back of her hand above the man's mouth to see if he was breathing, and I put my ear to his chest. Sure enough, his heart was beating. I looked across at Ellen, and she nodded. She slumped beside me, and I put my arm around her shoulder. Other people were coming forward now, eager to help, once there was little left to do. Someone handed Ellen a tissue, and another person brought a glass of water and a little food for the man. Very soon, an ambulance arrived, and the man was taken away. But just before the doors closed, we glanced inside to see if he was okay. Underneath the stretcher, well hidden from view, was the small dog. I turned to Ellen and smiled.

'You're a heroine,' I said. She looked at me, and I took hold of her hand. 'My very own Captain England!'

'Never heard of him!' she laughed.

'Her,' I replied.

Like most superheroes, as soon as we got back to the flat, we changed our clothes and had a wash. Ellen cleaned her teeth.

On the way back from the shopping centre, we'd stopped off at the local newsagent and rented a film. There was a substantial difference in our tastes and when it looked like neither of us were prepared to budge, we eventually opted for a compromise. The film we finally chose was a mixture of love story (Ellen's choice), horror (my choice) and action (both). Sitting in front of the television, we kicked off our shoes and lay back with our feet on the coffee table. Just as I was about to turn on the film, I noticed that the cricket had started, so I looked at my watch.

'Maybe we should wait a while,' I suggested. 'It's a bit early to start watching a film, don't you think?'

'Oh no, you don't, Thomas!' laughed Ellen. 'There's no way I'm going to watch cricket.' She could read me like a book. 'It's a ridiculous sport.'

We'd had this argument before. The problem for Ellen was that cricket wasn't like baseball. She couldn't understand why the batsmen didn't run every time they hit the ball, or why they did run even when they hit it behind. I'd tried to explain, quite poorly as it had turned out, but had finally conceded defeat.

'Why doesn't he just throw the ball at the sticks?'

'Why are all the uniforms the same colour?'

In fairness, I couldn't actually think of an answer myself. There doesn't always have to be an answer. So we turned on the film.

All things considered, it was pretty good, and by the time it had finished, I was really enjoying myself. Some of the more frightening scenes had caused Ellen to cuddle up to me and hide her face in my chest. I'd watched on stoically, refusing to flinch, though my secret was more down to trickery than to courage. Each time a frightening scene came on, I switched my focus from the screen to a small plant pot by the side of the television. It was impossible to tell that I wasn't watching the film. After years of horror films, I had deception down to an art.

'I'm going to get a drink,' announced Ellen. 'Do you want anything?'

I told her there was some beer in the fridge. I didn't usually drink during the day, not at the weekends anyway. I heard the fridge door opening, followed by the clinking of glasses, then Ellen asked if I was hungry. I was, although I couldn't remember if there was anything in the flat to eat. Perhaps some bread and meat, but that was it. For the next few minutes, all I could hear was the sound of cupboard doors being opened and closed.

'Not very organised, are you, Thomas,' she shouted from the kitchen.

'Only at work!' I shouted back, and I could hear her laughing.

Ten minutes later, she came back into the room carrying a plate of the biggest sandwiches I had ever seen. I asked her if she was expecting guests, but there was no answer. With her spare hand, she picked up a cushion and launched it at me, catching me squarely on the side of the head. It was an impressive shot, and I congratulated her on her aim, to which she bowed, nearly tipping the sandwiches onto the floor. I noticed that she'd forgotten the glasses, so I got up and went to the kitchen. There was another plateful of sandwiches by the kettle, like a pile of paving stones, and I wondered just how hungry she thought I was.

After half a sandwich, my jaw was beginning to ache. I'd read once that snakes could unhinge their jaws when consuming large objects. That would have been useful for me too. It was difficult trying to fit a sandwich the size of a shoebox into my mouth while at the same time smiling to show how good it tasted.

I couldn't help noticing that Ellen wasn't eating very much and wondered if this was another of her jokes. Unfortunately, my mouth was too full to ask. I had to drink a full glass of water before I could even think about talking. Massaging the sides of my mouth, I glanced over to her as she nibbled around the outside of her sandwich. Barely able to conceal her amusement, she took a drink of beer and asked me if I was feeling full.

I turned on the cricket.

'Thomas, can we see what's on the other side?'

'As soon as you've finished your sandwich.'

As a concession between overs, I flicked through the channels to show her all the programmes she was missing. I wanted to smile, but my jaw muscles were too tired.

At one point, as I flicked rapidly from quiz show to documentary, then news, and finally to drama, I happened upon a channel showing the American basketball league. Ellen shouted excitedly as it disappeared before pleading with me to turn it back on. When I refused, she offered me money, then all sorts of sexual favours, some of which I was sure she was making up. I politely refused. The cricket was at a very exciting point. Exciting for cricket, that is.

Half an hour later, I went for another beer. Ellen wanted one too. In the kitchen, there were dirty pots and half-drunk cups of tea on every surface. On top of the microwave was an old tub of spaghetti, with something growing around the edges. I picked it up and dropped it into the bin. By the sink was a cluster of old carrier bags, all empty, and to their right was a pile of dirty pans, several deep. Ellen hadn't been around for a few days, and I was embarrassed at how I'd let things go in the meantime. I'd always kept the place so clean and tidy when I knew that she was coming. I thought back to her making sandwiches earlier and my embarrassment deepened. By the kettle was the extra plate of sandwiches, neatly covered with cling-film to keep them fresh. Not once did she complain or utter any word of judgement. It wasn't often that the cleaning bug took hold of me, but on this occasion, it did. Rolling up my sleeves and pouring hot water into the sink, I set to work.

It took a while to bring the kitchen back to life, but when I'd finished, it was spotless. I looked around proudly and told myself I should do it more often. But I knew that I wouldn't. It was all just a bit too much trouble. Picking up two beers from the fridge, I turned off the kitchen light and went back into the living room. It had been quite some time since I'd heard anything from Ellen, and as I entered the room, I soon realised why. There she was, crouching in front of the television with the volume turned down, watching the basketball. At first, she didn't see me, but when she did, she stared at me all doe-eyed, like a naughty child caught in the act.

'Oops!' she said, and I started to laugh. It was impossible to be angry when she looked at me like that. Handing her a drink, we sat down on the sofa. I turned up the volume, and she flung her arms around my neck, planting a kiss on my lips. As I laughed even more, she showered me with kisses. And very soon I'd forgotten all about the cricket.

At seven o'clock, there was a knock at the door and in walked Sarah. It had been a while since I'd seen her, and I figured she must have had an argument with Gerald.

'Hi, Thomas,' she said, as she caught sight of Ellen. 'Oh, I'm sorry. I didn't realise you were busy.'

'It's fine,' I replied. 'We were just watching TV.'

Ellen gave a small wave from the sofa, then introduced herself as a colleague from the New York office.

'A colleague, eh?' remarked Sarah, with a smile. 'How very nice!'

The two of them grinned at each other, and Ellen invited her to sit down while I went to the kitchen for some drinks.

'No alcohol for me, Thomas,' shouted Sarah as I was opening the fridge door. 'I'm off it for a while.' I'd never known her to turn down alcohol before. I asked her if she wanted anything else and she replied that a cup of tea would be good.

The two women were chatting away when I returned to the room, and I was once again impressed by Ellen's ability to put people at ease.

'That's wonderful!' she laughed.

'I know,' said Sarah. 'I never thought it would happen!'

Handing her the tea, I sat myself down and asked her what had happened.

'I'm pregnant, Thomas!' said Sarah, smiling happily. I almost dropped my beer.

'Wow!' I exclaimed. It was all I could think of to say. Not the most fitting of best wishes, but it was as good as I had at that moment. I leaned over and gave her a hug.

'Stand up,' I said, and both of them looked puzzled. 'I want to see the bump.'

Ellen laughed. 'She's not that far gone, Thomas.'

I didn't know when a bump should show.

Pretty soon, Sarah was hugging me again. I could feel by the movement in her shoulders that she was crying, so I asked her if she was okay. She nodded, her head against my chest, and I squeezed her reassuringly. When she finally surfaced, there were small streaks of mascara running down her face.

'Look at you,' I said as Ellen passed her a tissue. 'All grown up.'

She laughed. 'Hardly!'

I smiled at her, waiting until she'd finished cleaning her face. 'You know, I always thought you were as messed up as me,' I said. 'But now you've fixed yourself. And I'm incredibly proud of you.'

She started to cry again, and Ellen looked around for some more tissues.

'You're pretty close to being fixed yourself, Thomas,' she whispered. 'You just don't see it yet.' At that moment she looked so calm and self-assured, with a determination I'd never seen in her before. My old Sarah was gone.

'Oh, and Gerald's asked me to marry him,' she said, as an aside. 'Next year.'

'I'd better buy a new hat then,' I replied, and we were all happy again.

For a couple of hours, Ellen and Sarah chatted about marriage and children while I searched for news about the cricket. It turned out that Sarah had been shopping earlier and had seen the commotion outside the health food store. She'd been in a hurry, so had carried on walking, but she asked now if we knew what had happened.

'Well....' said Ellen, and I knew we'd be there for a while.

Sarah listened intently, as Ellen chronologized the events of the morning, starting with my reluctance to get out of bed and ending with the collapsed figure of the man at the shops. Sarah laughed out loud as she heard about our meeting with Vera and congratulated Ellen on her ingenuity. She'd never liked Vera apparently. She then reprimanded me for having never taken her to the cafe, and I got the feeling that she was making fun of me.

When Ellen got to the final part of the story, I noticed a subtle reworking of events so that I appeared the hero, rather than herself. The sticky chest hair, the mouth-to-mouth, they were all there, but I was the protagonist, rather than Ellen. It made me sound rather impressive, so I decided not to correct her. When she'd finished, Sarah looked at me wide-eyed.

'Wow, Thomas,' she gasped. 'Unbelievable!'

I shrugged noncommittally, as if to imply that it was nothing special. Sarah winked at Ellen.

'No, Thomas,' she said. 'You misunderstand. I mean it's actually not believable.' The two women burst out laughing. 'You don't even touch door handles without first covering your hand!'

She was right about that.

Ellen spread her arms and smiled at me. 'Well, I tried,' she said apologetically. Sarah gave her a hug and told her she was amazing. She could never have done that herself.

To change the subject, I asked Sarah if she was hungry, and she replied straight away that she was. I announced that there were sandwiches in the kitchen, but before I had a chance to get them, Ellen had jumped up and was rushing past me.

'She's lovely!' said Sarah while Ellen worked away in the kitchen, re-cutting the bread into more conventional slices. 'Far too good for you, of course.'

I thanked her for her honesty, and she smiled, before telling me how happy she was that I'd finally found someone nice.

When Ellen eventually returned, she was carrying three more drinks and a selection of thinly sliced sandwiches. Sarah ate them all.

It was late before Sarah finally left. I offered to walk her to her car, and when she declined, I hugged her again, telling her for the umpteenth time how happy I was for her.

'I'm happy for you too, Thomas,' she said as we stood by the door. 'Don't you dare let her go!'

Before we went to bed, Ellen and I cleared up the living room. I apologised to her for the state of the kitchen earlier, but she just smiled and told me not to be silly, it wasn't as bad as I was making out. Even though I knew that it was. As we lay in bed that night, I asked her if she would stay the next day, and she replied that she would. That was good, I said, because I needed her to look at my car. There'd been something wrong with it ever since we'd got back from James's party. She laughed, but it was an exhausted sort of laugh. And before I could say anything else, she was asleep.

When Ellen and I arrived at the office on Monday, we were greeted with what can only be described as mayhem. No one was working, not in itself terribly unusual, but small groups had formed, and everyone was talking in hushed voices. Several people looked panicked. In the corner, one of the graduate trainees was crying, and by the vending machine, a senior manager stared aimlessly into the distance. I looked across at Ellen, and she shrugged, signalling with a nod for us to go to my office.

'No idea,' she said, before I'd even asked the question. We sat there in puzzled silence, then decided that it would be fun to guess what was wrong. I started with the death of a close colleague, but Ellen shook her head, saying that a colleague's death wouldn't affect everyone so badly. Her initial idea was that perhaps the Queen had died. It was my turn to shake my head. We moved onto weird and wonderful illnesses. Perhaps Ivor from marketing had contracted a disease on his recent trip to Nepal. He'd been looking very pale after all. No, not that. Had Sir Ian been embezzling the company pension scheme, so that we'd all be penniless in our old age? No, surely that could never happen. And as the guesses became more and more outlandish, we were suddenly interrupted by Henry and James, breathing heavily as they slammed the door behind them.

'That old bastard!' shouted Henry, sitting down in one of the chairs opposite my desk. He apologised to Ellen for his language. 'How dare he!'

So not an illness and not the Queen.

Henry's face was very red, much more so than usual, and worrying that he may injure himself, I told him to calm down, then to tell Ellen and me all about what had happened. It was

James who took the initiative.

'Sir Ian Walker,' he started. 'He's done us over!' It was evident that we had no clue what he was talking about. 'There's been an announcement. Haven't you heard?' We shook our heads.

'What have you been doing for the last twenty-four hours?' he demanded. Ellen smiled. 'Oh…well, never mind. He's closing down the London operation, that's all. Lock stock and bloody barrel!'

To my left, I heard Ellen gasp. Turning to her, I saw a look on her face which I immediately recognised— disappointment. I'd seen that look on many faces over the years.

'Did you know about this?' Henry asked, aiming the question firmly in Ellen's direction. 'After all, you're pretty close with Lady Walker. There's no way she wouldn't have had some involvement in the decision.' I'd never seen Ellen bristle before.

'I'm as shocked as you,' she said through clenched teeth. 'Do you really think I could have known this was going to happen and yet still drink with you, eat with you, Christ even sleep with you?' She paused, taking a deep breath. 'Well, do you, Henry?'

Henry looked suitably ashamed of himself and apologised immediately, taking great pains to stress that he'd never doubted her.

'I am, however,' continued Ellen, 'bitterly disappointed. As you know, Yasmine and I are close. Very close. At least I thought we were. But she never said a thing.'

I thought back to my talk with Yasmine, when we were sitting on the stone bench, and I recounted to the three of them what she had said: Ian does what he wants. He asks for my advice, but he's already made up his mind.

They looked at me in silence for a moment, then Ellen walked over and kissed me.

'Thank you, Thomas,' she said. 'I needed to hear that.'

'I'm annoyed with myself for even doubting her,' snarled Henry to himself, though it was unclear whether he was referring to Yasmine or Ellen.

For a while, we just sat there, each with our own thoughts, pondering our futures and wondering if anything, anything at all, could be done. London was the only office to be closed, with the primary operations moving to the States, where things would be ramped up. Ellen would be fine, of course. In fact, more than fine. It could only be a good thing for her as her star rose increasingly high on the other side of the Atlantic. But for the rest of us? Not great, it had to be said.

After a while, we decided to do what we always do when there's a problem—go for a drink. As it was early, and given the circumstances, we arranged to meet after work. A little food and a few drinks, then we would see how things looked. But, as Henry and James left my office, closing the door carefully behind them, I wasn't filled with confidence.

'I am so sorry, Thomas,' said Ellen, after they were gone. 'I really had no idea. I hope you believe me.'

The thought hadn't even crossed my mind. I didn't trust many people, but I trusted Ellen implicitly, and I was sad that she could even think such a thing. I could see that she was upset, so I went over to her and crouched down by her side.

'These things happen, Ellen,' I said. 'We'll be fine. Maybe it's the kick up the backside we all need.' She didn't look convinced, and in truth neither was I. The life I'd made for myself, whatever it was worth, was starting to fracture, and I was worried.

Ellen gently placed her hand on my cheek. 'There must be something we can do, Thomas,' she whispered. 'There must be.'

'We'll think of something,' I replied.

If we'd thought that more information would be forthcoming that afternoon, then we were to be disappointed. I'd expected some form of update now that the news was out, but we obviously weren't important enough for such courtesy. At least we now knew where we stood. Henry was in and out of my office for much of the day, grumbling about anything that came into his head, but in reality, he was just upset. Upset because he'd thought himself more important to the company than had turned out to be the case. To differing degrees, we were all guilty of that. We often believe we are indispensable, and it's a shock when we find out that we're not.

And so it was that the four of us left the office that evening, no wiser than we had been nine hours earlier. Outside the streets were already busy, with commuters heading in all directions, ties loosened, jackets unbuttoned. I wondered if perhaps some of them had received bad news that day, and whether, like us, they too were teetering on the precipice. But I didn't really care, not about them, their jobs or their lives. Just as they didn't care about us. Would I give up my job to save a hundred of theirs? Of course not. I turned to my companions, and I felt a solidarity. It was us against the world. And I had a hunch we were going to win.

Ten minutes later, we were sitting in Casa Mancini. I ordered a beer, as did Ellen. James and Henry ordered a bottle of wine each. At the table next to ours, a group of people in business suits laughed and clinked glasses, celebrating some good news or other, or perhaps a birthday. They were young, in their early twenties, and in each of their faces was a look of belief, a belief that life had great things in store for them. I remembered that look. It was on my face too until not so long ago. I'd thought I was destined for such great things, and the realisation that I wasn't was what stung me the most. I hoped it wasn't too late.

I suddenly realised that James was asking me a question, the look of amusement on Ellen's face snapping me back to the present. I'd missed what was being said, so I apologised and asked him to repeat the question. Ellen broke out into a huge grin, while James looked exasperated. Henry was reading the label on his wine bottle.

'Do you know how the company is structured, Thomas?' asked James.

'I don't know,' I replied. 'Rubber bands and chewing gum?'

Ellen shook her head and James told me to be serious. But I really had no idea. As far as I knew, I said, there was a board of directors, headed by Sir Ian, and they were the ones who made all the serious decisions, the rest of us merely following their lead.

'That's right,' said Ellen, coming to my aid. 'But the main point is that, unlike many companies, the majority of the issued share capital is in one person's hands.'

'Sir Ian Walker's, to be precise,' said James, finishing her sentence for her. So James had been busy and had done some research.

'So whatever Sir Ian decides, that's what happens,' said Ellen. It was her turn. 'Though here's where it gets interesting. I spoke to Bob Brewer this morning. He's on the board too.'

I knew that.

'And Bob says that the board was against the closure of London. It was Sir Ian who pushed it through. Without him, none of this would be happening.'

She paused for a moment, looking at each of us in turn.

'Such an asshole,' she said finally.

'It's arsehole,' commented Henry, looking up from his wine bottle.

'Really, Henry?' laughed Ellen. 'That's your input?'

'Sorry,' he replied. 'Just thought I'd point it out.'

It was Henry's opinion that whatever the makeup of the company, if Sir Ian Walker wanted London closed, then closed it would be. There was nothing we could do about it. And he was probably right.

'Anyway,' he said, 'more importantly, do you know this wine is fifteen per cent proof? No wonder I always get legless when we come here!'

Chapter 11

As if things weren't bad enough, news finally came through that Ellen was to leave. She was needed in New York—something about a big project. We all knew what that project was, and to make matters worse, she was to head it up. I would have laughed if it hadn't been so absurdly sad. On hearing the news, she'd immediately told me.

I remember the day well. It was a few days after we'd found out about Sir Ian's plans, and Ellen had stood in front of me, broken, like a small girl, lost and unsure what to say. There was nothing to say, so I'd hugged her while she cried. And all the hatred I'd felt inside burned incandescent, directed at a man I barely knew, a man who'd done many things to me, but unforgivably had made Ellen cry.

'I've got two weeks, Thomas,' she said sadly, wiping her eyes with the back of her cardigan sleeve. It was actually my cardigan, but it suited her much more than me, despite being far too big. 'Let's get away for a couple of days and go somewhere. Anywhere.' I nodded, reeling from the speed with which my world was unravelling.

I thought for a moment, then suggested that Prague might be good, or maybe Paris. Perhaps Berlin, but I'd never been there, so I couldn't vouch for it. But none of those were what she wanted.

'I want to see your hometown,' she said, after patiently waiting for me to finish my list of European capitals. I was lost for words. Morecambe? I asked her why. 'Because you speak so fondly and passionately about your childhood. And because I want to see the place that made you the man you are today. A good man.'

I hugged her closely once more, remembering what my father had once said to me: I don't care how I'm remembered Thomas, so long as I'm remembered as a good man.

Was I really a good man? I wasn't so sure, but if Ellen thought I was, then that was a good start.

So, it was decided—that weekend we were going home.

At nine o'clock on Saturday morning, Ellen and I were standing in the waiting area of Euston station, a small suitcase by my side and two very large ones next to her. Ellen's hair was in a ponytail, which I liked, and she had on dark jeans and a light blue T-shirt with a Batman motif across the chest. As for myself, not wanting to let the side down, I'd ironed my favourite black polo shirt and khaki trousers. There were several other polo shirts and similar trousers in my suitcase for when they were needed. I didn't have a clue what was in Ellen's cases.

'Do you really need to bring two cases?' I asked her, not for the first time. 'We're only going away for a couple of days.'

'I don't need two,' she replied patiently, 'but I want two.'

'You could fit a body in that one,' I said, pointing to the

large red case nearest to her. The one that I'd been carrying for the entirety of the journey so far, as well as my own case.

'Well, that can be arranged,' she said, a big smile on her face. But before she could add anything further, a voice came over the tannoy announcing the boarding platform for our train. After grabbing a sandwich and a cup of coffee, we hurried down the passageway to the train, Ellen graciously allowing me to carry both of her suitcases this time, while she took mine.

We found our seats with five minutes to spare, and Ellen was delighted to see that one of the seats was number A13. It was a good omen for the trip she said, then added that I'd have to sit in it, as thirteen was an unlucky number. I laughed out loud at that, receiving a stern look from the middle age man seated across the aisle.

The journey from London Euston to Morecambe was due to take around three hours, with most of the time taken up by the first leg from London to Lancaster. I usually slept on the train, but Ellen was having none of it, and she swiftly produced an old and battered pack of cards from her bag. She then proceeded to deal a hand to each of us. She was remarkably fast.

'You'd make a good croupier,' I said as the last of the cards landed.

'How do you know I wasn't one in the past?' she asked with a glint in her eye.

'Because you couldn't stay quiet for long enough,' I laughed, and she blew me a kiss.

Apparently, we were going to play a game her father had taught her—Dead Man's something or other. She briefly outlined the rules, and I was confident she was making them up. The object of the game was to collect the highest value cards in any given suit without having the king, which I assumed to be the Dead Man. It seemed simple enough, and though there were one or two rules I was unclear about, I was pretty confident I had the beating of her. However, thirty minutes later, as we passed through Milton Keynes station, I'd lost every game we'd played. And as we arrived at our first stop in Warrington, an hour and a half later, I'd won just once, a game that Ellen later admitted to losing on purpose, out of sympathy. By Preston I'd still only won once, and I was sure she was cheating.

'Are you cheating, Ellen' I asked finally as another game passed me by. I did my best to keep my tone jovial and without accusation.

'Yes, Thomas,' she replied with a smile. 'I am. But do you know how?'

I admitted I had no idea, and when asked, she refused to tell me. It was another thing her father had taught her, she laughed, as she slid the cards back into their old cardboard box. I told her that I'd like to meet her father one day, and I noticed a sad look on her face as she turned away, before putting the cards carefully back into her bag.

At last we rolled into Lancaster, historic city and home to my former school, the Royal Grammar School. Being a Saturday, it was lively, even as far from the centre as the railway station. Over the years, the student population from the local university had exploded, covering the city in an eclectic mix of colourful clothes and youthful exuberance. It was not at all the grey northern town I remembered from my youth. The trains to Morecambe were infrequent, so I asked Ellen if she wanted to look around the town before we left. She said that she would, so we left our bags in a locker and set off in search of what the town had to offer. First stop, Lancaster Castle.

'You may be disappointed,' I advised her as we made our

way up the steep hill towards the castle. 'It's very old, but not that big a building anymore.'

'You're kidding, right,' she said with a grin. 'I'm American. We love old buildings! Besides, here's your chance to boast about your history. Then you can tell me how insignificant ours is in the US.'

I stopped and adopted a statesmanlike pose, hands behind my back, chest sticking out. 'Even a history of one day can be significant', I said proudly. It made her smile, and we set off again, the warm feeling of her lips still fresh on my cheek.

The castle was closed. And as we stood there, me in embarrassed silence, and Ellen laughing out loud, I wondered how one of the town's biggest tourist attractions could be closed on a Saturday lunchtime. At the sound of Ellen's laughter, several nearby people cast curious looks in our direction, and we hurried away. It hadn't been the greatest of introductions to my birthplace.

The next train to Morecambe was not for another hour, so we decided to kill some time wandering around the town centre. It wasn't the biggest of places, so an hour would be more than enough. Makeshift stalls lined the streets, and as we made our way from one to the next, Ellen chatted happily with the stall owners. She was offered everything from smoking paraphernalia to scarves and drawings. I was happy to watch as she engaged with each one, leaving them smiling as she politely refused their offers. I had no idea how she did it.

Soon, however, it was time to head back, so we picked up a coffee and strolled slowly up the hill, back to the station.

On the platform, we sat in the sunshine, takeaway coffee in hand, as we waited for the train. Ellen was in good humour, reclining on the small metal bench we'd found and buoyed by the smiles and comments she'd received during our little expedition. With her head back, basking in the sun, she draped her legs over mine and sighed contentedly.

'It may be a cliché,' she said after a while, 'but this really is the life.' I nodded in agreement, though she didn't see. It felt like we were worlds away from the chaos of London, and that was a good thing. 'When did you lose your accent?' she asked, moving to position herself so that she could see me more easily.

'I didn't notice that I had,' I replied, 'until one day people started pointing it out when I came home.' I shrugged. 'I suppose it just happened.'

'A bit like me with my American accent,' she said playfully, and I laughed at the thought of her without that gloriously effusive accent of hers. Ellen and her accent were so intertwined, it seemed ludicrous that she should talk in any other way.

The train arrived on time, a tiny two coach affair with faded bench seats, and before long we were sitting at Bare Lane station. I told Ellen that when I was younger, there was a club not far away called The Bare Ladies Club, to which she laughed and accused me of pulling her leg. I assured her that I wasn't, but the more I thought about it, the more unsure I became. Perhaps it was just a thing which should have been, an idea I'd held for so long that in the end, I'd started to believe it. No one got off the train at that stop, and no one got on.

Five minutes later and we were pulling into Morecambe station, a small glass building with no visible door and no one inside. Not like the old station half a mile away, which had been a grand Victorian affair and now served as a pub. The dozen or so of us who were on the train politely queued to get off, and when we'd all reached the platform, I found Ellen not far away struggling with her cases. It was such a pitiful sight that I stood there for a moment to see how she'd get on. Behind her, I noticed an old lady giving me an evil look, so I hurried over to help.

And so it was that in just under five hours we had made our way from a busy, vibrant London to the idyllic serenity of Heysham village, our destination and the location of our hotel, a recently renovated pub with several rooms, in the heart of the old village. And it was perfect, with its newly whitewashed walls and bare oak beams. Polished brasses hung from the walls, and in the main drinking area, a basket of logs sat next to an open fire, patiently waiting for winter.

'It's perfect, Thomas,' purred Ellen after we'd collected our keys from the bar, which also served as the reception. I agreed, and she smiled, slipping her arm around my waist as we were shown to our room. The room turned out to have twin beds, rather than a double.

'It's a bit late to be shy about sharing a bed!' joked Ellen as I took the booking form from my pocket and checked the reservation.

Sure enough, I'd booked a double room, but rather than ask for a change, we decided it was fine. It would be cosy, said Ellen as she set about unpacking her cases. Articles of clothing appeared one after another, like rabbits pulled from a magician's hat. I watched her for a while, smiling as the wooden wardrobes creaked under the strain. Then I walked over to the large window by the beds. It had been opened slightly, allowing the warm afternoon air to flow into the room, and it felt good after the stuffiness of the train. Through it, I could see the small woodland area which surrounded the local church, separating it from the beach. The trees appeared so much smaller than I remembered. During the school holidays, I'd played there every day, climbing the trees and building dens. Ellen came over to join me, resting her head on my shoulder, and the two of us stood there in the sunlight, each lost in our thoughts.

'You know,' said Ellen after a while, 'at this moment in time, there's no other place I would rather be.' I couldn't have put it any better myself.

Just then, she reached out of the window and clasped her hand, before pulling it back to her chest. I asked her what she was doing, and she giggled. I noticed that she was blushing.

'When I was a child,' she said, 'a very young child, my father pretended to grab the sunshine when we were happy. He said that he was stealing it, so that we could keep it and always be happy. But I was tiny back then, and it looked like he was eating it. He'd laughed so much when I asked him why he was eating the sun. So from that day on, that's what we called it—eating the sun. Nowadays, whenever I'm truly happy, I still do it.' She looked at me and smiled. 'It's silly really.'

'It's not silly, Ellen,' I said. 'It's a memory, and memories are never silly.'

It was mid-afternoon by the time we left the hotel. We hadn't eaten since earlier that morning, so we stopped at the newsagents in the centre of the village to pick up a sandwich. We ate as we walked, Ellen repeatedly asking where we were heading, and me repeatedly telling her that she'd have to wait and see. The only clue I gave was that I wanted to show her a place which had been very dear to me in the past. She was not keen on surprises, so she grumbled all the way. As she chewed on her sandwich, small crumbs of bread cascaded to the floor in a most unladylike fashion.

In the end, she only had to wait a few minutes. We pushed open a small iron gate, its hinges quietly complaining and were greeted by a large expanse of well-manicured grass.

'You have got to be joking!' groaned Ellen, her mouth wide to reveal the remnants of her ham and cheese sandwich.

I laughed and kissed her firmly. 'Welcome to Heysham Cricket Club!'

The grumbling stopped, and she attempted a pout. But it didn't work–her eyes were smiling. She was never one to conceal her emotions, and as we walked around the paved pathway and passed in front of the old white-walled pavilion, a broad smile lit up her face, immediately infecting me. By the time we reached the small steps to clubhouse, we were both grinning idiotically. I didn't recognise most of the people outside, around thirty in all, but they nodded as we passed, before resuming their discussions. It was the same scene, repeated year after year, only the faces changing, and I remembered how many times my mother and father had sat here, on these same wooden seats, beer in hand as they chatted to friends. Only occasionally did they watch the cricket.

'Hello Thomas,' said a familiar voice as Ellen and I reached the top of the steps. I turned to find my old friend Mark Smith. In faded jeans and a black Van Halen T-shirt, he hadn't changed, despite the thirty years that had passed since we'd first become friends. A few more lines perhaps, and definitely more stubble. We shook hands, and I introduced him to Ellen. She smiled, and I could see she was having trouble understanding his accent. I thought about leaving them together for a while, but decided against it. It would just be mean. Funny, but mean.

Just then, there was a loud shout from the field, followed by a cheer, signalling the fall of a wicket. Someone nearby swore, and I laughed. I hadn't heard that particular word for a long time. I shook Mark Smith's hand again, and we went inside.

Nothing much had changed since my last visit, or indeed any visit before that, and the familiarity of the surroundings felt like an embrace. Small wooden tables and green padded bench seats hugged the edges of the room, while to the right of the door hung the old dartboard. On the far wall, next to a row of old black and white photographs, a television was showing repeats of old cricket matches.

'Christ, you must be in heaven!' said Ellen under her breath.

'I am,' I replied, and I smiled at her.

Surrounding the small bar, no bigger than my tiny bathroom at home, sat several people and one dog. Their conversations continued as Ellen and I walked over, with only the dog looking up. When it found nothing of interest, its focus returned to the chewed-up tennis ball at its feet. A couple of the men shuffled wordlessly to the right, allowing us access to the bar, and Ellen thanked them, receiving polite nods in return. And there stood Don the barman, looking straight at me, with his red hair and unkempt beard. He looked like a wildman.

'What can I get you, Thomas?' he asked as I leaned against the stained wooden bar. It felt as though I'd never been away.

'Two bitters, please Don,' I replied, and behind me, I heard Ellen cough.

By this point, the conversations around us had stopped, and the men by the bar said hello and asked how I was. I told them that everything was good, before introducing them to Ellen, who by this stage was getting the hang of the accent. She smiled and said how nice it was to meet them. I wasn't too sure who a couple of them were, but with the formalities complete, we took our drinks and went to sit at a small table in the corner.

'Are you sure you've not been here for a while?' she said.

'It's as if you've never been away.' I laughed and told her it was just how people were around here. I'm not sure she believed me.

Over the next hour, we discussed our plans for the weekend. Ellen had noticed a poster for a pub quiz at the cricket club. It was taking place that night, and she said that she wanted to go. I was happy with that, as I liked a pub quiz. We had a few hours to kill, so I asked her if she wanted to see my old school and the house where I'd been brought up, both of which were very close by. She said she'd like that a lot, so we finished our drinks and got ready to go. As we were leaving, Don asked if we were coming to the quiz that evening, and before I could answer, Ellen told him that she'd love to. He smiled and said that he'd see us later, before adding that 'the others' would be there too. I nodded, and we left.

Outside little had changed. Mark Smith was still there, and the cricket was moving along slowly. It looked like the same batsmen at the wicket, and I asked a middle-aged man how things were going. He apologised and said that he didn't know. He seemed more interested in his beer. I shrugged, and Ellen gave me a puzzled look but said nothing. As we left the cricket club, Ellen turned around and looked one final time at the men in white, standing like statues in the sun. Then she looked at me and shook her head.

'What do you think?' I asked her, and she laughed.
'Riveting!'

Once we were back in our room, I had a quick wash. The table at the cricket club had been sticky, and my hands felt uncomfortable. I asked Ellen what she wanted to do for dinner. There weren't any restaurants in the village, but the hotel did excellent food, so we decided on that. It would be a good idea to get a decent amount of food inside us before spending the evening at the cricket club. Ellen made me promise not to buy her any more bitter, so I asked her what she wanted instead.

'Not bitter,' she replied. And with that, we left the room and set off for the next part of our adventure.

The road from the hotel to my primary school took us through the centre of the village, which was no more than a newsagent, a cafe and bus stop. There was also a car park, with no cars in it, at the bottom of a steep hill. At the top of the hill was the school. Ellen held my hand as we walked, commenting on the beautiful old cottages as we passed them, with their colourful hanging baskets and small, deep-set windows. I'd thought about buying one of them a few years back but had found the low ceilings and small dark rooms oppressive, so had decided against it. Beautiful on the outside, scary within.

The initial steepness of the hill soon gave way to a gentle slope, and five minutes later, we were jumping over the small locked gate which served as the entrance to the school. Inside the main grounds, things looked very much as I remembered them, despite leaving over twenty years earlier. The junior block, an old stone building, stood next to the more modern upper school, with its flat felt roof and large glass windows. I'd worked on that roof during my summer holidays many years ago, with Mark Smith, whose dad owned a roofing company. It had been hard work.

The only real change as far as I could see was the dining hall, which had disappeared entirely, replaced by an area with swings and a climbing frame. Nearby, I spotted the old brick toilets, and I laughed as I explained to Ellen how my friend Mark Hutchens had once urinated over the top of the urinal wall, directly into the girl's toilets.

'I'm impressed,' said Ellen, though I could see that she wasn't.

A little further round, just past the new swings, was a set of broad stone steps that acted as seats overlooking the school playground. The dining hall had been directly behind, and opposite was a large wire fence, forming a barrier between the school and the council allotments behind. On one of the bleached white steps, someone had written in large black letters "Joe sucks donkey dick!" and Ellen and I both laughed like naughty children.

'Each to their own,' said Ellen once we'd calmed down, and we immediately started to laugh again.

'How far would you say it is from the bottom of these steps to that fence over there?' I asked Ellen after a while. She thought about it for a moment and then guessed about thirty metres.

'Well, as a child, I thought it was miles,' I said, thinking back to those heady days when everything had seemed so big and impressive. 'Mark Smith and I used to try to kick a football from here over the fence each day, and we never managed it. We thought it was impossible.' I looked at the distance now. It looked no distance at all. 'It seems ridiculous now, looking at it with grown-up eyes. I could do that without even trying!'

'Prove it,' laughed Ellen as she leaned back against the stones, soaking up the sun. She pointed in the direction of a grass verge to our left, and there amongst the weeds was an old leather football. I hadn't noticed it earlier, probably because I wasn't looking, but now it was hard to miss. Here was my chance. I wandered over and gingerly poked it with the toe of my shoe. The weeds gave way, and the ball rolled down the slope onto the playground.

'It needs inflating a bit,' I said, giving it several squeezes as if to prove my point.

'Getting your excuses in early, I see,' countered Ellen with a delighted grin.

She'd raised herself onto her elbows to get a better view, and her eyes followed me as I moved over to the spot from where I planned to launch the ball into orbit.

'Don't get too close,' I warned, 'or you might get sucked in.'

I squeezed the ball again, and I could hear her laughing behind me, then with a deep breath, I tossed it into the air and swung my right foot as hard as I could. A second later, it was soaring over the fence, away from the school and into the allotments. I turned around victorious. Ellen was on her feet, and there was a genuine look of surprise on her face.

'Christ, that was a long way!' she said and started to clap. It seems silly really, but with Ellen clapping and the ball rolling around in some old person's cabbages, I felt prouder than a grown man had any right to be.

And it felt great.

Half an hour later, with the heat dissipating and the sun beginning to fade, we were walking across the fields which separated the allotments from the housing estate where my family used to live. Though not big, they had been home to several horses, all of which had terrified me. I mentioned this to Ellen, and she asked if there were still horses there. I didn't think so, but wasn't sure, at which point we both quickened our pace. By the time we arrived at the wooden gate on the far side of the field, we were practically running. There was a metal bench on the other side of the road, so we walked over to it and sat down. And for the next few minutes we remained there, looking sheepish and more than a little out of breath.

From the bench, I could clearly see my old house, fifty or so metres away on the corner of the street. It had been a long time since I'd been back there and I must have looked reflective, because the next thing I knew Ellen was kissing me and smiling.

'That's it, isn't it,' she said quietly, and I nodded. 'Let's go and have a closer look'. I wasn't sure who wanted to see the house more, her or me.

It hadn't changed at all, at least from the outside. A different colour on the garage door and window frames perhaps, but in truth I couldn't really recall what colour they'd been the last time I was there. The front garden certainly looked the same, the huge rose bush by the gatepost still spilling over the low outside wall, and the lawn edged neatly like a lush green carpet. There was no car in the driveway, so Ellen urged me to go to the door to see if anyone was home. She said that we could pretend to be checking for undelivered mail. But it had been two years since I'd last been there, so I thought that would look odd. Nevertheless, as much to keep her quiet than for any other reason, I soon found myself walking up the short drive towards the house. Out of habit, I went straight to the back door, as it had always been the one we'd used. I looked up at the bathroom window, connected to the ground by a thick black drainpipe, and I recalled all the times I'd climbed up as a child, returning from school before my parents were home from work. The flat roof of the garage was another place I'd loved to climb up to. I'd thought it so high, but in reality, it was not much taller than me.

After a short hesitation, I gently knocked at the door.

'Unless rabbits are living here, no one's going to hear that,' said Ellen, and she banged on the door herself, this time loud enough to wake half the street.

'There's no one in, Thomas,' said a voice from behind us

and I turned to find Norman, our old neighbour, leaning over his fence, a pair of dirty gardening gloves in one hand and pruning shears in the other. 'They're away on holiday.' He smiled at me, a huge beaming smile that made me want to cry. 'How are you, my boy?'

Norman had been our neighbour for as long as I could remember, and despite his eighty-plus years, he seemed as active as ever. I'd spent many happy evenings with him, in the company of my parents and his late wife, as they drank whisky and tried their best to embarrass me. It was good to see him looking so well. We shook hands, and I introduced him to Ellen.

'Nice to meet you, love,' he said, then pointed to the house with his shears. 'Why don't you have a nosey through the windows. I know I would!'

'I'd love to,' laughed Ellen, and Norman smiled broadly before telling us he had to go finish his gardening before it got too late.

The next thing I knew Ellen was skipping across the back garden towards the kitchen window. By the time I reached her, she was already peering through the glass, her hand raised to block the reflecting sunlight. For the next fifteen minutes, we went from window to window, with Ellen asking questions as we visited each new room. For me, they no longer held any interest, rendered unrecognisable due to redecoration, but to Ellen, they were a source of fascination. As we passed each one, I told her a story about the room and the things I'd done there. By the time we were finished, she knew as much about the house and my life there as any other person alive.

We got back to the hotel at about six o'clock. Though we were both feeling tired, we decided to eat straight away, then head out for the quiz at around seven-thirty. The exertions of the afternoon, coupled with the two pints of bitter I'd drunk, had left me wanting a rest, but I knew that if I gave in, I'd be done for the day. So instead I busied myself with a wash and a shave while Ellen changed into her third T-shirt of the day.

We finished our food at around eight o'clock. We'd perked up a lot and chatted excitedly about the evening ahead. I teased Ellen about how she'd be expected to answer any question with a remotely American slant, and she replied with confidence that there were no questions about the US that she wouldn't be able to answer. As a result, I was hoping for a whole section.

Outside, it was a beautiful warm evening, and the small main street was deserted. Inside the tiny terraced cottages, lights had been turned on, and soft beams shone through the curtains, bathing the pavements in a multitude of reds and blues. Ellen smiled and said how it looked like a painting, so we slowed our pace, stepping from one coloured light to the next. By the time we appeared in the village square, it had been five minutes since we'd left the hotel, a walk that would usually have taken no time at all.

But there was no hurry. The quiz started at nine, so we decided to take the long route to the cricket club, back up the hill to my old school, and round past the old air-raid shelter. Along the way, I pointed out the houses of past school friends, and when we arrived at the school, we carried on along the road to where the old bus station had been. It was now just a circle of grass with a small glass shelter and a few boards showing bus times. At the top of one of the boards, someone had written that Jenny loved Ian, while further down someone else had announced that Ian was a dickhead.

'Such a polarising figure, this Ian,' said Ellen, before asking if I knew him. I replied that I didn't.

After taking a few minutes to catch up on the local gossip posted on the boards, we set off towards the convenience store. There had been two such stores next to each other many years ago, but now only one remained, the other seemingly converted into a house. The remaining one had been run for as long as I could remember by a formidable old lady, who must have been in her seventies even then. Subsequent generations had taken over, so that now the grandson, or great-grandson, was in charge. I had no idea what had happened to the old lady, but I could hazard a guess.

From there, we walked up a long pathway, its large concrete slabs worn and cracked from decades of use. Wide at the entrance, perhaps four or five metres across, it gently sloped upwards until suddenly it narrowed and the concrete gave way to grey patches of tarmac and gravel. Here, on either side, high stone walls ensured that no more than two people could walk together at any one time. At the far end was our housing estate, and I must have travelled that path many thousands of times in my youth. Ellen asked me if the path had a name, and I told her that we'd always referred to it as 'the snicket'. But I didn't know if that was a real word or not.

Towards the bottom, we passed an electricity generating station, and I recalled to Ellen how I'd been terrified of it as a boy, with its humming sound and small yellow sign portraying a stick figure being impaled by a lightning bolt. Even now, it made me uneasy.

Very soon, we came to the end of the path. Ellen immediately recognised the houses and pointed excitedly to my old home, as if I might have forgotten it was there. Next door, Norman's curtains were closed, and a faint light shone through a gap at the top. He'd be watching television, with a newspaper in one hand and a glass of whisky in the other, settled in for the night. This time, however, we didn't stop to look around but carried on along the footpath towards the sea, grey and shimmering in the distance. Far away, I could see the Port of Heysham, with several container ships and a large ferry, ready to transport people and freight the next day.

The path we now walked on hadn't changed in all the years I'd known it. As a boy, I remember thinking it the blackest, smoothest thing in the world, and when the skateboarding craze had first hit, my friends and I had spent hours on it, performing tricks and falling on our faces. The memory made me smile, and when Ellen asked what I was thinking about, I told her, and she laughed, unable to picture me with grazed knees and bruised elbows. Even to me, it seemed like a different person.

But soon, the memories made me feel sad. It had been a time of dreams, and it highlighted how little I'd done with my life. I decided it best to stop talking about the past.

We walked the rest of the way idly chatting, the North Sea wind pushing through the trees and into our backs, spurring us forward. We arrived at the cricket club just before nine, and as we walked up the steps and through the door, quiz papers were already being handed out. It was always a member of the previous week's winning team who put together the quiz, and this week it was my friend Declan who was in charge. He smiled at us as we entered.

'I thought you weren't going to make it.' he said.

'Not a chance!' said Ellen, and he laughed.

The dark blue rug which led from the doorway served as a path, guiding us to Don at the bar. He was moving quickly from one pump to the next and was sweating from the effort of having to deal with more than a handful of customers at any one time. He signalled to me, pointing to the nearest bitter pump, and when I shook my head and mouthed that one of the drinks would be a red wine, he stared at me, as though I was speaking in a foreign language.

There were around thirty people in the club that night, most of whom had come for the quiz and wouldn't be seen again until the next weekend. Several, however, were regular customers and it was two of these, Dean and Phil, who asked us if we wanted to form a team. Dean was a tall blond-haired man in his early thirties, who I'd known from my time at school in Lancaster, where we'd both been members of the school cricket team. I remembered myself as the superior player, though I'm sure Dean would have disagreed. Phil was older than us and had captained the local cricket team when I'd played there as a junior. He had long sideburns and a goatee beard, neither of which were there the last time I'd seen him. I introduced them to Ellen, and they both made the same joke about hoping for questions on America in the quiz. She didn't look quite so confident as she had done earlier.

The clubhouse bell rang, signifying that the quiz was about to start. The four of us made our way over to a small wooden table in the corner of the room and sat down, at which point Phil asked if anyone wanted to write down the answers. When no one replied, it was decided that the role would fall to him, and with it the task of deciding on the team name. He smiled to himself and immediately began scribbling at the top of the paper. His handwriting was barely legible, and we craned to see what he'd written.

'Pond lift?' I asked, somewhat mystified.

'No,' he said irritably, 'It's pond life! You know, to signify that we have people with us from across the pond.'

'It looks like lift to me too,' said Dean. 'No way that's an E.'

Phil shook his head, and Ellen leaned forward for a look.

'Port lift?' she said with a smile.

'Park life?' I added helpfully, at which point Ellen and Dean started to laugh. Phil smiled too, and taking his pen, he scribbled out the team name, changing it for another.

'Village Idiots,' he laughed. 'That seems more appropriate!'

When it looked like it would be another few minutes before things got underway, Dean asked Phil if he was in a better mood now. He nodded, and Dean explained to us that when Phil had arrived at the club earlier, he'd been in a foul mood. Ellen asked him what had happened.

'Some idiot kicked a ball into my allotment,' he said, a pained look etched across his face as he recalled the incident. 'Near on destroyed my cucumbers.' I watched as Ellen took a drink, and I could see her smiling behind her wine glass.

The club was now almost full, and the increase in sound meant that few of us heard Declan as he approached the centre of the room and called for everyone's attention. Slowly each table quietened down until at last, there was silence. Declan looked at me and winked.

'Question one,' he declared, and a small cheer rose from around the bar. 'In what year was Abraham Lincoln assassinated?' Dean, Phil and I stared intently at Ellen.

'Easy,' she said confidently. '1865.'

Phil's finger shot to his lips as he whispered to us that the room was full of cheats. Of which Phil was well known as being one. He carefully wrote down the answer, though it looked more like 1863 to me.

'Question two. What is the atomic number of gold?'

An old lady by the bar threw a beer mat at Declan, and the four of us sat back in our chairs. A man at the next table tried to steal a look at our paper.

'No idea,' sighed Phil. 'What kind of question is that?' Dean and I shrugged while Phil played with his pen, waiting for the next question.

'Seventy-nine.' The three of us turned to stare at Ellen. 'It's the number of protons in the nucleus of an atom,' she added. 'And for gold, it's seventy-nine.'

'How do you know that?' said Phil after a moment. It was clear he was impressed.

'How do you not know that?' replied Ellen with a smile, and Phil wrote the answer on the paper.

The rest of the quiz panned out in very much the same vein. Each of us participated at various points, but by far the greatest number of answers were provided by Ellen. And after the last of the fifty questions had been answered, we passed our paper to the nearest table and Phil went off to the bar for some drinks.

'Finally managed to clear the fence then!' said Dean, as Phil disappeared into the crowd. 'I saw you up at the old school earlier and figured the cucumber massacre was something to do with you.' Ellen and I smiled at each other. There was no point in denying it.

'I can't believe how far that ball went,' I said. 'And it wasn't even fully inflated!'

To my right, I could hear Ellen laughing.

'I think it's best if we keep it to ourselves, all the same,' laughed Dean. 'Phil was livid, though I'm pretty sure his description of the damage is open to interpretation.' As Ellen and I nodded in agreement, Phil reappeared carrying a small tray of drinks. A good amount of the beer had spilt onto the tray, though Ellen's wine seemed to have escaped unscathed. Under his arm, he was carrying three small picture frames, and as he settled the tray onto the table, he reached for them and laid them side by side in front of Ellen and me.

'Recognise anyone here?' he asked with a flourish of his hand. And I did.

The first picture was black and white, and showed my junior football team, taken over twenty-five years earlier. Ellen studied the image for a few seconds before pointing to a figure on the right. 'That's you, isn't it,' she said, and I nodded. 'So skinny,' she added, 'and all that hair!'

I smiled and assured her the hairstyle was all the rage at the time, with its long straight fringe and sides covering the ears. I pointed to one or two of the other people in the picture. In fact, everyone seemed to have the same hairstyle, even the adults. Next to me was a very young-looking Mark Smith, and it looked as though he'd been crying.

'Recognise him?' asked Phil, pointing to a boy on the left, with a shy smile and thick dark hair.

'Leigh, of course,' I replied. 'I'd know that face anywhere.'

'Who's Leigh?' asked Ellen, and Phil and Dean looked at me.

'My brother,' I said simply.

'What?' Ellen looked confused. 'You never told me you had a brother!'

I thought that I had, but apparently not. I explained that he lived abroad and that he didn't get back to the UK very often.

'He's an explorer,' said Phil, and Ellen stared at him. 'He discovered Guatemala.'

'You mean the Guatemala that was conquered by Spain in the sixteenth century?' asked Ellen, shaking her head. I thought to myself that would make a very good quiz question.

'Must be a different one,' said Phil.

The second picture, again in black and white, had me sitting in my cricket gear, padded up and with bat in hand. It was a team shot, in two rows, with the back row standing and the front row seated. I was in my late teens, and my features were already transforming into those of an adult. Regrettably,

I was also sporting a moustache, the kind of moustache which teenagers often grow, and adults often laugh at. It didn't take Ellen long to notice, judging by the howls of laughter. She mentioned something about Magnum PI, but I pretended not to hear.

The final photograph was taken in colour and showed a middle-aged couple standing behind the cricket club bar, smiling with their arms around each other. I recognised them immediately, and I looked at their faces, so happy and full of life. The man on the right, in his early fifties, wore a grey V-necked jumper, and his shirt was open at the collar. He was smartly dressed, and his dark smiling eyes contrasted with his lightly greying hair. Next to him was a woman, a few years younger than him, in a purple roll neck jumper with brown hair cut short at the shoulders. She was beautiful, and I felt a lump in my throat at the memory of her.

'We miss them too,' said Phil after a moment and I felt Ellen squeeze my hand. 'It's been a few years now, but we keep their picture behind the bar.'

My parents had served behind the cricket club bar in the years following their retirement. When times had been hard at the club, they'd lent some money to keep the place afloat. This had helped turn things around so that today it was in good health, both on and off the field. Now, holding that small photograph in both hands, I was surprised at how raw their deaths still felt.

'Anyway, enough of this,' I said at last. 'Time for another drink.' And this time, it was Ellen who disappeared into the crowd.

By eleven o'clock, the place was nearly empty. Numbers had thinned steadily after the quiz, so we'd relocated to the tall stools by the bar. A bottle of cheap red wine sat unopened on a shelf behind us, the spoils of our victory earlier in the evening. We'd won the quiz, albeit narrowly, and mostly due to Ellen's efforts. The job of creating the next one now fell to Dean and Phil, and it was clear that neither of them relished the prospect. Ellen had donated the wine to the bar, and Don had reciprocated by not charging us for any more of our drinks that evening. I'm quite sure they amounted to more than one bottle, but no one was counting by that stage.

At midnight, we were the only customers left, so Don decided it was time to close. Ellen went off to the bathroom while Phil rummaged around looking for his coat. He eventually remembered that he hadn't come in one. And while Don cleared the tables, Dean furnished me with advice. The kind of advice that all drunkards seem to possess.

'I know you both said that you're just good friends,' he said. 'But you're not fooling anyone.' He shook his head slowly, and I wondered if he was falling asleep.

'You, Thomas, are looking for something when you don't need to.' He was wide awake now. 'You may not know it,' he announced, 'but you have it all.'

Before I could say anything, Ellen had returned, and Don was ushering us unceremoniously through the door into the cold night air.

Phil seemed to have disappeared.

When I awoke the next morning, the sun was streaming into the room through the thin white curtains. Our train back to London wasn't until later in the day, so we lay in bed discussing our plans. As it was another warm day, Ellen wanted to take a walk along the promenade into Morecambe. From there we could catch a bus into Lancaster and have a look around, perhaps visiting my old secondary school. We'd have to come back to the hotel to collect our bags, before heading to the station, but I figured we had a good six or seven hours to kill. More than enough.

We showered quickly, and while I went downstairs to deal with the bill and to ask about leaving our bags for the day, Ellen busied herself with packing her two enormous cases. She hadn't worn anywhere near all the clothes she'd brought but had given it a good try. As for myself, I was now embarrassed by the small amount of clothing I had. It made it look as though I hadn't made much effort, when in reality I had. Like most things, there is a happy medium.

As we were about to leave, I joked with Ellen, asking her if she'd made room in her cases for a hotel dressing gown.

'Do you really think I'd steal anything from your hometown, Thomas?' she said, and it was clear she was disappointed that I'd even joke about it. She looked sad too, and I apologised.

When we were ready, we made our way outside into the morning sunshine. A cool breeze was blowing in from the sea, and we headed in that direction, turning left out of the hotel doors and making our way down the narrow street. Not far along, we came across the entrance to St Peter's church, its old iron gate rusted and pitted with moss. Grey worn gravestones lined a short winding path, and its gravelled surface crunched loudly as we made our way to the large church doors. The sound of singing grew steadily as we approached, and I smiled to myself recognising the familiar strains of a hymn I'd sung as a boy. Ellen held onto my arm as we peered around the door at the fifty or so people inside, now listening intently to the words of the old man at the front. An old man I recognised at once. It was Mr Timperley. He'd been the vicar when I was a child. I marvelled at how old he must be now. He'd seemed old back then.

Ellen tugged at my arm and signalled silently for us to go. It felt like we were intruding on their devotion, so we left, quietly closing the heavy oak door behind us. Back in the sunshine, she commented on how old the church was and how beautiful, with its high ceiling and ancient dark beams. I laughed and took hold of her hand, gently pulling her up a path to the left, which rose steadily before vanishing into the trees. A minute later, we were out of the trees and standing at the top of a rocky outcrop overlooking the sea. Below us were the green fields of The Barrows and to the right, the promenade, arching into the distance before eventually disappearing from view.

'That's not the old church,' I said at last. 'This is the old church!'

Standing next to us, barely noticeable at first, were the stone ruins of a building no more than a few metres in length. Two of the walls had disappeared entirely, but in a third, a small arched opening overlooked the sea. In front of it was a large brown plaque, with the history of the church etched in bold, dark letters.

'Christ!' exclaimed Ellen, before quickly apologising. 'It says here that this place is nearly fifteen hundred years old!'

'Yes,' I replied. 'The new church is only about a thousand.'

We stayed at the old church for about half an hour, sitting on the grassy ridge watching the seagulls circling overhead. Far below us, the waves slowly rolled in against the shore, the sound hypnotic and soothing. When we were ready to go, I pointed out the steps to the promenade and gathering up our things, we set off.

It should have taken us thirty minutes to get into Morecambe, but on this occasion we took about an hour, stopping every few hundred metres for Ellen to read one of the many historical plaques which lined the way. At one point we came across a public warning sign attached to the metal railings which separated the promenade from the beach. It showed a hand emerging from a pool of water in the sand, with the words "If the tide doesn't get you, the quicksand will!" printed below.

Ellen burst out laughing.

'Not the greatest marketing slogan for a town!' she said, which made me laugh too. I'd never thought of it like that.

A little further on, we reached the border between Heysham and Morecambe, marked in this instance by a modern-looking cafe selling ice creams and drinks. The lure of an ice cream proved too much. I decided on chocolate—it was always chocolate for me. Ellen went for rum and raisin, which sounded disgusting. She watched on as I requested extra chocolate sauce, as well as a chocolate flake, and she laughed as the chocolate sauce dripped down my chin.

We continued our walk until soon we came across a small jetty which protruded no more than a few paces into the sea. Ellen asked what it was, and I told her it was all that was left of the West End Pier, which had been destroyed by a storm decades earlier, along with its many shops and amusement arcades. She shrugged and said that it was a shame, as she'd have liked to have seen a pier. When we arrived at a similar jetty, half a mile further along the promenade, I smiled and told her that this had been the location of Morecambe's Central Pier.

'Storm?' she asked.

'Yes,' I replied simply, 'though this time with added fire.'

Ellen thought about that for a while. 'I take it Morecambe isn't known for its engineering prowess?'

'No,' I said, 'it's known for its prawns.'

The bus ride into Lancaster took around twenty minutes and was very busy indeed, which was odd for a Sunday. We sat on the top deck, at the front, which in my opinion was the place with the best view. It also provided a good vantage point from which to see all the people who were waiting at each bus stop. A little into the journey, I noticed that many of the people getting onto the bus were overweight, and I wondered why. I was about to point it out to Ellen when a very large couple came up the stairs and sat on the seat to our right, breathing heavily. Before long, the man reached into a plastic bag he was carrying and produced two large meat pies, one of which he handed to his partner. Therein lay the answer to my question.

Not much later, we pulled into Lancaster bus station. We followed the couple to the narrow stairs, taking great care not to stand on the small pieces of pie which now covered the floor. Ellen insisted I go first, and she placed both of her hands on my shoulders as we descended the stairs. We waited at the bottom, to allow several old ladies to disembark, with their wheeled shopping bags and thick overcoats. And when we finally got off, I looked across at the big clock situated high up in the centre of the station. It was just past midday, and all around us, people hurried back and forth, going from one place to another, just as they did every day. Gone were the times when the town went to sleep on a Sunday.

When we reached the town centre, things seemed just as they had been twenty-four hours earlier. The early afternoon streets, bathed in warm summer sunshine, teemed with shoppers, and the numerous coffee shops overflowed onto the white pavements. Somewhere in the distance I could hear a busker, singing a cover of a Beatles song. He was so bad that I couldn't make out which song it was meant to be. And on a corner, by the new Carphone Warehouse, a group of students stood with their faded jeans and unkempt hair, passing the day in idle debate.

Ellen had already made her way over to the canvas-covered stalls lining the main shopping street, and I watched her as she held up one T-shirt after another, appraising each before handing them back. I walked over, and she smiled. She then pointed to another T-shirt and asked me what I thought. The shirt was a vibrant royal blue with the Captain America emblem across the chest. I thought it looked too big for her, and I told her so, which made her laugh.

'It's not for me silly!' she said, before holding the shirt up against my chest. 'Perfect,' she declared and handed it to the stall owner, along with a twenty pound note. I thanked her, and she handed me a paper bag containing my new top.

'You're most welcome,' she laughed, linking her arm through mine. 'A shirt fit for a hero.'

The primary purpose in coming to Lancaster that day was to visit my old secondary school, situated up a steep hill about a mile outside of town. Ellen wanted a drink before we headed out, so after several minutes of searching, we eventually found ourselves in a tiny coffee shop. I'd never been there before, located as it was down one of the many back streets which covered the old town centre. The place itself specialised in milkshakes, so we each ordered one, mine being chocolate, while Ellen went for vanilla. I could see that she wanted to say something, but for once, she kept her thoughts to herself. A member of staff came over to give the table a wipe and to ask us if we wanted anything to eat. He was in his late twenties with long black hair and a neatly trimmed beard, and it was noticeable that none of his questions were directed at me, his full attention being reserved for Ellen. After he left, I mentioned this to her, and she said that she hadn't noticed. But I knew that she had.

It was another hour before we made it to the school. The hill seemed much longer and steeper than I recalled, and by the time we reached the top, I was beginning to wish we'd brought a bottle of water with us. I remembered that there'd been a small shop just before the school, but when we got there, all that we found was a house with lace curtains and a bright red door. And with that, another of my childhood memories disappeared into the ether.

The school itself was a sprawling affair, made up of two large stone buildings, one on either side of the main road. Over time, several other buildings had been added further up the hill. In the end, it had become an eclectic mix of architectural styles, functional and wonderfully diverse. Ellen seemed fascinated and poked her head into any opened door or darkened corner she could find. With each place we visited, she would ask me questions about my own experiences there, and I would delve deep into my memories to recall anything of interest. And in this way, we slowly, very slowly, made our way up the hill.

At the top was the science block and next to it the old house where my schoolmates and I had been taught Latin, compulsory from the second year. Why I'd continued studying Latin right through to A-Level was still a mystery to me. I was never very good at it. No, worse than that, I was actually terrible at it. But I liked the teacher, and my best friends also studied it. With hindsight, perhaps not the best reasons to take a subject.

As I stood there, looking up at the old place, Ellen held her hand to a window, peering through to see if she could spot anything of interest. She was to be disappointed. She was hoping for slate tablets and quill pens, but all that she found were empty desks and neat piles of books. On a blackboard at the far end of the room, someone had written the words "Praesis ut prosis".

'What does that mean?' asked Ellen.

'Lead in order to serve,' I replied, quoting the school motto. She looked at me as though I'd just deciphered the Rosetta Stone, and I smiled sagely. Every old boy of the school knew the translation, but she didn't need to know that.

A new glass extension had been added to the far side of the building, so we moved around for a closer look. Inside were neat rows of wooden tables and chairs, with overflowing bookshelves lining the far wall. I wondered if they were the same books I'd studied, Catullus and Tacitus, with their deep red covers and unintelligible texts. A little further along had been the biology department, at the time no more than a row of prefabricated huts, but now replaced by a brick-built cube, with polished metal doors and large rectangular windows. Inside each of the windows was a cream coloured blind, and it was much to Ellen's frustration that they were all pulled down, revealing nothing of the wonders hidden inside. From memory, old Bunsen burners and broken test tubes.

There was little else to see there, so we left the area through the main gate and walked further up the hill, approaching the boarding houses on our right. Before we reached them, we turned into a small car park. To the left had been the boarding masters' houses, and as we passed them, making our way up a narrow path to the sports fields, a familiar voice called out from a nearby car.

'Thomas! Is that you?'

The car was small, and it took some time for its occupant to prise himself out of the tiny front seat. It was Mr Douglas, my old physics teacher, and though he was now in his eighties, he was just as I remembered him. Once out of the car, his body seemed to unravel, as if the minuscule proportions of the front seat had forced him to fold in on himself. He was tall, much taller than I remembered, and the antithesis of my other youthful recollections.

'Christ, how tall is he?' gasped Ellen.

I wasn't too sure.

'About nine feet,' I said. At least that's how it seemed to me. 'I think teachers never stop growing.'

With thin strands of white hair covering his bald head and spectacles perched at the tip of his nose, Mr Douglas was an imposing figure, despite his rakishly thin frame. He strolled over to us, and I shook his hand firmly. He laughed when I called him 'Sir', insisting that I use his first name. Which, of course, I could not. A teacher will always be a teacher. We chatted for a few minutes, and I introduced him to Ellen, who was the epitome of good manners and charmed him thoroughly. Just as he was leaving, he turned to me and asked if we were there to see the cricket. I smiled and said that we were, but Ellen didn't smile.

'You have got to be joking,' she said as Mr Douglas disappeared along the path. I assured her that I knew nothing about the cricket, but it was obvious that she didn't believe me. Even though it was the truth.

It was such a lovely day that we ended up spending much longer than expected at the school, lying together on the grass bank by the new pavilion. The sun was hot overhead, and around us, small groups of people chatted together and spread blankets on the grass. Ellen and I watched them for a while, then did what most people do at school cricket matches—fell asleep. I don't know how long I slept for, but I was suddenly woken by a small fly landing on my nose. I turned to see if Ellen was still asleep, but she wasn't. Instead she was propped up on one elbow looking at me and smiling.

'You were snoring!' she said, a long strand of blond hair dancing in front of her face. I told her that I didn't snore, and she laughed. 'Of course not, Thomas!'

The big clock on the pavilion announced that we'd been

there for nearly two hours, and that we were now pushed for time. We quickly gathered our belongings and headed back towards the small path on which we'd encountered Mr Douglas. It took us a great deal less time to get down the hill than it had to get up, and within twenty minutes we were at the taxi rank by the bus station. There were still a couple of hours before our train, but we had to get back to Heysham, collect our cases, then return to Lancaster, so bus travel wouldn't work. As we waited our turn in the queue, Ellen turned to me.

'You know, cricket's not that bad after all,' she said.

'How much of it did you actually see?' I asked, and she smiled.

'None at all.'

The journey back to London passed uneventfully. We decided to upgrade our tickets, so found ourselves for most of the journey in a near-empty first-class carriage, with enormous leather seats and free coffee and biscuits. It had been a while since we'd eaten, so the biscuits were dispatched immediately, and when the attendant came over to ask if we'd like anything else, we picked up a sandwich each and two bottles of water. Ellen asked if I fancied a game of cards and laughed when I declined. There was a newspaper on the table, so we decided to attempt the crossword instead. Not the cryptic one, as I was terrible at those. Sometimes a crossword reveals how much we know and at other times, how little. This was one of those occasions which left us feeling very intelligent, so Ellen decided to try the cryptic crossword. I marvelled at her ability to unwind words from the most peculiar of clues. And in no time at all that too was complete.

'What would you like to do now?' I asked as the train sped through Wigan station, the light outside beginning to fade as the sun disappeared below the trees.

'This,' replied Ellen, and she leaned over and put her head on my shoulder. Within moments she was asleep, and that was how she remained for the rest of the journey.

Arriving back in London, I asked Ellen if she wanted to go for something to eat, or perhaps a drink. I could phone Henry and James if she liked, they would undoubtedly be up for it. But I could see that she was tired and when she said that what she most wanted to do was to go back to my flat, I was more than happy to oblige. This weekend had been our swansong, all about us and enjoying our last few days together. It had started with just the two of us, and it was fitting that it would end in the same way. It had been perfect.

Chapter 12

'What should I wear for my leaving drinks?' said Ellen as we made our way back from work. The drinks, and a meal, had been arranged for the Friday. 'How about the black dress I got last weekend? Do you remember?'

Of course, I remembered. We'd been out for the day in the centre of town, doing the things tourists do, like visiting the British Museum, the Houses of Parliament, and so on. Later we'd gone to the theatre, which if I'm honest, is not really my thing. But Ellen had enjoyed it, so we'd both been happy. As we'd walked along the streets that night, dodging the tourists, we'd held hands and vowed to keep in touch once she was back in America. We'd visited gift shops and clothes stores, all of which stayed open until late in the evening. And when we'd finally got back to my flat, Ellen had put on a new dress, though I'd no idea how, or where, or even when she'd got it. It was black, and she looked like a blond Audrey Hepburn. And she was stunning.

We were walking slowly, much slower than the rest of the

people around us, hurrying as they were to get home, or to get a decent place at a local bar or restaurant. Their leather briefcases and designer handbags bashed against their legs as they walked, and I wondered once again why everyone was in such a rush. Did a few minutes really make that much difference? That had been me until recently, and I struggled to recall why. Why had I rushed to places that I didn't want to get to? But now I just strolled, with nowhere to hurry to, chatting with Ellen, and pointing to this and that as we discussed the events of the day at work. It seemed so natural now and so normal.

As we approached the Underground, the tall office blocks stood out like reprimanding fingers against the sky, and I took one last look around. I was Orpheus, standing nervously at the fiery gateway. Ellen noticed my hesitation and asked me what was wrong.

'Nothing,' I replied. 'I just feel anxious for some reason.' She said nothing, just squeezed my hand reassuringly. And then we descended the stairs, leaving the warm air of the street for the even warmer air below.

The rocking of the train was always a double-edged sword. On busy days, when there were no spare seats, and I was forced to stand, squashed between strangers, it was not a pleasant experience. But on those rare occasions when I could find a seat, I'd feel blessed as I sank into the well-worn cushions, the carriage gently rocking me from side to side, the very definition of contentment. And today was one of those days. Ellen and I found ourselves next to each other, legs touching in the tiny seats, as the roll of the carriage went to work. I heard Ellen sigh gently next to me, and I asked her if she was okay. She announced that there could be no better example of luxurious travel and we both laughed at how true, and at the same time how ludicrous, that was.

Opposite us was an enormously fat man, his legs spread wide so that his neighbours were forced to sit at uncomfortable angles. With each movement of the carriage, his giant chest would wobble back and forth. I quietly pointed it out to Ellen, pretending to be discussing something altogether different.

'You sod!' she said, as she started to giggle, her red lips pursed tightly in a vain attempt to contain her amusement. I knew full well that she wouldn't be able to control herself for too long, so I sat back to see how things would unfold. Barely a minute later, she pinched my thigh, quite painfully as it happened, and announced that we'd be getting off the train at the next stop. I told her she was being ridiculous, to which she replied that it was my fault and stood up to go. Reluctantly, I got up too, and as we made our way unsteadily to the exit, several passengers lunged for our seats. And for the next few minutes, until we rolled into the station, I found myself sandwiched against the train door, with hot metal to my right and a sweaty body to my left. Unfortunately, it wasn't Ellen's.

'I believe I have learned another valuable life lesson,' I announced as we made our way up the worn stone staircase to street level.

'I very much doubt it!' Ellen laughed.

She had regained some natural colouring to her face by this stage, following the bright crimson of the train. And as we reached the top of the stairs, we were both laughing. Ellen turned to me and shook her head, smiling broadly as she linked her arm through mine. And like that, arm in arm, we made our way down the busy road in silence, enjoying the warmth of each other and without the need for words.

After ten minutes or so, it was becoming clear that I had very little idea where we were. Ellen asked if I knew where we

241

were going and I admitted, with some embarrassment, that I didn't. I was in completely unfamiliar territory, with no landmarks to guide me. Not that I was surprised. I'd never been one for exploring. And I wasn't unique in that. When people move to a new city, they don't explore much beyond their new home or place of work. The city becomes like a number of small pods, a mile or so in diameter, linked by public transport. There are the home and work pods, as well as a few pods for socialising, but outside of that, it may as well be a different country. And that's where I found myself now—in a different country.

We were making our way down much quieter streets by this stage, when suddenly we came across a large pub, set back from the road, with a large patch of broken gravel for a car park. It looked nice, all hanging baskets and painted signs advertising upcoming football matches. Inside, I could see tables surrounded by families, and towards the back was a long bar, propped up by a group of middle-aged men, deep in conversation. I was about to suggest to Ellen that we go inside for a drink, to discuss a plan of action, when all of a sudden, a car pulled into the car park. Out jumped its occupant, a tall thin man in his early thirties with glasses and neatly combed hair. He was looking at his watch and muttering something about being late, and it was evident from the speed with which he entered the pub that he was in for a spot of bother.

He seemed to have forgotten to lock his car.

Ellen watched as he disappeared through the wooden door, then turned to me and smiled.

'What's that road number near your flat?' she asked. I must have looked puzzled. 'You know, the A something or other?'

'Thirteen,' I replied, though I had no idea how I knew

242

that. It wasn't the kind of thing I would normally know.

'Haha!' laughed Ellen. 'Just like our train seat!' She sounded very pleased with herself, though she was trying very hard not to show it. But before I had the chance to say anything, she'd pulled me over to the car and was telling me to get in.

'For old times' sake!' she said as she opened the door and jumped in, urging me to follow. I shrugged and joined her, the two of us finding ourselves in adjacent front seats, her the driver and me the confused passenger.

'Well this is nice, isn't it Starsky?' I said as I watched her tugging violently at the steering column. Seconds later, its plastic covering was lying in my lap, and several coloured wires were poking out. The starter, ignition and battery wires, I later found out. I'm not sure what she did next—some form of trickery—but very soon we were cruising down the road, Ellen beaming with pride and me fumbling with a map, desperately trying to locate the A13.

As we drove, I quizzed her about how she'd been able to start the car so quickly, and she reminded me of her father's side-line as a car mechanic. He'd taught her for years how to make her way around a car, and she'd learned all that she could. 'You never know when things might come in useful,' she laughed.

'Yes,' I replied. 'You never know when you might need to steal a car.'

The A13 led almost directly to my front door, but we parked the car a few streets away so as not to give any clues as to who'd stolen it. I'd taken a tissue out of my pocket and cleaned any surfaces for fingerprints, much to Ellen's amusement, and she'd spent the next ten minutes calling me the Pink Panther, which seemed to amuse her a lot. By the time we finally got back to my flat, it was around seven-thirty, and it had been a long time since we'd eaten.

'I'll make us some sandwiches,' offered Ellen as we walked through the door. I could see the beginnings of a smile.

I returned her smile and told her that would be nice. She eyed me suspiciously, and I could see that she wasn't sure if I was joking or not.

So I turned on the TV.

'And then we can watch highlights of the cricket.'

Chapter 13

We arranged a goodbye meal for the Friday evening.

'Do you have everything packed?' I asked as we sat in the office. Henry and James were unusually quiet, and I knew they were sad to see her go.

'Pretty much,' she replied, staring out of the window.

It was another hot day, and the sun shone straight into the room, making it humid. The space inside my chest was so stuffy I could hardly breathe. Ever since the announcement of her departure, the atmosphere in the office had taken a definite turn for the worse. It was Thursday, the home straight of the week, and the time when most of us came to life. But nobody seemed in the mood to celebrate, least of all me. Ellen's departure would be leaving a gaping hole in the office. At least until it was shut down. Henry had described her as a bright light where it was needed the most, and I couldn't have put it better myself. If it were up to me, I would have asked her to stay. But it wasn't up to me. And with the recent announcement, we all knew this wasn't the place for her.

'You know, we'll all be sad to see you go,' said James quietly. For once, he wasn't wearing his brightly coloured braces and bow tie. I found myself wishing that he was, as the funereal atmosphere of the last few days was beginning to take its toll.

'Thank you,' whispered Ellen. She was wearing a blue dress, with her hair tied back, and while she was still beautiful, some of the radiance had gone. It made me think of autumn, my least favourite time of the year, when all the joys of summer disappear, leaving only memories, and the uneasy feeling that the best times are behind us.

I didn't really know what to say. I'd been in a bit of a daze the last few days and had decided not to talk about her leaving. As if by not mentioning it, it may not happen. I joined her at the window, and we both stared silently at the street below. Outside, life carried on as normal, and I looked at the people, ambling from one place to the next, oblivious to the day-to-day problems of every single person they passed. Was this what normality looked like? The combination of a thousand problems, mixed together to form everyday life—calm on the outside, turmoil within. I couldn't help but feel sad, not only for myself, but for my friends too.

Though mainly for myself.

As we stood there, the sun appeared from behind the building opposite, and the sudden surge of heat caught me off guard. I could feel the blood pounding in my temples, and I suddenly felt tired. If it hadn't been for Jane coming in, I was sure I would have fallen asleep. She smiled amiably and offered us all a coffee. I told her about Ellen's meal. And after that, we all went back to work.

That night, Ellen stayed over at my flat. We would say our goodbyes at the meal the next day. She was to spend her final evening at the Walkers', which was probably for the best. I'd never been one for prolonged goodbyes.

I'd arranged to meet Yasmine on Saturday for a coffee.

'You look beautiful, Ellen!' said Jane as we entered the restaurant. James and Henry were there too. Alongside Henry sat Beth, a big smile on her face, mirroring the one on Henry's. Ellen and I smiled to one other. Ellen hugged everyone in turn, before finally we took our seats. I'd been afraid that the evening might turn into a sombre affair, but I needn't have worried. We don't do sombre very well.

The women were talking about Ellen's stay in London, and I noticed how happy Ellen seemed as she recalled our trip to Leeds, then the visit to Morecambe. She looked across at me, and I reached for her hand under the table. Henry and James were discussing the wine. Henry had put on his glasses and was pointing something out. Both of them looked well on the way to being drunk. It wasn't until we were starting on the main course that anyone mentioned the elephant in the room. Of course, it had to be Henry.

'Ellen, I really wish you weren't going,' he said. 'You've no idea what your being here has done for us all.' Ellen smiled at him, and I could see how sad she was. For once, it was my turn to help her out.

'We can't be selfish, Henry,' I said. 'Ellen's got her own life in America.'

He seemed puzzled, so I explained about her fiancé and their plans to marry when she got back to America. It was difficult for me to actually say it out loud. But it was all I could think of to say.

Jane looked confused. 'I didn't know you had a fiancé,' she said, and Ellen stared at me in surprise.

'Of course, you did!' I interrupted, before Ellen could say

247

anything. 'I overheard the two of you talking about him at James's party.'

Now both Ellen and Jane looked surprised.

'I wasn't talking about him,' said Ellen, and she looked embarrassed. Everyone stared at me, as if they'd just discovered the biggest idiot who had ever existed. I wondered to myself if they might just be right.

The silence stretched out for some time, and it was James who eventually broke it. He wanted to know what time I was taking Ellen to the airport. When I said that I wasn't going, they all stared at me again. It was the same look as before.

'What?' screeched Henry. 'What better thing could you have on than seeing Ellen off at the airport?'

I felt like I was on trial.

Before I could say anything, Ellen explained to them about our desire not to prolong things and also that she was required to spend the night at Sir Ian's. The merest mention of his name set Henry and James on edge. Here was my chance to deflect attention away from myself.

'Anyway, enough of that,' I said. 'A toast to Ellen!'

And with that, I was off the hook.

For the next half an hour, Ellen and I were bombarded with questions, and it quickly became apparent that we sorely lacked answers. We hadn't really discussed what would happen after she returned to New York. Most likely, she'd get married, and I'd be alone again. Even more alone, now that Sarah was getting married. But deep down, for me at least, I hadn't wanted to think about it. I hadn't asked because I was scared of the answer. Maybe there was nothing 'after', and I wasn't ready for that.

'Most unsatisfactory!' declared Henry finally.

I couldn't have put it better myself.

James was having trouble processing everything he'd just

heard.

'So…' he said slowly, as if trying to convince himself of what he was saying, 'Ellen's got a fiancé, and is going back to America to marry him.' I nodded. 'And you are…' He paused for a moment, as if searching for something nice to say. 'Doing something else?'

I shrugged.

'Short straw anybody?' said Henry, though he wasn't smiling.

'I suppose so,' I replied.

That just about summed things up.

The rest of the meal passed uneventfully. Ellen made everyone promise not to talk about her leaving, and we all agreed. This evening was for her after all. It was a celebration of her brief time with us, and we wanted her to be happy. It was as simple as that. Tears and regret were for another day.

And so, the evening came to an end, and with it, everyone's time together. Ellen didn't want to be late getting back. And while Henry, James and I went outside for a cigarette, the three women hugged and said their goodbyes. When we got back, Jane was crying. Over the last few weeks, she and Ellen had become close, and now, standing there, she looked suffocated with emotion. James put his arm around her shoulder.

In typical English fashion, Henry and James shook Ellen's hand and wished her all the best. As a nation, we've never been good at that sort of thing. She kissed them both on the cheek and told them to look after themselves. Then it was my turn. I walked over to her, and at first we said nothing, just stood there staring at each other. I took hold of her hands and kissed her.

'Look after yourself, Ellen,' I whispered.

'You too, Thomas,' she said, attempting to smile. 'You're not such an arsehole after all.'

'It's asshole,' I replied.

Throwing her arms around me, she kissed me on the lips and hugged me for what seemed like hours. The others looked away, a final gift of privacy. And as she slowly drew away, I could see that she'd been crying. So had I.

As her taxi departed, she waved to me through the back window.

And then she was gone.

'Do you feel like going for a drink, Thomas?' asked Henry, breaking the silence.

I smiled. 'No thanks, Henry. I think I'll go home.'

Sitting on the steps to my flat, I lit up a cigarette and watched the smoke as it rose slowly into the air. It was like a ghost disappearing into the night. In the pale light, the houses, with their grey roofs and painted fences, seemed abstract and unreal. It had been a strange evening.

I turned the key and let myself in. It was dark inside the flat and a ray of moonlight peeked through the curtains. There were two cups on the coffee table, cups used only that morning, as Ellen and I had chatted about our time together.

'If this is it, Thomas,' she had said. 'It was a ball!'

I smiled as I remembered how she'd flung her arms around me and kissed me so hard that I couldn't breathe. I wanted that again.

It only took a few minutes to tidy the flat. I carefully washed the two cups and placed them back in the cupboard. I was feeling drained, so I took off my clothes and got straight into bed.

Tomorrow was a new day.

When the alarm went off, it felt like minutes since I'd

gone to bed. It was ten o'clock, and I was still tired. I reset the alarm and went back to sleep.

At one o'clock, the alarm rang again, and this time I got up. It was the latest I'd got up since my university days, and I felt mildly ashamed of myself. As I wasn't due to meet Yasmine until seven, I had most of the day ahead of me, so I wandered around the flat, moving things from one shelf to another. After making a sandwich—thinly cut—I settled in the living room to read yesterday's newspaper. For once, I decided to forego my Saturday trip to the cafe. Somehow, I didn't fancy the idea.

I finished the paper, then watched television until five-thirty, at which point I went for a shower. It never took me long to get ready, as most of my clothes were the same style, and my short hair managed itself. I then had a shave and cleaned my teeth, the whole operation taking no more than thirty minutes. And that included the shower. I thought of the shower situation in Leeds, and I smiled to myself.

At half past six, I was walking across London Bridge on my way to the office. I'd somehow lost my ID card the previous evening and was hoping to find it in my room. Typically, this would have irritated me, but not today. I was in an odd mood.

Peter the Porter was waiting behind his desk when I arrived, and we exchanged greetings.

'Working on a Saturday, sir?' he said as I neared his desk.

'I could say the same to you, Peter,' I replied.

'No one at home waiting for me.'

I frowned. 'Me neither, I'm afraid.'

Inside the office, it was dark. Fortunately, most of the furniture had been stowed away neatly, so I arrived at my room unscathed. It didn't take long to find my card, lying there on top of a pile of papers. I should have looked at them that week but hadn't got around to it. I took the card and slotted it into my wallet. Just as I was leaving, I noticed a photograph sandwiched between two files on my desk, and I picked it up. It had been taken at James's party, just after Ellen and I had come back from his neighbour's house. We were hugging each other, and as ever, Ellen was smiling. I was trying to look cool, but it wasn't really working. Our clothes were covered in dirt, and I looked as though I'd been dragged through a hedge. As usual, Ellen looked fantastic. I smiled at the memory, then carefully propped the photo against my computer and left.

Outside, it was cloudy. The setting sun had stained the skyline red, and the tall buildings resembled huge stone knives, dripping with blood. I pulled my jacket close, and for the first time in weeks, I was cold.

The coffee shop where I was meeting Yasmine wasn't too far away, and as I arrived, I could smell the aroma of pizza from a restaurant across the street. It had been a long time since I'd eaten, and I suddenly felt hungry. Incredibly hungry.

'What can I get you, sir?' asked the waitress as I sat waiting for Yasmine. She was like a little roll of fat, nearly all body, with very short legs. And she reminded me of food, so I wanted her to go away.

'Coffee, please,' I said quickly, and she disappeared.

It was a busy place, and it took her nearly twenty minutes to return, by which time the coffee was cold. I took a sip and grimaced. Noticing, she immediately apologised.

'I'm sorry,' she said. 'I got chatting and forgot all about the coffee. Can I get you another?'

'Well, I appreciate your honesty,' I laughed. 'Yes, another would be good. Thanks.'

She was much quicker this time.

It was already a quarter past seven, and there was no sign

of Yasmine. By the time half past arrived, I knew she wasn't coming, so I got ready to leave. No doubt she had a good reason.

Just then, the door opened and in walked Henry and James. I'd told them I was meeting Yasmine but had no idea how they'd guessed it would be here. They were dressed casually, much more casually than I'd seen before, and when I noticed that Henry wasn't wearing socks, I nearly burst out laughing. I was about to make a sarcastic comment when I saw the expressions on their faces. Something was wrong.

'What's going on?' I asked, at once becoming concerned.

It was Henry who answered. 'I'm sorry, Thomas,' he began. 'I've got some bad news.'

'What bad news?' I could feel myself shaking.

'There's been an accident.' He hesitated for a moment and looked across at James. 'Sir Ian's been involved in a car crash. I think he's dead!'

And then there was silence. Henry and James looked anxiously at one another. While neither of them held any love for the man, no one wanted him dead. Henry especially looked shocked, and I wondered if he was going to be all right. As for myself, I didn't know what to say. There was nothing I could say. The two of them sat down, and I don't know how long we sat there before I eventually asked what had happened. It was James who replied this time. Sir Ian had lost control of his car and had crashed into a wall. Early reports were that the brakes may have failed.

'Do you want a drink, Thomas?' asked Henry, our stock question in most situations. I thanked him but said that I wanted to go home. The two of them nodded, and while I tidied my coffee cup and saucer, James ordered a taxi.

'Who'd have thought?' sighed Henry as we were leaving.

'Who indeed?' I replied, buttoning up my jacket. The taxi

was waiting outside, and we all got in. First stop, my flat, then off to the others. I suddenly realised that I didn't know where Henry lived. I'd have to ask him one day.

None of us spoke much on the way to my flat, and when we arrived, we shook hands, and I got out. And just as I'd done the night before, I sat down on the steps and lit up a cigarette. The smoke danced for a moment, before drifting away on the breeze. There was a light on across the street, and through the window I could see a family eating. It reminded me again how hungry I was.

Unlocking the door, I walked into the flat. Several candles flickered by the window, and the smell of food floated from the kitchen.

Ellen got up from the sofa and came over to greet me.

'I heard the news,' she said.

We stared at each other for a while, and in the end, it was me who spoke. 'Brake failure, or so I'm told.' I paused and looked at her. 'Though I'm no car expert.'

She shrugged.

'At least Yasmine's fine.'

'That's good.'

And then she smiled at me. That beautiful smile I'd come to love so much, a smile that said everything was going to be all right.

'You must be hungry,' she said, kissing me and taking my hand.

I looked at her and laughed. 'I'm starving!'

I'm not sure when I fell in love with Ellen. At least, I don't think so. I want to say that it was as soon as we met, but things don't really work like that. Not for me anyway. Whenever it was, it didn't take long. Perhaps it was the moment she saved me in Leeds, even though she'd manufactured the situation. She had come to my aid, and she's been saving me ever since.

And I don't know when Ellen fell in love with me. I've never asked. I'm not sure I need to know. I'm happy just to know that she did. That works fine for me.

I didn't think about Sir Ian at all after he died. In truth, he was a bit of an arsehole. Or asshole, if you prefer. He had no thoughts for us, so I have no thoughts for him. Yasmine was due to be with him on that fateful drive, but for some reason, she decided to stay at home. She went for a walk with Ellen instead.

All work at the company stopped for a while, as a new structure was put in place. Yasmine took control, as the beneficiary of her husband's controlling interest. And very soon, the company was heading in a completely new direction. It turned out that we needed London after all. Yasmine asked Ellen to stay, to help steer us through the turmoil, and she did. Very soon, we were living together, though in reality that had been the case for a long time. The flat was too small, of course, but we liked it all the same. And later that year we were married, it finally dawning on me that her fiancé wasn't real, made up for convenience when she'd first arrived in London. She'd always assumed that I knew. But I can be a bit slow sometimes.

James and Jane are still together, as are Henry and Beth, remarkably. Neither men have changed, and I doubt they ever will. We still work together, go out together, get drunk together. Except that now there are six of us. A much better number.

Things have worked out pretty well.

Chapter 14

It was a warm morning yesterday as Ellen and I made our way up the steps to the gallery. With us was Matthew, our son. He's six. I hate going to galleries, but Ellen thinks it's good for Matthew and probably for me too. The upside is that afterwards we go for ice-cream. Matthew and I like that.

We'd been wandering around west London for what seemed like hours and had succeeded in doing very little. I was in an excellent mood, and Ellen and I were laughing together about something that had happened the night before. Henry and Beth had been over for dinner, and Henry had brought with him a very expensive bottle of wine. He'd showed it off like a newborn child but had got drunk and knocked over his glass, so that it emptied into his soup. He'd looked like he was going to cry.

It was a big hall, covered with pictures by well-known local artists. So well known that I hadn't heard of any of them. I soon found myself wandering around, searching for distractions. A little while later, I noticed Ellen and Matthew staring in confusion at a large picture. Ellen waved to me, and I ambled over to take a look.

'What do think this is, Thomas?' she asked. It looked a bit like a building.

'A penis?' I ventured.

She pinched my arm playfully and gave me a kiss.

'What do you think, Matthew?' I said, pointing to the picture. He had about as much idea as his parents. Suddenly, his eyes lit up.

'Ice-cream!' he shouted.

Grinning, I picked him up and set him on my shoulders. He wasn't at all interested.

'One day, he'll have children of his own,' laughed Ellen, as I put my arm around her waist. 'And then he'll realise that there's more to life than ice-cream.'

I smiled and turned to face her.

'Rum and raisin?' I asked.

She thought about it for a while, then gave me another kiss.

'Chocolate, please.'

Printed in Great Britain
by Amazon